'*Moxyland* does lots of things, masterfully, that lots of sf never even guesses that it *could* be doing. Very, very good.'
William Gibson

'A Technicolor jazzy rollercoaster ride into a dazzling hell.'
André Brink

'A rare treat. Reminiscent at times of Neal Stephenson's *Snow Crash*, *Moxyland* is funny, gritty, imaginative and, ultimately, deeply disturbing. A politically charged urban speculative thriller that will leave you wanting more.'
Obrigado

'*Moxyland* makes a refreshing and thought-provoking debut. It shares the jazzy language associated with early masters like Gibson and Sterling, but the technology in her world is necessary for survival, sometimes a point of pride, and often dangerous.'
Strange Horizons

'*Moxyland* is bewilderingly fast-paced, slick; a next-generation cyberpunk that gets the heart pounding. I can't wait to read the next one... definitely a must-read.'
Hub

'Lean, sharp, and tightly written, *Moxyland* keeps raising the stakes, from the opening chapter to the uncompromising finale. And with its electronic panopticon, it gives us a dystopia to rival *1984* or *Stand On Zanzibar* – a future horrifying for its very plausibility.'
Gareth L Powell

LAUREN BEUKES

Moxyland

**ANGRY
ROBOT**

ANGRY ROBOT
A member of the Osprey Group

Lace Market House,
54-56 High Pavement,
Nottingham
NG1 1HW, UK

www.angryrobotbooks.com
Your government lies

Originally published in South Africa by Jacana Media
(Pty) Ltd 2008
First American paperback printing 2010

Distributed in the United States by Random House, Inc., New York.

ISBN 978-0-85766-004-6

Printed in the United States of America

9 8 7 6 5 4 3 2 1

For Keitu

Kendra

It's nothing. An injectable. A prick. No hospital involved. Like a booster shot with added boost.

Just keep telling yourself.

The corporate line shushes through the tunnels on a skin of seawater, overflow from the tide drives put to practical use in the clanking watery bowels of Cape Town – like all the effluent in this city. Like me. Art school dropout reinvented as shiny brand ambassador. Sponsor baby. Ghost girl.

I could get used to this, seats unmarked by the pocked craters of cigarette burns, no blaring adboards, no gangsters checking you out. But elevated status is not part of the program. Only allocated for the day, to get me in and out again. Wouldn't want civilians hanging around.

As the train slows, pulling into the Waterfront Exec station, it sends plumes of seawater arcing up the sides. In my defence, it's automatic; I lift

7

my camera, firing off three shots through the latticed residue of salt crusted over the windows. I don't think about the legal restrictions on documenting corporate space, that this might be provocation enough to revoke the special access pass Andile loaded onto my phone for the occasion.

'They don't like that, you know,' says the guy sitting across the way from me. He doesn't look like he belongs here either, with his scruffy beard and hair plastered into wet tufts. Older than me, maybe twenty-seven, twenty-eight. He's wearing a damp neoprene surf peel, a surfboard slung casually at his feet, half blocking the aisle.

'Then I'll delete it,' I snap. It's impossible, of course. I'm using my F2, picked up cheap-cheap along with my Hasselblad at the Milnerton market during the last big outbreak, when everyone thought this was really it. It's oldschool. Film. You'd have to rip it out the back, expose it to the light. But no one's ever sharp enough to notice that it's analogue.

'Kit kat,' he says, 'I was just saying. They're sensitive round these parts. All the proprietary tech.'

'No, thanks. Really. I appreciate it.' I make a show of fiddling with the back of the camera before I shove it in my bag, trying not to think that

I'm included in that definition now – just as much proprietary technology.

'See you around,' he says, like it's a sure thing, standing up as the doors open with an asthmatic hiss. He's left a damp patch on the seat.

'Yeah, sure,' I say, trying to sound friendly as I step onto the station platform. But the encounter has made me edgy, reinforced just how out of place I am here. It's enough to make me duck my head as I pass the station cop at the entrance – behaviour the cameras are poised to look for, not to mention the dogs. The Aito sitting alert and panting at the cop's feet spares me a glance over its snout, no more, not picking up any incriminating chem scents, no suspiciously spiked adrenalin levels or residue of police mace. His operator doesn't even bother to look at me, just waves me through the checkpoint with a cursory scan of my phone, verifying my bioID, the temporary access pass.

It's only six blocks but my pass isn't valid for walking rights, so Andile has arranged an agency car, already waiting for me on the concourse. I nearly miss it, because it's marked only by a VUKANI MEDIA licence plate. The name means 'Awake! Arise! Fight!', which makes me wonder who they're supposed to be fighting. The driver chuckles wryly when I ask her, but doesn't offer up a theory. We travel in cool professional silence.

Although my hand itches for my camera, I manage to restrain myself as we pass between the rows of filter trees lining Vukani's driveway, sucking up sunlight and the buffeting wind to power the building. You don't see filter forests much, or at least I don't. They're too expensive to maintain outside the corporate havens.

Inside, the receptionist explains that she'd love to offer me a drink, but it's not recommended just before the procedure. Would I like to have a seat? Andile will be only a minute. And would I mind checking my camera and any other recording devices? I don't have to worry about my phone: they've got app blockers in place to prevent unauthorised activity.

I reluctantly hand over my Leica Zion, and after a moment's hesitation, the Nikon too.

'It's got half my exhibition on there,' I say, indicating the F2.

'Of course, don't worry. I'll stash it in the safe,' she says, against a backdrop of awards – gold statuettes of African masks and perspex Loeries with wings flung wide.

I take a seat in the lounge, feeling naked without my cameras. And then Andile arrives in a fluster of energy and hustles me towards the lift. He's got the kind of personality that precedes him, stirring up the atoms before he even enters the room.

'There she is. Right on time, babes.' He honestly speaks like this. 'You get in all right? No hassles?'

'It was fine. Apart from nearly being ejected because I took a photograph of the underway.'

'Oh babes, you got to rein in those urges. You don't want to look like one of those public sector activists with their greater-good-tech-wants-to-be-free crap. Although those pics will be worth something when you're famous. Any chance I could get a print?'

'To go with the rest of your collection?'

His office on the seventeenth floor is colonised by an assortment of hip ephemera, a lot of it borderline illegal. The most blatant example is the low-fi subtech on his bookshelf, a cobbled-together satellite radio smuggled in from the Rural in defiance of the quarantines, which probably only makes it more valuable, more flauntable. It all goes with the creative director territory, along with the pink shirt and the tasteful metal plug in his right ear. The stolen photographs of the underway would fit right in.

What doesn't fit in is the contract. The wedge of white pages on the desk among the menagerie of vinyl toys seems antiseptic, too clinical to gel with all the fun, fun, fun around it.

The bio-sig pen I signed with (here, and here, and here) had microscopic barbs in the shaft that scraped skin cells from the pad of my thumb to mix with the ink. Signed in blood. Or DNA, which is close enough.

'Adams, K.?' A woman steps through the doorway from the boardroom, all crisp professionalism in a dark suit, holding a folder with my name printed on it in caps.

'I'm Dr. Precious. We met before, during the pre-med?' Through the floor-to-ceiling windows behind her, the southeaster bunches and whirls the clouds over Table Mountain into candyfloss flurries. *Spookasem* in the local. Ghost's breath.

'Can you roll up your sleeve, please?' She's already prepping the autosyringe.

Dr. Precious is here on call. Even ad agencies with big name biotech clients on their books don't tend to have in-house doctors. Andile claims it's because, 'The labs are so impersonal, babes.' But I suspect that it's easier to bring her in here to shoot us up one at a time than to get the necessary security clearance for twelve art punks to enter a restricted biomed research facility.

Not that the rest are art punks necessarily. All Andile will say is that they're hot talent. Young, dynamic, creative, on the up, the perfect ambassadors for the brand.

'You know the type, babes,' he said in interview #1, when I was sitting in his office, still reeling from the purgatory of dropping out, my dad's cancer, wondering how I got here.

'DJs, filmmakers, rockstar kids, and you, of course,' he winked, only emphasising that this is all a mistake, that I am out of their league. 'All Ghost's hipster chosen.' But we don't get to mingle until the official media launch party.

'Just in case one of you goes into meltdown,' Andile said in interview #3, when it was already too late to pull out. As if I'd even consider it. 'Ha-ha.'

Dr. Precious loads a silver capsule like a bullet into the back of the autosyringe. She's too smooth to be a doctor-doctor. She's not worn hollow from the public sector, new outbreaks, new strains. Inatec Biologica it says on the logotag clipped to her lapel.

Before interview #1, I thought their line was limited to cosmetics. I imagine her in a white coat and face-mask in a sleek lab that is all stainless steel and ergonomic curves, like in the toothpaste commercials. Or behind a cosmetics counter, spritzing wafts of perfume and handing out fifty-g samples of the topshelf biotech creams (one per customer, please). This isn't so

different after all. It's just that the average nano
in your average anti-ageing moisturiser acts
only on the subdermal level. Mine, on the other
hand, is going all the way.

'Don't sweat it, Kendra,' Andile said back in
interview #3, seeing my face. 'The chances of
meltdown are like zero. They've been using the
same tech in animals for years. Cop dogs, the
Aitos, you know, guide dogs, those helper mon-
keys for the disabled. Well, not quite the same,
obviously.'

Which doesn't mean that the contract didn't
include a host of clauses indemnifying Ghost,
their parent company Prima-Sabine FoodSolu-
tions International, Vukani, Inatec Biologica
and all their respective agencies and employees
against any unforeseen side-effects.

'So, how long before the mutation kicks in?'
I ask, acting like it's no big deal, as Dr. Precious
swipes at the crook of my elbow with a disin-
fectant swab, probably loaded with its own
nano or specially cultivated germ-eating bacteria or whatever new innovation Inatec's come
up with specially.

'Oh babes,' says Andile, mock-hurt. 'Didn't
we agree we weren't going to call it that? Promise me you won't use that word in the
interviews.'

'What did you have for breakfast?' says Dr.

Precious unexpectedly. But her question is a ruse. Before I can think to answer (cold oats at Jonathan's apartment, no sign of Jonathan, but that's not unusual lately), she snaps the autosyringe against my arm like a staple gun. And just like that, three million designer robotic microbes go singing through my veins.

It doesn't even hurt.

Considering the hype, the bulk of the contract, I am expecting nothing less than for the world to rearrange. Instead, it's like having sex for the first time. As in, is that it?

'That's it. It'll take four to six hours for the tech to circulate. Do you want me to run through it again? You may experience flu symptoms: running nose, headaches, sore throat in the first twenty-four hours. Then it'll stop. Enjoy it. It's probably the last time you'll ever get sick.'

'All perfectly normal, babes. Just your body adjusting,' Andile chips in.

Just my immune system kicking into overdrive to war with the nanotech invasion. But it's only temporary. People adapt. Evolve. It's all in the manual, although I haven't read all the fineline. Who does?

'I'll see you here for a check-up next week.' Dr. Precious ejects the silver capsule from the back of the autosyringe and slots it carefully back into the case with the other empty shells. Can't leave that stuff lying around. Light catches the gleaming shells, the reflection of Dr. Precious stretched thin like a Giacometti sculpture.

I'm already planning a timelapse, to capture the change. Only the top three layers of the epidermis, Andile was at pains to point out, a negligible inconvenience to carry with you for a lifetime.

If I could embed a camera inside my body, I would. But all I can do is document the cells mutating on the inside of my wrist, the pattern developing, fading up like an oldschool Polaroid as the nano spreads through my system.

My skin is already starting to itch.

Toby

Her timing is perfect, as always. My motherbitch manages to call bang in the middle of my morning streamcast. On an everyday, this wouldn't bug me – motherbitch is one of the favourite recurring characters on my cast, according to my Comments section, but I'm supposed to be hooking up with Tendeka to plot our criminal adventure, so it's inconvenient deluxe.

'You were late fifteen minutes ago, my darling,' she says by way of greeting and it's true, I've forgotten that she's scheduled one of our 'we have to talks' over a civilised brunch, but with the amount of sugar I'm doing, she's lucky I can remember the colour of my eyes without a mirror. I've *told* her to upload appointments to my phone. Whore.

I smoke some more on the way to the Nova Deli, just to bring me up enough to handle, and switch my BabyStrange, currently displaying images from the gore folder, to record. You'd be amazed at what compelling viewing even the most arb of daily interactions can make – or then, if you're watching this, maybe you already know.

I take a shortcut through Little Angola, which I only realise is a terrible mistake when I'm hit a double blow by the smell of assorted loxion delicacies and the chatter of warez in the overbridge tunnel market.

The warez are outmode. It's not just that they're cheap useless, cos who really needs a tube of bondglue or six, except for the street kids, and there are better highs for less, but cos they're all fucking chipped. This is non-reg, but the cops have better shit to worry about, especially when it doesn't impact the corporati.

The whole audio chipping thing was outlawed almost as soon as it hit. I mean, it was bigtime initially, with cereal boxes and toys and freeware and fucking appliances all chirping their own self-importance, jingles, promos, sound-effects, celeb endorsements, so that house spouses had to wear ear blanks to get through the supermarket. It was only a matter of time before the multinationals made it illegal, or specialised use only, but then notions of illegal don't extend to the developing. Most of the stuff now comes down from Asia or central

Africa, so the chips in here aren't even speaking
English or Xhosa or any of the other eleven na-
tionals; it's all Cantonese and Portuguese and
Kinyarwanda.

It's ugly, but the effect, even cumulatively, is
nowhere near as annoying as the relentless
twitter of the motherbitch. I pause at a stall selling plastic belts and cellphone covers and Fong
Kong sunglasses to get her a talking Hello Kitty
taser that yelps for 'help' incessantly in five different languages. The vendor tries to sell me
one from under the table, rather than the
squawking sample that got my attention. Once
they're activated, he says, you can't turn the
damn things off. Better take a new one, still in
the box. But I tell him it's absolutely perfect and
transfer the full asking to his phone, not even
bothering to haggle. He can't even keep up the
pretence of being offended. Cash talks, baby.

Between the short cut, dodging the herd of
cyclists who try to run me down on the prome-
nade, and stopping to check out the surf –
negligible; the sea stretching between Mouille
Point and Robben Island looks greasy and flac-
cid, but that doesn't mean it won't be cooking
on the corporate beaches – I'm already an hour
late.

I slide into the motherbitch's usual booth at
Nova Deli by the window, playing it charming,

even patting that disgusting mutacute she insists on carrying around with her, draped off her neck like an albino tiger slothmonkey scarf. It bares its neat little teeth at me, the only thing at this table brave enough to express how it really feels.

'Oh Pretzel, stop that.' Motherbitch taps it on its nose and it starts making these grovelling, warbling, purring sounds. I wish she could have settled on one species or two max. These multiple mash-up jobs make me queasy.

She is sucking on a nutradiet. She blows a punctuation mark of vitamin-enriched smoke in my direction. 'Did you call the Sunshine Clinic?'

'Oh, hey, I'm fine thanks, mom. Just great. Thanks for asking. Got a regular DJ gig now, Thursday nights at Replica. Met a cute girl. Several, actually. Nothing serious, no grandkidlets on the way or anything, sorry to say. Swivel's cool, bit disarrayed, but it just hasn't been the same since you stopped paying for my cleaning service. All ordinary, you know. Oh, and you'll be happy to know my ratings are up. Who said I have no ambition? Well, apart from you, obviously, but in light of this, I really think you're going to have to reconsider. I'm streamcasting live now, by the way. So if you have anything particularly entertaining to say, go right ahead.

This is a good time. And how is Tyrone? Or was it Wynand? I do struggle to keep track. Which reminds me, I bought you this. In case, you know, you need to put one of them in his place.'

I slide the Hello Kitty taser across the table towards her. It's still bleating. 'That's "help" in like five different languages, right there.'

The waiter materialises with two rooibos lattes, like I even drink that herbal shit. While he's fussing with the coffees, motherbitch plucks up the cartoon cat canister in her napkin and drops it neatly onto the waiter's tray, with the same cool efficiency she used to dispose of the rain spiders that probably still hang out in the kitchen.

'Your father and I have been talking.'

'That's a first time.'

'We've managed to agree on your problem.'

'Can I have one?' I ask, reaching for the pack of nutradiets.

'No, Tobias, honestly. They're calibrated for my bio-rhythms exactly. They'd just make you sick.' Which is a lie straight up, although of course they are personalised for her nutritional requirements – she pays extra for that – but at least we're communicating now.

'So what's the problem?' I say, taking one anyway, igniting it with a light tap on the table.

'Oh my darling.'

'No, seriously.' I take a drag and the micro-
nutrients kick up the sugar by 100 degrees. I am
intensely interested, blisteringly smart, devastatingly witty.

'Your habit.'

'Which one?'

'Toby, please. You make me terribly tired. It's
unconscionable. We've decided.'

'And that's it?'

'Well, of course you have a choice. If you'd
bothered to phone Sunshine… It's just that we
won't be enabling you anymore. We've already
advised the trustees.'

I take another drag of the nutradiet. I think
it's the zinc that does it, that complements the
sugar, I mean. You have to watch it though, because vitamin C will kill a buzz dead.

'Oh for god's sake. You're on something now,
aren't you?'

I lean back, put my feet on the table to a jangle of cutlery and crockery, cos there's not really
space for it. If I can get her to cry, points go to
me and everything else is annulled.

'So, how is father? Still fucking his boss?
What's her name again?'

But she just looks at me.

'Really, darling.' Even the squashy-faced mar-
supial is the image of bored contempt, digging
under its armpit with its perfect little teeth.

Chalk this one to her.

By the time I get to Stones, my mood has not improved. The pool bar is not, shockingly, exactly jamming at eleven a.m. on a Sunday, even though it's one of the few places in Long Street that's still general access. No corporati pass or proof of income required, and the cams don't work too well. Which goes a way to explaining the general dinginess and a clientele that leans towards the undesirable side of the LSM spectrum – and also qualifies it as the ideal venue to plot Tendeka's next outrageous, which he's being generous enough to allow me to guest on.

It's a mutual beneficial. I score some quality vid that'll push up my streamcast's rankings, and he gets his exploits recorded for posterity, faces blanked out, of course. Not like those fucking idiot thug-lifers in Baltimore who were IDed and arrested by their uploads, in high-def. Tendeka and Ash are in the middle of a game, but when he sees me, he sets down the cue and crams me into a back-slapping hug of camaraderie, or maybe that should be comrade-ery for the Struggle revivalist over here. He's such a wannabe, so born fifty years too late. His dreads shoved up against my cheek smell of too much ZamBuk wax.

'Toby! We thought you weren't coming.'

'What, and miss all this?' I gesture at the near-empty pool hall, inhabited only by Tendeka and his go-everywhere accessory, Ashraf, a couple of oldtimers wedged in the corner, sinking their fifth beers already and not even lunch time, and the bartender, of course, who is tuned out to the soccer. The irony is lost on Tendeka.

'Can you tone down the coat? We don't want to draw too much attention,' he says, conspiracy quiet, as if he's telling me I have bad breath. Can I tell you how crazy it is that the visuals are freaking him out when they didn't make the motherbitch so much as flinch?

My BabyStrange is set to screensaver mode, so it clicks into a new image every two minutes. Here's a random sampling to give you an idea of what's displaying on the smartfabric that is so bothering Ten: close-ups of especially revolting fungal skin infections, Eighteenth Century dissection diagrams and, for a taste of local flavour, a row of smileys – that's sheep's heads for the uninitiated – lips peeled back to reveal grins bared in anticipation of the pot.

'No, see, Ten, that's where you're wrong,' I explain. 'It's camouflage, hiding in clear sight. By drawing loads of attention, I actually avert it.'

'You're not going to turn it off?'

'That's right.'

'Uh-huh,' he says, flat. And just in time, Ashraf swoops into the rescue, reprising once again his role as long-suffering BF and keeper of the peace. Mister fucking UN.

'We've got a lot to get through, Ten. C'mon,' he says, nudging him back to the table.

Tendeka goes grudgingly. Cos the fact is, kids, they need me. Can't do it without me. Security on the adboards is tighter than a nun's twat unless you've got a connection. Of course, I still have to *convince* my connection, but they don't need to know that sweet Lerato isn't on board yet.

Ten scoops up the balls in the plastic triangle with a neat click-clack and picks out four to map out the plan. 'He's the eightball, naturally, I'm solid orange, the blue stripe is some polit-ec student they've got tagging along, a girl apparently, who better be cute, and Ashraf as the white ball to counterbalance.

There's lots of actiony stuff, leaping about on rooftops and crawling under fences and avoiding cameras and Aito patrols. I stop paying attention five minutes in. I think we've just got to the part where we have to run across six lanes of highway, judging by the way Tendeka has the balls leaping over the cue laid across the table, when this incredible girl walks in, all juiced to kill, to give focus to my distraction.

Even by the competitive standards of Long Street, being this city's hipster capital and all, this girl is styling, with her hair streaked in fat chunks of copper and chocolate, dirty cream boots and a charcoal cowl-neck dress over jeans, overlong sleeves dangling over her knuckles – this despite the soaring Celsius outside. I'm so preoccupied figuring out if I actually know her or just from the scene that I miss what she says.

'Sorry, what?'

'Do you mind?' she says again, already reaching into her back pocket for her phone, hung skate-rat off a silver chain from her belt, to log twenty rand to the table to get *tata machance* on the next game. 'I mean, if you're not busy?'

Ten scowls, but what's he gonna say? Fuck off, we're planning the insurrection? That's the problem with pool halls: they're not exactly discreet. And who else is she going to play? The geezer alcoholics in the corner?

Besides, Tendeka's already chalking his cue, just in case you thought anyone else was going to game-on. I'd point out that a real general would let one of the footsoldiers take care of this little nuisance – like me, for example, cos I could think of some ways. But his logic's going to be to get rid of her as quick as possible, and the truth is, kids, he's the most qualified.

Ten could wax us all six-love, baby, with one arm amputated. He's that guy who carries his own cue around, the kind that snaps together like a sniper rifle in a war movie. He's also that guy who's not going to cut a rookie any slack.

It's too entertaining to pass up. Surreptitiously I hit the record button on my cuff as I hand over the stick to the girl.

'Your massacre, kid.' But as she takes it from me, her sleeve slips back and I catch a glimpse of a faint glow. I knew something was up. Long sleeves in the height of the heat don't cut it. I've seen enough light tatts on the little trendies in the clubs to know, even from a glance, that this here is the coke. The real thing. And when I twig that I saw her a week ago in the eastern seaboard executive zone, which is strictly corporati only, it all clicks into place.

It's the first time I've seen it. First time anyone I know has seen it. It's a riff on the standard dark marketing shit. Hand out free stuff to the cool kids and hope everyone else is paying attention so they'll run out and buy it. Ordinarily, this would be out of my interest field. My streamcast is called Diary of Cunt, not Diary of Ad-wank. Your weekly round-up of Toby's astounding life: good drugs, good music, sexploits with exceptionally beautiful girls, regular skirmishes with the motherbitch, and, most

recently, some para-criminal counter-culture
activities compliments of Mr. Steve Biko-
wannabe over here with the pool cue.

588,430 unique hits daily, as of this morning's counter. It's not shabby, but let's just say
it's not BoingBoing. Or the baby animal cast.
Or even that flavour of the viral week, that MIT
girl who builds robots and casts pornos of them
screwing her.

But that could all be set to change.

There's been lots of big talk about this on the
rumour blogs, but no images. It's so new on the
scene, how could there be? Which means an
exclusive. Bigtime traffic. Hits galore. Maybe
even syndication.

It's a close one. Make no mistake, she's playing catch-up, but the girl has some skills. Forget
whatever you picked up in the conspiracy forums on the fringe, it's not comic-book
superpower shit. It helps you focus, like that
zone thing athletes get into. Faster, slicker, more
productive.

It's beautiful to see it kick in. Someone who
wasn't paying close attention, someone without my consummate experience, might not
even have registered. But I am and I do. It's a
textbook special. The breath catches in her
throat as it hits, her shoulderblades tightening
like she's been punched in the chest, and then

it starts to fray away into her system and she goes all loose.

I am overwhelmed with jealousy. Even occasional viewers will know I'm a waster – in more ways than solo, if you were to ask my mother-bitch. But I'm functional skeef. It's not like I'm the kind of junkie freak sporting a tongue-piercing applijack. But I have notched up most of the pharmacologicals. Supersmack, kitty, halo, you name it. I can ID the flavour of the bliss by the rush. But in truth, it's all cheap shit. Black-market. Ill legit. Not like this girl's high.

And maybe Ten catches a snatch of this, something in her face that reveals that all is not exactly halaal, cos he catches her by the arm.

'Hey. Are you okay?'

She snaps to attention, all hyped-up reflexes. 'Yeah. Good, thanks. Do you mind if I take this shot?'

She folds over her cue, Bruce Lee in the intensity of her focus. She slides the cue back over her knuckles, once, twice, and then pops the white so hard it leapfrogs the eightball snookering her path and whacks her last remaining ball into the pocket. The white dives right in after it, so it's not quite the perfect shot. And who's to say the girl wasn't capable of doing it on her own, sans a sweet little neural turbo-boost?

But even Ten's noticed that she's not playing straight. Her pupils are waxed full moon. He snags her sleeve as she moves to give him room to play his shot.

'You tweaked?'

'What? No. And even if I was, how would that be anything to do with you?' There's just enough of a catch of self-defence in her voice to spur him on, evangelical recovering that he is.

'Hey listen, you want to get off that shit. You think I don't know the signs? I've been there. I can help you.'

'Would you give it a break? Jeez. I'm not on drugs.'

And now, with all this fast-escalating tension, we are starting to draw attention. The bartender snipes, 'Keep it cool, peeps.' Not that he has any intention of coming round from behind the bar.

Ashraf steps in. 'It's not important, Tendeka, just leave it.'

'Yeah, back off, okay? I don't even know you.' But Tendeka is still holding her wrist as she twists away, and her sleeve slides up, exposing the green fluorescent.

'What is *that*?' Tendeka snaps. Now that he's spotted it, he won't let go. 'What the *fuck* is that?' He yanks up her sleeve to expose her wrist, and one thing is clear – this is no rinkadink glowshow. None of the signature goosebumps of an LED implant blinking through the ink of a conventional light tattoo. Cos this isn't sub-dermal. This is her skin. The double swirl of the Ghost logo in mint and silver shines luminously from cells designer-spliced by the nanotech she's signed up for.

'Get off!' She shoves him away, a little too hard, maybe inspired by the nano-enhanced hormone soup sloshing around in her head, but hard enough so that Ten staggers back and catches the edge of his beer on the corner of the table. He's a big boy, heavy enough to break a glass easy, and a snick of it jams into his palm. Spilt beer and fat glops of blood spatter the floorboards.

'You fucking sell-out!'

She steps to the side, putting the pool table between them. How could she have known he would take this so seriously?

'Do you know what that shit even does? You're a fucking lab rat. A corporate bitchmonkey! You make me sick!' Tendeka vaults over the table towards her. She grabs the cue and swipes it at him, more warning than weapon. I'd intervene, but where's the fun in that?

With all the shouting, no one notices the bartender reaching under the counter to activate the panic button, or barely more than a minute later, the tromp of big police boots and padded paws mounting the stairs at pace.

The girl turns her head to the door, almost as if she's anticipating it, as the cop and the Aito come ploughing into the room. She drops the cue and raises her hands in a neat physical dissociation from the scene. The cue rolls scuddering across the floorboards and comes to a stop by the stairs, where the dog sniffs at it once, and dismisses it with a whuff.

'Oh, and is this your private fucking sponsorbaby security force?' Tendeka says, whirling on the cop, who is already aiming his scanner at him. He couldn't be more off. The poor schmuck is obviously just a garden-variety citicop, unlucky enough to draw the Long Street patrol.

'Come to protect the technology? Cos that's all you are, baby. A freakshow prototype.'

The Aito barks in warning, echoed by a bleep from Ten's cellphone as the cop isolates his SIM from all the others in the room with the scanner.

'Yeah, fuck off! Don't you fucking log a warning on me. I have the constitutional right to express my fucking opinion. Ever heard of fucking freedom of expres–'

The cop doesn't bother to register a second warning. He goes straight for the defuser. Higher voltage than necessary, but when did the cops ever play nice? Tendeka drops straight away, jerking epileptic and setting off the damn dog with excited yipping. I'm reckoning that's 170 to 180 volts right there. Anything over 200 requires extra paperwork to justify the use of potentially lethal force, but that doesn't mean the cops don't push the limits.

Some wasters I know set off their own phone's defuser, on low settings for those dark and hectic beats. Even rhythm can be induced, kids. But it's not easy. You have to hack the hardware, and if you don't know what you're doing, it'll crisp you KFC. Or worse. It's a disconnect offence to tamper with a defuser. You can't play nice by society's rules? Then you don't get to play at all. No phone. No service. No life.

Tendeka judders and spasms at the cop's feet, his phone seething and crackling, while the damn dog yelps an over-excited accompaniment, like it's really getting off on this. Not even Ash dares to intervene. Eventually, the citiprick takes mercy and hits endcall, and it's all done for the day, baby.

'Anybody else?' he asks, snapping his fingers at the modified dog, so that it shuts up instantly. Ten manages to raise himself to his knees, pale and heaving for breath.

'How about you? You want some more, boy?'

Ten shakes his head breathing heavy and a little too desperate. Ashraf kneels next to him and

slowly, very obviously, hands him his pump.
Ten takes a gulping greedy hit. Really, he should
have his asthma registered on his SIM. Medical
pre-conditions mean they have to go easier on
you.

'Yeah, thought so. Just remember, I've
logged your SIM. You even think about causing any more shit, it's disconnect, china.' The
citicop steps neatly out of the way as a horde
of VIMbots scoot out from under the bar,
scrambling to sop up the blood and glass and
spilled liquor.

'And here I was so hoping for a quiet day.' He
tucks his scanner into his belt and rattles his
chem mace cheerfully at the bartender. 'You let
me know if this guy gives you any more trouble. I'll be happy to sic /379 here on him.' The
bartender grunts and raises a hand. Playing it
cool, as if he weren't the guy who 911-ed the
citiprick in the first place. The cop whistles, two
notes, and the Aito snaps to attention and pads
out down the stairs after him.

Ashraf hefts Tendeka to his feet, cursing soft
and furious in between wheezing breaths as his
asthma meds kicks in. Game over. Please upload
more currency. The oldtimers in the corner turn
away pointedly.

The girl looks on, wan and shocked. It's the
perfect opening.

'I don't know about you,' I say, 'but I need a drink.'

'Aren't you with that guy?' She turns to me, incredulous.

'Nope. I mean, I know him, but you know, we're not tight or anything.'

Ashraf gives me a poisonous look over his shoulder as he levers Ten towards the stairs. But c'mon, he's got Tendeka in hand, and I'm not going to get dragged into his ridiculous mess. Not when there are more interesting messes to be involved in.

'Sorry. He's like this hardcore activist or something. Let me buy you a drink. Make up for it. I'm sure he'd offer himself, but, well…' But well, he's a little indisposed. A little crisped. A little out the door.

I steer her towards the bar, easy in her condition. She's looking almost as strung out as Ten.

'Cause any more *shit* like that, girl, and I'll call in a crisp on you too,' warns the bartender.

'Hey, easy now. Everything's sony. Just want a drink. You do serve drinks? Ghost for her, and same for me, shot of vodka on the side. I'm Toby, by the way.'

'Kendra.'

The bartender sets two cans down in front of us. Kendra doesn't even wait for the glass, just cracks it open and practically downs it, with a neat little shudder, as if she's hitting the hard stuff.

'You don't mind if I mix mine? I don't think I'm scoring the same benefits.'

'Do what you like.'

I tip the vodka into my glass and fill up with Ghost. It comes out of the can the same pale shade of green as her eyes. I wonder if they were always that colour or if that's another side-effect of the tech. I lean on the bar and just spit it out. Coming on candid tends to surprise people into surprising answers. 'Can I see?'

She looks at me, scoping my motives, and then slides up her sleeve and turns her arm over to reveal the glow on her wrist.

'Nice. Did it hurt?'

'Funny you should ask.' The girl is flying now, or drowning, in all the opiate happinesses the body can generate: endorphins, serotonin, dopamine, the Ghost binding with the aminos. Tiny biomachines humming at work in her veins. Voluntary addiction with benefits. All free if you qualify for the sponsor program. Apply now, kids, while stocks last. You'll never afford this high on your own change.

'Why do you do that?' she asks, nodding at my BabyStrange, which is back in display mode, with a new addition to the gallery of a close-up of a blood splat on green pool-table felt. 'It's really gross.'

'Would you rather I displayed logos?' I tap the cufflink with my thumb, zoom in on the can of Ghost, snap it, and wallpaper it solid over the smartfabric.

She laughs in a brittle, self-conscious way, but the conversation flows easier after that. She's a photographer, and she uploads a flyer for a group show at Propeller to my phone. I trade her an invite to the Replica Insurrection party. Provided I don't get too fucked, I might even DJ. But I hold back on the plus one. I'd prefer her to rock up solo mission. She tells me about a set of photographs she took in the loos there, photographing streaks of light under the doors, of all the things to document in club culture.

She's annoyed at the suggestion. 'I specifically didn't want to photograph the usual club crap. It was about decontextualising the space.'

'Maybe you could come down and decontextualise my space sometime,' I say, and she rolls her eyes, but it's the good kind of rolling.

Those of you who have been paying close attention may have noticed that I haven't mentioned my streamcast. This is not an accidental omission, kids.

Down the other side of the bar, one of the oldtimers orders a Ghost. Just to see. Cos maybe, just maybe, it's in the secret ingredients, right?

'I feel like everyone's watching me,' she confesses.

'Course they are. You're splinter-new, novelty deluxe. And the burning question on everyone's lips is, what does it feel like?'

'Like taking drugs?'

'That's probably the most generic description I've ever heard. I'm not buying that.'

'Okay, okay.' She laughs, openly, warmly, very hot. 'I'm just... improved. It's like, everything's running better, like I've had a tune-up, you know? The world seems sharper. Or fiercer. As if someone's pulled the focus. Like in photography, hyper-realism?' She catches my blank look. 'Where everything is intensely real. It's super-defined.'

'Sounds hectic.'

'Yeah. Although, you know, I'm not entirely convinced I'm not imagining it.'

'What?'

'Everything. All of it. That it's some dumb psychology trip they've got us on, to get us to drink the stuff. And all the rest of you.'

'Hey, don't knock the product. It's not bad, although they could tone down the lime. You should speak to them about adding some flavour variants, if you're gonna be drinking it forever.'

'Yeah.'

'And you seemed to handle Tendeka pretty
well.' I wave away her concerns, cut her off before she can launch into an apology, as if she
was the one in the wrong. 'No, don't worry
about it, he had it coming. He can be a right
sanctimonious dick. And besides, that game was
fucking tight.'

And besides, it's apparent to sundry all that
she's rushing off her face. It's definitely physical.

'But that's the thing. I'm pretty sharp at pool.
Maybe not that sharp, and it's been a while, but
I reckon I could have taken him on a good day.
And maybe this just happened to be… Oh, don't
look so sceptical. I used to play league in Dur-
ban.'

'Chill, sweet K. I believe you.' And to prove
it, I lean forward and pull into her.

Initially, she kisses me back. But then she
flinches away from me, total panic stations. 'I'm
sorry…'

'Don't be sorry.'

'No, I have a boyfriend. I, uh, I can't. Okay?
I'm flattered and…'

'It's okay. I was trying my luck. Look, I've
backed off. We'll just reset the timer to zero.
Sorry if I freaked you out.'

'It's fine. Thanks for the chat. It's nice getting
to talk, to connect, you know?' She's talking too

fast, already up, slinging her bag over her shoulder.

'Yeah, yeah. Okay. I know.' I'm grinning at her fluster, which only makes her more so.

'And tell your friend, I'm sorry. I didn't mean… He was an asshole, but he didn't deserve that. The cops and–'

'I'll do that. But don't stress it. Like I said, he had it coming.'

'And forget what I said about it being psychological. I talk too much sometimes. It's not… I mean, of course it's genuine makoya.'

'Sure. No worries. And come to Replica next Saturday. That's a free entrance on your phone.'

'Thanks. And Toby?' She pauses in the doorway, but the camera catches me unawares. It's an oldschool design, clunky and cumbersome, but I'm too preoccupied, caught in the flash, to catch the make.

'If you wanted me to model, you only had to ask,' I snip, but she's completely composed now, as if it's the camera rather than the nanotech inside that smoothes out her edges.

'Thanks. I'll see you around.' She winks, which is so cute, it physically hurts. And then she vanishes down the staircase.

Tendeka

INCIDENT REPORT

South African Police Services
FILE SAPS-CITI
430/77
LOG – CTC Public Disruption
Occurrence No: *94-1678*

ACCUSED_____

(surname, first name)   (alias)
Mataboge, Tendeka   **N/A**

(sex)   (DOB)   (Age)
M   **05.06.86**   **32**

(Place of Birth)   (ID number)
HARARE   **8606050112291**

(cell SIM ID)   (prior?)   (criminal registration)
062-699-1359   Y   #2291-1359-470

(residential address)
Last known: 43 subC, Berlin, Khayelitsha, Cape Town, 7948

(height/weight)   (hair)   (eyes)   (complexion)
1.94m/94kg   dreadlocks   brown   dark

(ID status)
Civilian. LSM (Living Standards Measure): 6

(marital status)
Married.
Emmie Chinyaka. Malawi national.
3/8/2018

(identifying marks)
Tattoo on left shoulder, thick black rings or 'bull's-eye' pattern. Black band tattooed on right bicep and wrist.

(occupation)   (employer)
NGOs, charitable   self-employed
fund-raising/events

(biological verification)   (date)   (time)
              N   N/A   N/A

(priors)

- 23/2/2018 – CC 279 (a) Public disruption.
  Participating in unlawful, unlicensed protest
  march.
  Loc: Parliament.
  Defuse. R5000 fine. 24H disconnect.

- 29/12/2017 – CA 415 Defacement of corporate
  property.
  Loc: V&A Mall Christmas display.
  Defuse. 24H disconnect. 16 days corporate
  service.

- 18/7/2017 – CC 279 (a) Public disruption.
  Loc: Vanguard Drive, Langa.
  Defuse.

- 22/11/2013 CTTD 80 unpaid underway fare
  fines. Amount settled in full.

- 4/2/2008 CSP 121 (Juvenile) Possession of
  narcotics with intention to distribute. 150
  grams nitra-amaldrine (street name Bliss).
  Sentenced to eight months in Boys Town
  juvenile facility. Six months probationary
  surveillance.

- 17/10/2006 CVC 3A (Juvenile) Breaking and
  entering.

Loc: 28 Roberta St, Bonteheuwel.
Suspended sentence.

OFFENCE_____

CC 279(a) Public disruption

(offence time)	(offence date)	(location)
11h23	**17/9/2018**	**Stones Pool Hall, 181 Long Street**

(conjoined with)
CC 592 (b) Aggravating behaviour

OFFICER'S NOTES_____

Disruption alert logged 11h20 from Stones' Pool Hall (Premises ID 33CBD-Long181). Officer and Aito /379 responded.

On arrival found subject shouting threats and acting in aggressive manner.

A scan of the subject's SIM ID register revealed that the subject has recent priors including previous public disruptions and a juvenile record.

Subject failed to respond to officer's verbal warning or warnings uploaded to his phone.

Activated a defuse to subject's phone.

Defuse < 200 V. Non-lethal voltage.

Defuse lasted approx 2.5 minutes.

Subject adequately subdued.

Officer left premises without further incident.

Subject's SIM logged on SAPS watch-list for period of twenty-four hours.
Temporary disconnect.

'Sorry, Ten,' Ashraf says, flicking his screen back to show me. The log is already live on SAPS.co.za, and this is what's so truly fucked up, that government inc. thinks this level of transparency automatically rules out repression. If it's all out in the open, it has to be above board.

'But what did you expect?' Ash says, like this is the time to be griefing me.

'Fuck!' He flinches as I slam my foot into a cold-drink can, sending it clattering down the street. At least it's not a Ghost can – that would have been too much. skyward* is going to be seriously pissed.

The worst is confirmed when we get to the entrance to the D-line underway stop on Wale Street and my phone won't scan. Or, rather, it does scan and blocks me outright in response to the police tag on my SIM, to the tremendous amusement of the leisure-class kids overdressed in their ugly expensive clothes. Bastards. Bastards. Bastards. I suck at my palm, which still stings, even if it's stopped bleeding. At least the fucker didn't mace me, else every biogen dog in the city would be trailing me like I was a bitch in heat.

We cruise down Adderley towards the station, past the Grand Parade, and the blaring logos and adboards squatting on the façade of the old library like parasites. And what really grinds me is that it was supposed to be ours for Streets Back. We'd rounded up a bunch of kids from the Castle Street shelter with this plan to do graffiti murals. It was a way of letting them make a mark on the city that usually filters them out like spam. It was all legit. We had the permits and everything, with a small development grant Ash set up, from an Italian org complete with our own Italian liaisons. It all got fucked up, though. The Italians came out to make a documentary of the whole spiel, and then got all pissy when it wasn't happening. Like it's my fault we ran out of money.

First up we had to pay for chatter flyers, because how else are you going to reach illiterate kids who can't read a poster? So the audio chips were crazy expensive, then the freebies we got from the paint company were all reject stock, broken nozzles, dried-out paint, two years past their expiry date. By the time we'd bought our own paint and masks and overalls and food for all the kids who showed up instead of just the ones who worked on the murals, our budget was gone. I tried to tell those Italian amigos that

these kids had been let down so often, the one
thing that would have a real positive impact on
their lives would be an established routine and
adults who stick by their promises. They were
all, like, terribly sorry to hear about our trou-
bles, very understanding, but we have to
understand there are so many other projects
just as worthy, all desperate for cash, and they
have to support the ones that can show sustain-
ability.

I sent the hombres a real nasty email afterwards, telling them exactly what neo-colonial
cocks they were, coming in here, raping our re-
sources and fucking off again. I thought Ash
would appreciate it, but he got in a real mood
about him being the money guy, the business
manager, and I should stick to being the passionate poster boy, and besides, 'hombres' is
Spanish. Whatever. And if he could have handled it, then he should have fucking done it.
Pricks. I hate it when people fake being on the
level, all global village-ing when they're the
ones raking in fat salaries, and we're the ones
living hand-to-mouth with a soccer club and
Emmie's baby on the way.

Now Ash has this big plan all laid out with
some corporate sell-out buddy, who says he can
get the project into his company's CSI program,
no problem. Like getting some big dick to

sponsor the whole thing isn't a total violation of everything we do.

We have no choice but to head up to the taxi rank, cos the minibuses aren't as regulated as the trains. You don't get the corporates taking taxis, putting up with shoving in among twenty-four people packed into a space officially licensed for sixteen, or dealing with the strikes or the gun fights when the taxi wars get too heated. And some of the gamchees are willing to look the other way for a small fee, purely administrative. The trick is to do it out in the open, as if it's a normal transaction. My wallet is locked out along with all the other functions on my phone, so Ashraf transfers five times the going rate to the gamchee manning the taxi at the head of the Khayelitsha line.

We cram in next to a mama with a week's worth of groceries and a two year-old spilling out of her lap and a guy who is too beat down to be gangster – probably just some poor asshole riding the job-hunt bus to nowhere. Not likely he's going to get anything with what's clearly a knife scar striped through his hair above his ear, which pegs him as loxion. Could be worse though, he could be disconnect. He could be living Rural or in Zim, that other suburb of China.

'*Yey! Diskonneksie. Geen moeilikheid nie, ne?*' The gamchee waggles a finger at me. At five times the fare, he knows full well I'm not gonna be any trouble at all.

I feel like shit. I'm still not breathing 100% and the muscle in my eyelid keeps spasming. It's driving me crazy, although Ash says he can't see it.

'That's one of the things I'm talking about. The shit we can't see. The tech was only approved, what, eighteen months ago? How do they know what the long-term effects are going to be? And here they are dishing out defusings like it's a party game. It's like shock therapy, you know, dampening down excitable behaviour, frying our brains, flattening us out, so we're all unquestioning, unresisting obedient model fucking zombie puppydog citizens.'

The mama rearranges the child on her lap uncomfortably, and Ash beckons for me to lower it a decibel. He always gets embarrassed when I talk too loud in public. It's not like anyone can hear me above the driver's bhangra rock blaring from the speakers or our greedy gamchee friend hoping to pick up a couple more fares, screeching 'Kaaaaai-ee-leetsha!' out the window in case there's any uncertainty about our route.

'Ten. If it was about brainwashing, they'd just dose the water supply. Don't you think? Chill out, baby.'

I lower my voice slightly.

'I'm not talking brainwashing. I'm saying it's electroshock lobotomy. Government endorsed. And the whole water supply thing? Please. Too easy to test for. The international enviro agencies would pick that up in a second. Unless they paid them off. I mean, anything's possible. They're all corrupt, all of them.'

Ash is wearing that humouring-me smirk.

'Okay, okay, fine. You're right. Conjecture hurts the cause. Enough with the conspiracy talk. But you know it's true.'

The taxi rockets around Hospital Bend, which used to feature an actual hospital, home to the world's first heart transplant, before it got turned into luxury apartments, past the nice middle-class burbs, Obs and Rosebank and Pinelands and Langa, and into the loxion sprawl proper. Don't be fooled by the cosy apartment blocks lining the highway, it's all Potemkin for the tourists. You just need to go a couple of blocks in to find the real deal, the tin shacks and the old miners' hostels and the converted containers now that the shipping industry has died together with the economy. All the same shit they've been promising to fix since the 1955 Freedom Charter or whatever it was. And despite the border patrols, the sprawl just keeps on spreading. You can't keep all of the Rurals out all of the time.

The taxi pulls over to let us out at the circle at the entrance to Berlin, named like so many of the districts, Kosovo and Barcelona and Joe Slovo and Mandela Tribute Park, for the headline news. We get out by the massive and so very conspicuous SAPS station, and walk the rest of the way back to the club, past the tourist zone, where the rubbernecks come to get their taste of poverty and their photographs with the kiddies, maybe some love muti from the sangoma, or a taste of mqombothi beer shared around in a can between men who are only there to lend the scene authenticity, to earn a little cash to buy a Zamalek, real beer in a real bottle, because no one cares about tradition anymore. The tourists don't venture too deep into the heart of it, which means they're missing out on the drop toilets and spiderwebs of illegal electricity connections in the newest parts of the sprawl, where council hasn't got to yet.

Ash would point out the good stuff they're missing too, the stuff he tried to show our hombre friends, the barbershop strip in Chinatown and jazz at the shebeen and the soccer club and the boxing society and the entrepreneurs hawking minutes on their cell phones (illegally with the new SIM ID laws in place) and the sense of community and how transformation has been real and important. Like it's not a total wank, where people are just as economically fucked as they were before, only now they're sick as well, or, worse, trying to escape being sick and bringing it in with them from the Rural. And that leads to spates of outbreaks all over and crackdowns, just as bad as those bad old days when the police came storming in to quarantine and deport whole neighbourhoods.

Ash takes my hand as we reach the soccer pitch next to the club, really just a scrap of dirt that the community housing committee cleared for development, so uneven that the ball catches on clods and goes wide or random. It's good practice for the kids, Ash says; when they get to play on a real field, they'll have the advantage. We're trying to get it permanently instated, which requires more funding, more waiting, more neo-colonial cocks, no doubt.

He fiddles with the ring on my finger. 'Do you really have to wear that?'

'Don't start with that now, please,' I say.

'But all the time?'

'And what am I gonna do when Home Affairs comes knocking? And interrogates me on why I'm not wearing my wedding ring?'

Ash snorts. 'In light of all the other transgressions? The heady whirlwind of the entire week-long romance before you got married? Or that she lives in a totally different part of the

city? Or, you know, that minor detail about you
not being female-inclined? I'm just saying.'

'Then you don't need to be uptight about it.
Jesus, Ash. She's a fucking refugee. Have some
compassion.'

The club smells decidedly funky, like too
many sweaty kids have simply dumped their
gear post-game in a pile, which turns out to be
exactly the case. Ash starts plucking up the
shirts and pants to take to the laundry vat just
down the way. The place is looking more run-
down than usual, the Kaiser Chiefs poster
curling at the edges from the damp seeping
through from the DIY-rigged shower next door.
It's been like that for eight months already.
We've applied for additional funding to get a
real one, after the uniforms, after we get Streets
Back back on schedule.

I go into our room to find Zuko playing video
games on my machine, when he knows full well
it's only available for homework, and besides,
I'm supposed to be meeting skyward* online.

'Uh-uh, bro. Off. On the pitch. You can round
up some of your playmates and practise for a
couple of hours.'

'What about the thing?' Zukes asks, because
he's tagging along tonight. Ashraf doesn't like
me to involve him in the extra-mural, being a
minor, but between the soccer and our 'special

projects', I keep him distracted, off the streets, out of the kind of trouble I got into at his age.

'Don't sweat it,' I tell him. 'We got plenty time. We're only leaving here at nine-thirty. So hit the field already.'

'What?' Ashraf freezes mid-scoop, sweaty crumpled shirts dangling from his arms. 'We're not still going?'

'Chill, baby. Toby's got a friend who is going to sort it one time. I'm not going to let a disconnect stop me. It'll be smooth sailing. Promise.'

'After that stunt at Stones, you're still counting on Toby?' Ashraf is about to get majorly wound up, but then he slices his eyes meaningfully in Zuko's direction. 'I'm gonna do the laundry. We can talk later,' he says.

But it's good for the kid to know what's on the level and in the open. You can't hide shit behind closed doors.

It's better that Ashraf is off to do the laundry. He takes it as a personal affront that I spend so much time in Pluslife. 'Our life not good enough for you?'

But before skyward*, we were Disney channel, strictly kid's stuff. We gotta step it up if we want to be taken seriously. I plug in the headphones, ignoring the huffiness in the background as Ash slams the door behind him, connect to the Plus server and I'm gone.

Skyward* is waiting for me in Monomotapa, which is what I call my house in Avalon. With 59.3 million registered users, it's one of world's favourite virtual escapes, which makes it easier to blend in unnoticed.

Despite the Euro-traditional name, Avalon is Asia-centric, so the game world is six to eight hours ahead and more than half the population don't speak English, which suits me perfectly. What's the point of escaping to Plus if the world is too close to the one you just left? And besides, you can make an okay living, earning Avalon guinees (guineveres, current exchange G7.26 to the ZAR) teaching other residents English.

skyward*'s avatar is looking uglier than usual, a stubby obese woman with a lumpy bald head and features on the wrong side of a mix of Asian and black. He says it's so people underestimate him, because even in game space everyone wants to be skinny and beautiful. I couldn't be bothered with the customising, I just uploaded a photograph and skinned it direct to my avatar. It's more honest.

I spent more time on doing up my place. It's pretty humble, designed to be bio-friendly, all recyclable materials, solar panels on the ceiling, a wind farm in the garden. Not that you need to generate energy in-world, but it's the principle. It's a shining example to throw into contrast the kind of excesses the neighbourhood attracts, which is why I chose this location specifically.

It's a recreation of the LA hills, which pulls in celeb wannabes by the dumpload, all avatared to resemble their current favourites, living or deceased, the Cary Grants and Tupacs and Gwyneths and Engelica Ks. The fankids go totally overboard, doing all this research online, re-creating every detail, right down to the brand of soy milk their celebrity keeps in the fridge or the mosaic tiling in the bathroom or the guest lists for their parties. Sometimes there's more than one celeb clone in the neighbourhood, and then they get into this bullshit competitive crap about who's keeping it more real. It's a symptom of everything that's wrong with our culture.

I click the conversation window, and immediately, skyward* throws up a personal firewall that locks us into private chat.

>>skyward*: hey.

>> 10: Sup in the Dam, my man? Listen, I'm thinking of calling it off, I got watchlisted today.

>> skyward*: you're gonna have to be more careful. come on, we should take a walk.

>>10: Yeah. Okay.

It's dead quiet this time, past midnight in Japan, so only the most devout of players are online, and I don't know why skyward* is antsy about eavesdroppers, especially in my home. But I'm not gonna take issue if he wants to play it noir. Avalon LA lends itself to that. We step outside my domicile and walk down the driveway into the night, which is far brighter than realworld, every star visible, every orbit hotel and satellite.

We set off into the wilderness around the apartments, modelled on an idealised movie versioning of Mulholland Drive, so no gated communities, no Mexican labour riots, and there are even virtual coyotes, although I have yet to see one. Some of them are people too, playing out an entirely different kind of alternalife, which I can relate to far more than the celeb clones.

We head up towards a hill, the one furthest from the civilisation, which sometimes means the pixels drop off the page. Gamespace maintenance doesn't pay that much attention to the uninhabited areas, not in a freeworld, anyhow. If we were on premium subscription base, we might have justification to complain.

skyward* picks up the conversation only when we reach the top, looking down on the lights glittering in the dark. There are several parties happening in the valley tonight, no doubt careful re-creations of the real deal, thumping bass drifting up. I pull up my private settings, toggle the ambient audio to lock out the human-generated, so the incessant doefdoef vanishes immediately, leaving us with the sound of crickets and wind in the grass. Not that the grass is actually stirring – too much render time for my connection speed to handle.

There's a flickering on the horizon, and at first I think it's some bug in the software, but as it spreads, multi-coloured, I figure that someone has hacked the sky. It's doing a northern lights thing. And that's the beauty of Pluslife. That here you can actually have an influence on the world.

>> skyward*: i'll be straight with you. calling it off is not an option.
>> 10: It's not a cancel. It's a raincheck.
>> skyward*: it's critical we go ahead.
>> 10: Hey, man. I got crisped and marked once already today. I'm down for twenty-four hours as it is. And I can't do fucking anything. I'm impotent here.
>> skyward*: think of it as a test. prove to me that you're NOT impotent. that you can get around. how am I going to trust you with bigger ops if you can't handle a minor setback? you do still want in on the heavy

impact stuff, don't you, 10? stop splashing around in the kiddie pool.

>> 10: Don't hardball me. This is serious shit. If I get picked up in criminal activity during a watch period, that's a fucking disconnect offence!!!!!! It's easy for you to kick back in fucking Amsterdam and be telling me I have to risk a disconnect in Cape Town.

>> skyward*: you're right. it is serious shit. either you can handle, or you're just playing. i don't have time for dabbler wannabes.

>> 10: ...

>> skyward*: well?

I watch the northern lights flickering above our avatars, the digital representation of myself and a dumpy woman who might or might not look anything like skyward*. The sky loops in fractals of colour, pale-blue fire washing into acid green and purple like tie-dye. Just lines of code, really. Some bored programmer, a kid with extra time to waste. No different from the wannabes re-creating some rock star's mansion. It's pretty. But empty. Just a distraction.

>>10: Okay.

Lerato

Gaborone has all the soul and personality of a strip mall, or maybe the teenage blank-heads who hang out in strip malls all desperately trying to conform. It feels like a shabby wannabe cousin of Jozi – trying too hard, too much hair gel.

This must be what Americans go through, the sour disappointment, expecting to encounter the exotic when it's all the same homogeneous crap the world over. Only it's Mugg & Bean rather than McDonald's. And this is what we are striving for? Give me Lagos any day, screw the crush and the dirt and the traffic. It's better than that blandly innocuous dust-pit.

Did I mention the dust? I arrived with a minor chest infection, but it's like breathing silt; the air is thick with it. And it's stinking, sticky humid. Two days in, negotiations are fraught, Mpho is on the verge of a breakdown from the tension, which makes me wonder why I even need a design architect along if he can't take the pace, and I'm getting uncontrollable coughing fits for ten minutes straight. I had to excuse myself from the Bula Metalo meeting. Khan-Ross sent his PA to come see if I was okay.

The whole thing was hideous. The city. The coughing. Mpho getting all clingy. The problem. It took us four working days to resolve it, and it all came down to the technicalities. My department. Pure fluke that the channel code our push ads were coming in on just happened to be identical to within a digit of the Botswana police authority's defuse signals. Sorting out the code was simple: it was the PR that was a total nightmare, not helped by the fact that Mpho has the EQ of a gecko. Sweet, but not exactly socially adept. He hasn't caught on, for example, that our little sexual sojourn was a one-time limited offer, valid for this particular business trip only – and only then because there's fuck-all else to do in Gaborone except fuck.

Mpho's about as good in bed as he is a systems designer. Same technique even – mechanical as a piston shaft and unwavering from whatever approach worked last time. And it'll work this time too, if only because he'll eventually wear you down.

It meant I had to do a shit load of managing in both scenarios, especially with Bula Metalo. Let's face it, I can get myself off, but soothing feathers that weren't so much ruffled as plucked (because Mercedes is a major Bula Metalo client, and they were not pleased that their customers were being electrocuted by their advertising) took a lot more time and effort.

So eventually, it was all sorted, and we're on our way home, flying deluxe economy, which is one more reason I have to get a new job, but I'm still coughing like I'm about to hack up a lung, and this fat chick across the aisle keeps giving me these dirty looks, and I know exactly what the paranoid wench is thinking. Don't think I didn't notice her call over the flight attendant, the fervent whispering.

It's no surprise then when Customs pulls me aside at OR Tambo International, ready to slam me into quarantine with the rest of the medical refugees in the camps converted from hangars. Which is not great, considering I have a sort-of illegal (in the sense of sort-of dead or sort-of pregnant) cellphone nestled in the lining of my suitcase. A chipped one – defuser-free. Needless to say, Mpho is completely ignorant of this, and manages to make the situation worse by working himself into a state of outrage on my behalf.

I'm not concerned. A dry cough isn't exactly a typical symptom, but I am not in the mood to play coy with Customs, even if they should be commended for being so vigilant. I have my trump card. Why take the path of least resistance when you can simply eliminate it?

When the uniform at the counter asks me for my immune status, I snap, 'I think you'll find my company does regular, Health-Dept approved screenings,' and slap down my Communique exec ID, which has the intended effect. Which is that they back the fuck off and fast-track me into the priority queue, the Customs guy apologising all the way. 'We're so sorry, Ms. Mazwai, if we'd known, it's just the risk, and there's been an outbreak in Tanzania; they've closed down Dar es Saalam...' Like I care.

'It's so boring,' I tell Mpho, who agrees absolutely with whatever I say. 'You'd think they could just formalise the process and issue us with corporate passports. Or segregate the flights, like they do on the underway. How much is that to ask, really?'

Two hours and seventeen very mellow minutes later, thanks to a combo of Dormor and vodka served on the connecting flight, we arrive home courtesy of the corporate underway door-to-door. Mpho tries to grope me in the lift, a clumsy invitation to spend the night in his apartment, but I'm too exhausted to break it off or even avoid breaking it off with a mercy fuck. Besides, my apartment has a better view. It gives me obscene satisfaction that I'm one floor above him in the Communique residence, even if his is a single pad.

The door opens to my SIM ID and total cacophony. Jane twitches guiltily. home™ is in rebellion, the system flopping between settings like a dying fish, desperately trying to accommodate all our personal pre-programming at once. The stereo is genre-blending, overlaying the banal pop she likes onto the frantica dub I got compliments of Toby, bass lines colliding with the alarm.

I can't say it's not interesting, but it's wrecking the effects of the Dormor, especially with the lights strobing, caught between the sheerday blue I prefer and the warm orange plush Jane's convinced she likes after she read some colour-therapy article in the pushmags, and plunging sporadically into darkness as some kind of compromise.

Jane is the kind of desperately depressing unattractive that would be borderline pretty, if only her nose didn't resemble a ski-jump or her jaw weren't so pointy or her hair wasn't such a stringy orange, just for example. Nor, sadly, is she the kind of girl whose personality makes up for her physical limitations. As far as I've paid attention, Jane's tastes seem to be a pastiche lifted from pushmag articles, TV makeover shows and social networking recommendations that keeps her comfily secure within her own genre.

Oh, and did I mention she's in Accounts? And let's face it, at thirty-four, way too old to be stuck in middle management. Catch me still hanging around as executive programmer eight years from now.

Infuriatingly, Jane hits the off switch on the remote.

'Oh nice, Jane. Give me that. How am I supposed to restore the settings if it's off?' I turn it back on and click onto the menu. 'Christ on ice. What have you *done*? Pass me the keyboard.'

'I'm sorry. I was only trying to record *Ángeles de la Calle*,' which is the soap Jane is happily addicted to, a remake of a 1951 Mexican telenovela, only sexified, modernised, stripped of context and colour. A bit like Gaborone. A real bleach job. And particularly perverse, considering you can stream the original on the Retro channel. Okay, so it's unwatchable, unless you're a total fanboy or an academic, or alternatively, stoned with the subtitles turned off.

'I already set that up for you.'

'But with the rugby–'

'It's a clever system, Jane. It would have registered the reschedule automatically. Oh, never mind.' I reboot home™ manually, so it defaults back to the original settings. God only knows how she managed to do so much damage with the remote. 'There. It's all set up for you.' But I do it in such a way that it's going to cut off the last two minutes of the episode, overriding the download manager that normally insures against such eventualities. And you know what these things are like. Can you say cliffhanger? She's going to die.

'Can you do me a favour and *not* touch anything in future?' I snap. Jane looks so miserable, I almost recant, until I open the fridge and see that she hasn't bothered to place a grocery order.

There's only ice cream. Thank God Communique has twenty-four hour chefs, which is one major benefit (apart from the sea view, of course) that made defecting from New Mutua all worth it.

I don't ask if there's anything Jane wants, although when I place the order with the kitchen, I throw in a side of avo maki. Keep your friends close and your enemies and all that. I'm just going to ignore the contradiction in how this philosophy pertains to my ruining her soap. The rules of contempt decree that you have to play nice occasionally.

I take a shower and decide the only way I'm going to get the dust (and okay, that man) out of my hair is to cut it off. So when the doorbell goes ten minutes later, I'm busy hacking through my braids with a pair of sewing scissors. Naturally, I assume it's my sushi. But home™ logs the SIM as Toby. I waver about whether I really want to let him in, whether I can handle him right now, decide what the hell, and instantly regret it as he lopes in still wearing his peel, fresh from a surf on the Communique beach. He's soaked. And his backpack is squirming.

'You're dripping on my carpet.'

'Nice hair,' he responds with real admiration, and leans down to kiss me on the mouth, a little too intimately. I shove him off, but, unlike Mpho, he's not bothered by the rejection. 'Gotta towel?'

Jane steps into the lounge to see who it is, and her face clouds. She and Toby share a prickly antipathy, although she flat out refuses to admit it's because he's not corporate. She's internalised enough feel-good talkshows to know you should never confess to being a bigot.

I've been cohabiting with her for eight months now, assigned as live-ins according to synchronous personality matching by Seed. The overlap of our schedules is usually only an hour or so a day, not including weekends. I don't know how she manages to be so bad at number-crunching that she has to work overtime so frequently. Maybe she's trying to impress someone, get that promotion which is always and forever going to pass her by in favour of a smarter, better, more attractive candidate.

Not that I'm complaining. It means we stay out of each other's way, and she's oblivious to how I really spend my down time. (I could even confess to having maybe given Seed a little nudge in this direction, but hacking Communique's central database would be a violation of company protocol, and subject to a downgrade at the very least.)

Toby is still bitching. 'What is up with the security pricks? Like I haven't been here a squillion billion times before. Scratch that your visitors should have free rein.'

'Yeah, but then who knows what kind of streetside degenerates would wander in.'

'People like me, most probably,' Toby grins.

This is old routine. Even though I've hooked Toby up with a Communique Preferred Visitor's card, he has a habit of losing it. I don't let on how much this irritates me, because then he'd only do it on purpose, the same way he always ups the slang to get under my skin.

'Poor baby. Lumped in with the civilian dregs again?'

'Separate entrance and all. Back of the train. Can you tell?' He sniffs himself suspiciously and then flumpfs into the couch, still wearing his peel. Jane bites off a little squeal of dismay.

'But never mind my travails. How was Gabs?'

'Shit. Thanks. It's this big push on Push–' Toby snickers gratifyingly. 'But their cellular network is a shambles. It doesn't have the band-width to cope with the content, and there have been horrendous glitches with Bula Metalo's ads conflicting with the defusers. So it's ads or social control. Your choice.'

'Sounds like a good time to be a criminal in Botswana.'

'Uh, yeah, apart from that whole death penalty thing.'

'Hectic. Forget the work shit. I only asked to be polite. Did you get it?' Toby grins lopsidedly in that way that girls find attractive, although, honestly, he's more interesting than beautiful, especially since he's started cultivating his beard.

Jane is still hovering in the alcove anomaly squeezed between the kitchen and the lounge, which is but one of many factors that reveals our apartment was originally intended for one inhabitant and then converted, which only makes me more bitterly resentful about being lumped in with tedious finances girl.

'C'mon, let's get you that towel,' I say, down-playing his comment, and because I'm dying to see what's in the bag. And yeah, okay, because otherwise Jane is going to have a coronary about the couch. I'm not completely heartless.

'Should I call you when the food is here?' she chirps.

'You got edibles coming?' Toby perks up. I might have suspected he would have the munchies.

'Straight from Communique's premier chefs.'

We traipse into my room and I close the door. Toby unpeels, weaseling out of the skintight suit that protects him from all the pollutants in the water. He's not wearing anything underneath.

Jane assumes we fuck, but Toby and I worked that out of our systems years back. And besides, he's too promiscuous. I know that sounds hyp-ocritical coming from me, but I'm careful. I throw the towel at him.

'You're still not eating enough.'

'Girls like a boy on the skinny. And besides, it's not insufficient food. It's oversurplus drugs.'

'Speaking of which.'

Toby grins, and like a cheap magician, sum-mons a joint of sugar between his fingers. But when I reach for it, he holds it above his head.

'Uh-uh. Did you get it?'

'Maybe. You gonna tell me what's in the bag?'

'Maybe,' he shoots back. I pass him a lighter, and all play is put aside as he sucks the joint to life.

'Do you ever worry about her?' He jerks his head at the door.

'Uh. No.'

'Surely, *surely*, sugar and, hmm, let me see…' He sniffs delicately at the length of the joint, takes a long drag and smacks his lips together, playing connoisseur. 'Just a hint of vanilla and a touch of bliss isn't exactly on the employee pre-approved list?'

'Stop fooling and hand it over.'

'Only if you tell me you got it.'

'Only if you tell me what's in the bag.'

'Ah. Seems we're stalemated.' He waggles the joint. I ignore it, nudge the neoprene with my foot. Then I look up at him coyly through my lashes. This is an old game we play, practically choreographed.

'What do you think?'

He tackles me, knocking me back onto the bed and pinning my arms above my head. 'You incredible woman.' He moves as if to kiss me, trying his luck as if the final play wasn't already pre-determined, and I twist my head away and take a drag from the joint still pincered between his fingers instead. He mock-sighs and lets up. 'You used to be so much fun.'

'And you used to be not such a drugged-out freak. Put that away. And put some clothes on. I assume you brought clothes?'

He gets sulky and crouches down beside his pack, turning his back on me. As he starts unzipping the bag, it jolts and struggles. A scrimmage ensues.

'Shit!' Toby falls backwards onto his ass as a VIMbot shoots across the room and under my bed. I yelp and pull my feet up, laughing. 'Toby! What was that?'

'My new friend. I liberated him.'

'How do you know it's a him?'

'I would never have gone for a female. Too troublesome.'

I stick my head over the edge of the bed. The VIMbot is already at work, rustling the dust bunnies.

'Tobe. I can't help but notice that this particular VIMbot appears to have the Communique logo on it.'

'Yeah, like I said, I liberated him. Just like I'm gonna liberate you one day: storm into the cursed citadel, slay the vile monsters or, you know, Jane, and carry you off.'

'To your shitty swivel with the rest of civilian humanity.'

'Hey, don't knock the swivel. I get a view at least a fifth of the time.'

'And motion-sick the rest.' His rotating apartment, designed to maximise space, makes me dizzy.

'I like the revolving. It's like being on a ride. All the time.'

'Thanks for the offer, the noble knighthood thing. But I'll pass.'

'Okay, you wanted to know my motivation? It's revenge.'

'Oh. Right. I see. You kidnapped a VIMbot because you resent Communique's security policies?'

'Not just Communique, Lerato. Every corporation! Let every multinational conglom quake in fear, for the people have spoken! Dredge humanity is banding together, taking a stand for freedom, truth, equality – and the right to buy Fong Kong brands.'

'A noble cause indeed. But I'm not buying the whole Fong Kong cheap rip-off pledge, considering you're wearing a thirty grand BabyStrange chamo coat. Please.'

'Okay, all right. I needed some help in my apartment. It's a mess. And this little guy... I just know he wants to help out.'

'All right, all right. I concede. You can have the damn thing. But let me neuter the little bugger first. Pass it here.'

Toby scrabbles under the bed and yanks out the bot, which is buzzing hysterically, desperate to get back to vacuuming. They're pretty dense. You can't interrupt them mid-task. He hands it to me, and I snap out my toolkit and unscrew the faceplate underneath it. It takes less than ten seconds to over-ride the GPS tracking program and the homing instinct. It's not like a cleaning bot is exactly a priority.

'What about the vocal responses? You want 'em?' I ask Toby, who is now pulling on his jeans.

'What does it say?'

I click through the options. Even less than you'd expect. It's such a simple piece of tech and they're not expected to last long, so they're pretty limited. 'Error, please try again,' it chirps mechanically. 'Property of Communique Inc.,' and, lastly, a really cute 'All clean.'

'*Mal*,' Toby says, so I leave the vocals operative and hand over the bug, which is now sitting quietly on best behaviour.

'Oh, crap, speaking of my BabyStrange, know anyone who might be keen to buy it? My parents cut me off. Again.'

'Is that your way of asking for a loan? Least you have parents, big boy.'

'Is that your way of turning me down? Aw, poor little orphan girl in her subsidised beachfront corp apartment and cushy job.'

'You are such an ass.'

'That's still a no, then?'

'I have an idea. I know it's out there. Why don't you try working for a living?'

'I would, but my allergies. No, okay, I've got something hooked up with a games merchant, but it's been a while since I played with a joystick. Well, apart from this one.' He touches his crotch. 'Point is it's gonna take a couple of days for anything to come through.'

'This is only because I pity you and your delusions of splendour,' I sigh, pointing my phone in the general vicinity of the item in question, but really at his phone. 'Check your account. I've transferred 5k for you. Which I expect back, Toby. Seriously.'

'Truly, you are a generous corporate bitch-monkey,' he says, putting his hands together and bowing. I throw a pillow at him.

'Oh, and still on the subject of the BabyStrange. Now that you've saved it and, not uncoincidentally, my streamcasting career, I've got something to show you.'

He plays back a weird mash of some almost bar fight, which ends tediously and predictably in a defusing. It's not overly interesting, until he points out the big guy with the dreads, his would-be revolutionary friend.

'Is that where you're getting all the political doggerel?'

'Yeah. Along with the winning phrase "corporate bitchmonkey." We're having a protest party. It's the new theme night at Replica. Insurrection Saturdays. Awesome DJ playing.'

'You, you mean?

'You should come. It's going to be toyota. I can comp your phone, plus one, if you want.'

'Toby. You know I can't attend those sorts of things.'

'Not even to show solidarity with your generation? Okay, okay, chill. It's just a bash. No one actually gives a shit about protesting against the system, except Tendeka maybe. But I did want to ask if you wanted to make a contribution.'

'What kind of contribution?'

'My beauty, your genius? The perfect pairing.'

'I can't do this guy's phone if that's what you're asking, especially not if he's just been defused.'

'So, what about switching off the security on an adboard? I can get you the exact GPS. It's just temporary.'

'Oh. I don't know. What's temporary?'

'Long enough.'

'For?'

'A little outlaw smear campaign.'

'What would you do if you didn't know me, Toby?'

'I'm sure the world would be hugely improved.'

'Whose board is it?'

Toby sucks intently on the joint, all the better to avoid meeting my eye. 'Fuck knows. I don't keep track.'

'Well, where is it?'

'N2, near Roodebloem Road. Smack in the middle of the highway.'

'You know that's a Communique board.'

'Your employers would disapprove terribly.'

'It's a serious offence, Toby.'

'Worse than the tamper job you just did on this little guy?'

'Oh, please. That's the equivalent of stealing stationery. Aiding and abetting a hack job on corporate property? That's a whole other category. That's goodbye plush apartment and cushy job. Firing offence, no written warning required.' I have to feed him the lines, cover up the snap of excitement. It's like finding the wall blocking your way in a dead-end alley is only made of cardboard, that you can push right through it. I know exactly how to use this.

'You could have just come out with "no",' says Toby, pulling his shirt over his head. It

clings to the damp on his back, so he is all elbows tangled in rumpled cotton.

I yank the tee down to his chin, so he can see
me, see how serious I am. His lanky arms are
still caught in it, sticking stiffly above his head,
like he's being robbed.

'I didn't say I wouldn't do it, Toby. I just want
you to appreciate the risk I'm taking on your
behalf.'

'Okay. Got it. Muchos graçias, scary intense
girl. Can I have my t-shirt back?'

I step back so he can finish getting dressed.

'And speaking of dangerous favours…' I rum-
mage in my suitcase for his present and toss it
to him. He stashes the phone just in time, as the
door cracks open.

'Uh-oh,' Toby stage-whispers, 'evil house-
mate alert.'

Jane pokes her head in, bearing gifts. 'Oh,
hey, your food is here. What are you guys
doing?'

'Fucking,' Toby says brightly. 'You wanna join
us?'

Kendra

As soon as I step out into Long Street and the warm sheet of rain that soaks through my clothes, I realise I can't face going back to the loft right now. Not because of the gaping holes in the walls where the builders have knocked through the kitchen, or the dust that the absorbent tarps are supposed to sponge up right out of the air, but because it's too weighed down with memories.

The way your brain works it's always rewiring itself; the layers of association tangled up with different people and places recontextualised by new experiences. You can map out a whole city according to the weight of memory, like pins on the homicide board tracking the killer's movements. But the connections get thicker and denser and more complicated all the time.

I feel like the tarps sop up emotional residue along with the dust drifting down to settle on the carpets, filming the walls; the shouting matches we degenerate into at two in the morning when he stops in for a 'chat' after a night out with his friends – and wants to leave straight after. Five months ago, I liked the glamour of being a kept woman. It made a change from being just another impoverished Michaelis student. But now it just seems stale and tired and terribly naïve.

I walk down the steps to the underway, below the new deco curls of the signage that says 'Long' and 'D', and stand on the platform along with some kids who epitomise the Michaelis breed, with their overtly punky hair and ramshackle clothes, cultivating the ugly look for the shock value.

The tunnels rumble and shush with far-off trains. It's 98 seconds till the next connecting train to Chiappini Street. If it wasn't so humid and soggy, I'd walk.

The rumbling amps up and the train rides in, sending plumes of water skating up on either side of it. The plastech doors slide open and I push past the crowd to slide into a seat while there's still one going. The train rises slightly, hissing as the hover reinflates, and glides off, the neon lights on the tunnel walls slipping into blurred darts as we pick up speed towards Adderley Station.

I've got several spools to drop off with Mr. Muller. It was a mission to find someone who still dabbled in oldschool processes like film. If I were a real artist, Jonathan teased me, I would have done it myself as a point of pride.

Four Ghosts down, the sense of panicky urgency has eased up. Andile didn't tell me it would be like this. That I would have to placate it. Or maybe it's just the residual humiliation of Toby trying to kiss me. The pathetic truth is that Jonathan would probably encourage it.

I take out my Leica Zion, my everyday filter on the world, and start clicking through the memchip, past the people framed in the window of the Afro Café and the unfinished graffiti on the Parade clustered between the adboards, past the pictures of bridges from the negative space binge I went on last week, until I come to the images of my wrist.

Four thousand one hundred and twenty photographs over the time it took to develop, like film. Played back in timelapse the bruise blossoms and bursts, resolving like a Rorschach into the logo. It's the exact colour of the phosphorescent algae shimmering in the waves on the beach in Langkawi, where Jonathan took me after the agonising slow-mo months of my father's death.

I spent an hour looking at my skin this morning, studying my wrist, my face. The cosmetic effects are the most obvious, but it's the stuff you can't see that counts; the nano attacking toxins, sopping up free radicals, releasing antioxidants by the bucketload. It's a marathon detox and a fine-tune all in one. And the nano's programmed to search and destroy any abnormal developments, so I'll never have to go through what Dad did, the cancer chewing its way through his stomach, consuming him from the inside out.

No promises, said Andile, before he made me sign the contradicting waiver: 'The applicant understands that any claims made by Inatec staff regarding medical or health benefits are based on preliminary findings from testing in animals. The applicant understands that the Inatec nanotechnology is still in the prototype phase of development and, based on this information and understanding, accepts full responsibility for all the risks inherent, etc, etc.'

I don't mean to be dismissive of the etceteras or the risks inherent. I know exactly what I'm in for, despite what that freakshow from the bar might think. Or my shrink, who believes I'm just doing this as a way of asserting myself in the whole bang shebang with Jonathan.

I'm a demo model for their demographic. An angel of aspiration. A guinea pig for an appropriate alliterative beginning with *g*. Ghost, I guess. Only once removed on the food chain from the kids who sell space on their chamo, adblips playing out on the plastivinyl of tees and jackets like walking projectaboards, only with more 'risks inherent'.

And my skin does look amazing, like it's been buffed and scrubbed and moisturised within an inch of its life, all velvaglow and radiant, even though the only cosmetic in the apartment is Jonathan's aftershave. It's been almost six days now with no side effects, or only good ones, apart from the first few miserable days when the flu and achiness hit. But then maybe that was self-induced. Maybe all of it is.

It's a shock to find Jonathan at the gallery, but really, what did I expect? He and Sanjay are examining my prints, laid out on Propeller's floor in a blunt mosaic. They weren't supposed to start the selection without me. Sanjay is squatting, shuffling like a crab between the prints. He's already set two aside. He flashes a smile at me when I come in, slightly strained at the edges.

'Hey, sweetness.' Jonathan gives me the full-body up-down, like he does to the models in castings. It's an old habit, he's told me, from the

job. As in, don't take everything so personally,
Kendra.

On any other day, the cigarette dangling off
his lips would have annoyed the hell out of me,
when he's supposed to have quit again, but my
secret makes me feel smug and secure, counter-
balancing the elation, like a fish jumping in my
chest, that I can't keep down at seeing him.

'You shouldn't be smoking over the prints.'

'Don't be so tense, baby. It's not going to hurt
them.' He starts to reach for my shoulder, to
knead the knots in my neck, but I brush his
hand away, irritated.

There are to be three of us in the group exhibition: Johannes Michael, who does intricate
paperwork mobiles on a massive scale, taking up
Propeller's entire second floor; and Khanyi
Nkosi, a legend at twenty-six. I am either privi-
leged to be sharing a space with her, or at a
serious disadvantage because no one is going to
pay the slightest bit of attention to my work with
her audio animal installation in the room. She's
only bringing the thing in at the last minute, because of all the controversy around it.

It's the first time I've seen all the prints laid
out together and, despite my anxieties about co-
exhibiting with Khanyi Nkosi, I'm deliriously
happy about how they've come out. I've already made my final selection, although I'm

glad to see Sanjay and Jonathan have picked out the portrait of the drag queen, caught bumming a light from a garage attendant at 3 am. I've blown it up, so that her face is all texture, the make-up caked in the lines around her pursed mouth, lit up by the flame cupped in her hands. It came out surprisingly perfect considering no one knows how to use film anymore.

The others have not, and Sanjay is still wary about the whole thing. The over- and under-exposed, bleached, washed out, over-saturated with colour, blotches and speckles and stains like coffee-cup rings, or arcs of white on white where the canister has cracked and let the light slip inside.

My shrink tells me I'm co-dependencing; my father's death means I'm paralysed, afraid to make my own decisions, so I defer to Jonathan because it's easy, and this is my core problem. Well, actually, he didn't; he let me figure that out for myself, which cost a little more, a few months more of therapay, more wasted time, when apparently he had the answer all along.

What he does tell me of his own accord, after this revelation, is that I should move out and cut Jonathan off, get some distance to regain my equilibrium, to recover a sense of self. He uses a lot of shrink-speak that doesn't translate, like it's only applicable to someone else's ordered life, where the rules work.

So I'm still speaking to Jonathan, still hanging out with him, still sleeping with him – when he comes round. Still deferring to him on the important stuff. Because he's the guy orchestrating all the moves. Because I don't have his pull or his contacts, like Sanjay, for example. Sanjay is a major name on the international art scene, responsible for launching the trajectories of people like Susu Ngubane or Cameron Sterling, whose sculptures now sell for in the region of seven hundred grand. Jonathan deals with Sanjay on all of the details of the exhibition. Or should that be exhibitionism? Because isn't it my soul being laid bare here?

I know he's been seeing at least two other women in the times between, when we are off, on, off. Because we are just 'casual', as he calls it, because quantifying something puts it in its place. But sometimes I feel like he's reminding himself rather than me. Maybe that's just wishful thinking.

I met the one, Stacy, at a party. One of those awful media blitzes, hanging off him like she was his handbag. Old bag. Cos she was – thirty-eight at least. An editor at one of the pushmags he works for occasionally. One of the perks of the job, fraternising with the help. Of course, Jonathan is thirty-eight, so he's right up there with her. Closer to her than me.

I asked to take her picture, to Jonathan's delight. 'You cunning little fox,' he whispered, kissing my shoulder, as if we were all supposed to pretend I didn't know they were fucking. 'You just guaranteed yourself a publicity splash, sweetheart. We'll have to make the event worthy of the write-up.'

But, really I was more interested in reducing her to planes of colour, the hard sculptural bones offsetting the flicker of pity in her eyes.

The print I went with was an accident, a misfire while I was adjusting the light settings. It shows her sitting on the edge of the fire escape stair, on the balcony outside the apartment. The focus is on the shapely knot of her knee, one hand resting in the dark fall of her skirt, a black blur. You can only see the angle of her jaw tilted out of frame. It makes her look vulnerable.

When I confronted him about her later, sitting in the window of his loft, the night bitter cold against my naked back and the traffic streaming below, he ducked and evaded. But I know I am cast in the role of Poor Thing. The doomed unrequited who can't quite let go. And it is my fault that we still fall into bed. His mercy fuck. But really, I think the word should be mercenary, for all the benefits I score: the loft, the career guidance, this show.

'Do you love him?' my shrink asks, and I feel angry because it's so obvious, and is this really what I'm paying for? But I don't have a coherent response. I love his ferocious confidence, the way he charms strangers, so they flock to him like tame little birds to peck at the compliments that drop from his lips. And the way you know it's only crumbs, and long for more.

But I have a greater sense of his physicality. The image I have of Jonathan, one of the first, which I have tried to document on film countless times, but also keep in my head, are the lines that crease the corners of his eyes in bright sunlight when he smiles. Why this and not any of the other details – the triumvirate of moles in the crook of his arm; his lips, slightly too plump, too voluptuous for a man; his giant hands with knuckles like the knobbly skulls of little animals – or the whole, I don't know. But then Jonathan says that's just like me, to take in the partials rather than the composite.

The shrink doesn't even bother to make notes. When he gives me the bill, I include it in my expenses, and Jonathan pays it without comment.

'Hey, dreamy girl,' Jonathan waves impatiently from the other side of the room. 'This is your exhibition, you want to pay attention?' I set down the print and drift across the room.

Not telling him about the branding feels like
my counter to the Stacys, to all the times he
doesn't answer his phone. An amulet of protection.

'Babes, you can't be serious about this,' he
says, tapping one of the photographs, already
mounted and leaning against the wall.

It is my favourite.

'It's really childish.'

They are both waiting for my reaction,
Jonathan irritable and Sanjay polite, but evalu-
ating at the same time, like he already has the
measure of my work, but not yet of me.

'What do you think?' I ask him.

'No ways. You're deluded if you're making
that the centrepiece, sweetheart. It's not right.'
Jonathan interjects, but Sanjay gives me a little
nod of approval.

It's like the night dive Jonathan and I went
on in Malaysia. It was only my eighth dive, and
I wasn't qualified for it, but for five hundred
bucks, qualifications can mysteriously be over-
looked. In the boat, over the nasal whine of the
engine and the oxygen tanks clanking against
their restraints, Jonathan teased me about being
scared, winding me up about how claustropho-
bic, how suffocating it would be.

And it was terrifying when I rolled off the boat
backwards, and the shock of water engulfed me,

but not because the darkness closed in. Because it made the sea wide open.

Visibility limits your imagination of the ocean only as far as you can see, ten metres, fifteen at a stretch. But it's only in the utter black that you can feel the true scale, the volume and weight of that gaping unknowable drift between continents.

The photograph is called *Self-Portrait*. It is a print from a rotten piece of film. Two metres by three and a half.

It came out entirely black.

Toby

I'm stoked with my stash, kids: new illicit phone that's immune to defusings *and* capable of reading illegal downloads (let's try not to spread that around too much), and a spiffing VIMbot to restore my swivel to the state of superclean it hasn't seen since my old lady first picked it out of the catalogue. Not that I've ever been especially bothered about fighting the good fight against creeping entropy, but it'll make for a change.

I spill the VIMbot out of my pack onto the bed and it goes zooting between my Pumas, breaking for the corridor and nearly gets away. Luckily the door has already started to rotate away. A lot of people don't like this whole cog system of floors, the entire building like a gyroscope in perpetual motion, but, hey, it saves space on doors and it just saved my VIMbot from bolting.

The little fucker just misses the gap and thwacks off the wall, tipping itself over and lying with its legs twitching frantically, a fantastic dirty sound emanating from its inner devicings. If a robot could grind its teeth, assuming they had teeth, that's what it would sound like. It's the kind of sound that's eminently sampleable.

I like to mix it up eclectic, got over 150,000 songs on my phone, ready to download to the decks and about nine and a half thou records in the mix. Everything from spectro to new bliss jazz, and some oldtime stuff too. And my brand spanking handset will double that capacity, now I'm free to loot and plunder without the digital rights malware blowing up in my face.

I set the VIMbot down on the kitchen counter, holding it down with one hand, and sample that deliciously awful sound directly to my phone. I can already hear the track unfolding in my head, with that metallic teethedge in the backbeat.

I play around with that for a while, thinking about how I really like sweet-K, and what a bad sign that is. The last person I was this interested in was Tamarin, and she was psycho deluxe, especially when she bust me and Nokulelo together. But what was she expecting when I was still with Jenna when we hooked up?

Forget the rational; they always think they can change you. Rearrange the furniture. What is it with that?

If I'm going to do this Kendra thing properly, I'm going to have to upgrade my gear. The way I'm figuring it, fuck *Boing Boing*, I'm gonna syndicate this straight to CNN or Sky News, then hit up some funding to do a proper documentary or a feature, and land a sweet deal on a major cast channel. MicrosoftTimeWarner or Al Jazeera.

I'm going to need a decent mic, a broadcast-quality lens, and to stock up on extra memory – and the fridge while I'm at it. It's glaringly empty, like my bank balance, which is already looking unhealthy deluxe, even with Lerato's loan. My mother doesn't realise how much maintenance my accustomed lifestyle chows up. She would have to cut me off mid-month. Cunt.

So it's off to hook up with Unathi and make some quick cash-in-phone. When I finally make it through the traffic, it takes me another half-hour to find his dockside squat among the derelict buildings. It's borderline illegal, mainly because of the health hazard he and his slum-friends pose, but at least they're not drug dealers or human traffickers or anti-corporate terrorists, which are all the cops really care about. Occasionally, they'll get harassed, mainly

for tapping into the grid and using juice they're
not paying for, and they've had to move twice
already in the last six months, but it's all par for
the lifestyle, kids. Take note before you consider
a career in the lucrative but feckless world of
underground game-dealing.

A shaven-headed someone, so nondescript I
can't distinguish if it's guy or girl, opens the
door without so much as a heita, then vanishes
into the maze of backrooms which smell of
burnt rice and that heavy sour smell of humanity that hasn't had access to running water for
a while.

Unathi doesn't bother to surface from the sag-
ging wallow of the couch, which is the only
furniture in the room, apart from a deflated
beanbag and the scramble of consoles and
wiring and six different screens blaring a mash
of content into the lounge, providing the only
light. He's wearing the same leopard-print vest
I saw him in last time, which was at some LAN
party, but when I rib him about not having any
other clothes, he claims it's just cos he's got
three of them. He's also shaved his head, so between him and the androgynous thing at the
door, it's beginning to look like a real cult
around here.

'I don't know, man. When was the last time
you played?' he hedges, fiddling with the frayed

tassle of the shweshwe throw that has solidified from unidentified spillage like a topographical map.

'Cut the sceptical, man. You know I can handle it.' The truth, kids, is that I can't remember. 'I've been busy, man. Diary of Cunt takes up most of my day. Have you checked it?'

'No.'

'And I've been working the decks, sampled a VIMbot earlier, which was mental.' I half raise my phone to transfuse him a copy of the Replica invite, but he's not keen. Never one for the social. 'And girls,' I add, cos I can't resist the dig at him nesting in this shithole, pre-demolition, twenty-four/seven by seven, getting it on only in Pluslife. 'Uh-huh. Maybe you could bring 'em round some time. Get me a piece of your pie. For once.'

'Sure, man. I'll do that.' And this is a lie deluxe and we both know it. Although at least it resolves the gender question of the nondescript baldy.

'Yeah, that'd be *kif*.'

'*Kif* like a spliff.'

'Want one?'

He tosses me a baggie of sugar, A-grade, and isn't it always the way that someone who never even fucking leaves the house should score the premium? I start rolling while he plugs into my data.

'You're way outdated.'

'So?'

'My clients won't dig that.'

'If I can get the shit, who cares about my track?'

'It's real competitive, Tobias. Real lucrative.'

I don't say anything. Lick the ends of the paper to fuse 'em together, which is a waste of effort when the paper's self-adherent, but fuck it. I light up, take a toke, and pass it on. Unathi takes a deep hit and shows no sign of passing it back.

'How about we start you off easy?'

'Whatever.'

'There's a new weapon in *Nemesis Redux* that everyone's after, but I doubt you're up for that right now. Doesn't look like you played it before either.'

'Fuck you. I can handle.'

'Uh-huh. How about *Kiwi Pop*?'

'What, the kid's game?'

'You'd be surprised how many parentals want to indulge their kiddies' every heart's desire. It's war out there, 'specially in virtual mutacute land.'

'Isn't there an age protection plugged in? Precisely to stop people like me from amokking among the kiddies?'

'Yeah, but I got a hack. Like candy, baby. How could you resist?'

'Exactly. I just wouldn't feel right.'

'Coming over all moral? Spare me.'

'Don't you have anything else?'

'How do you feel about meatspace? There are some interesting ARGs happening at the moment.'

'Alt reality? I don't know. Do I have to dress up?'

'You'd look so cute with pointy ears. Or fangs.' He wiggles his fingers in front of his mouth all nosferatu.

'Not a chance.'

'Okay, okay. There's a new title, just hit the market a couple of months ago. *Scorpions Elite*?'

'What's the concept?'

'Pseudo-cop shit. Mix of gamespace and meat. In game, it's busting heads, fragging bad guys, typical shooter. Real world is mainly detective work online, collaborating with wikis to solve clues, but also field action, shaking down informants kinda thing. It's quite kif, cos it's not only game employees, it's other players too. It ties into *FallenCity Underworld*, so you have other people playing bad guys. Oh yeah – and some gun battles in publisher-approved location. Although it might be too complex for you. Bit rof when you've been off the circuit so long.'

'Piss off, Unathi.'

'Yeah, I think we'll kick you off gently. Till you get a feel for it again. Here's your user ID.' He flips me a game token marked with *Kiwi Pop*'s mascot, a pink and yellow dino-beastie thing with a toothsome grin and beady black eyes that goes by the name of Moxy. I only know this from too many afternoons spaced out with kiddies' TV.

'I got an order for a purple Blinka Stinka. It's worth two-eight. That's fourteen hundred to you. And yes, that means I'm taking 50%. It's a sliding scale. The rates will get better if you do.'

'I gotta tell you, Unathi, if I wanted to get fucked, I would have stayed in bed.'

'Yeah, screw you, Tobe. Purple, okay? Any other colour is not gonna cut it. It's somewhere on North Island, level six. Apparently. Shouldn't take you longer than a couple of hours.'

'Easy. But let's ask Moxy, shall we?' I flip the game token into the air and slap it down onto the back of my hand, heads or tails, Moxy or the game-co logo. I peel back my fingers, take a peek. The little dinosaur fucker grins up at me.

'I'm going to take that as a good sign.'

Kendra

It's almost dusk by the time I reach Mr. Muller's apartment block in District Six. I feel a twinge of guilt – I should have called first. But the elevator recognises my SIM on the approved guest list straight away, slides open, and drops me to level minus-four, sending a notification to his home™ automatically, so that when the door swings open, he is already brewing the ultra-caffeine.

He's got his wall2wall set on Karoo; pale light over scrub hills complete with a windpump, metal blades turning idly in a breeze you could almost convince yourself you felt. It's an idealised version of the Rural, peaceful, as far removed from the real thing as you can get. At least Mr. Muller keeps the display reduced, so it only takes up half a wall, more painting than wraparound. He doesn't like to forget that it's not legit. He says it's just another kind of sedation. A lulling, he calls it. 'Watch out for the lulling,' he says sometimes, like it's something profound, especially if a commercial sets him off. Commercials really get to him. He says you used to be able to skip them, just prog them right out of your recording, but it's hard to imagine that now. Then he'll launch into a rant on how the world has evolved for the worst, although at least crime is down. But the truth of it is he likes to yell at the television, and I should just leave an old grouch and his foibles in peace.

He turns, two cups already in hand. 'Hello. I wasn't expecting you today. You're looking well. Got something new for me?'

I swap him a cup of ultra for two spools of film. He puts them on the counter as if they are holy artefacts. The counter is already looking frayed, the plastic peeling, even though the sub-terr is only a couple of years old. The whole thing makes me depressed, but Mr. Muller likes to joke that he's just in touch with his body. It's dragging down with age, so he's moved below ground to keep up with it. 'This way, they won't even have to bury me,' he says. 'Just lock the door and be done with it.'

Of course, he's joking. The property in this neighbourhood is far too valuable, even the swivels and the subterrs. There are a lot of old-sters living below ground, but the wall2wall scenics make it more bearable.

The major advantage, he says, is that there is no natural light to interfere with his darkroom. It's really his bathroom, the entrance hung with a tunnel of black recycling bags, because even the fake light from the projected vistas can mess with the process. The problem is getting the chemicals. He has to get them shipped in from a guy in Nairobi, which takes weeks with all the new security checks.

I had about thirty rolls already by the time I found Mr. Muller. Didn't have the slightest idea what to do with them, because there was only one lab I could find up in Jozi, and it would have been impossible for me to be involved in the process, or to fly up every time I wanted to develop a new spool. I'd gone completely overboard with the film. Partly it was the find, picking up the thirty spools for next to nothing at the market, and what else was I going to do with them but shoot? But it was also the mystery, a grand experiment. When I told him this, when I found him, Mr. Muller knew exactly what I was talking about. 'It's an alchemy,' he said. 'As much in your head as the camera.' Unfortunately, it's also horribly expensive, especially now I have to buy my film from a specialist supplier via the Net, and Mr. Muller doesn't cut me any slack.

His wife left him seven years ago. Although he doesn't go into the details, I get the idea that there was an affair involved, maybe even on his side. That's when he picked up on his old habit. There's not much call for film development these days, but he's taught me tons I didn't know from digital.

If I catch him in the right mood, he'll haul out his portfolio from back in the days when he was a photojournalist for the *Cape Times*, which, endearingly, he insists on keeping hardcopy. We'll flip through thousands of portraits of politicians and public figures, jazz concerts and crime scenes and the Quarantine Riots.

My favourite is the mangled wreckage of a truck engine embedded in the sludge of a dried-up irrigation pond, framed by grape vines shrivelled from the temperature rise none of the farmers wanted to believe in. It's the result of a car bomb set off by a bunch of right-wing students in Stellenbosch, who thought they could do a better job than government inc. with the drought and the superdemic. The only thing they managed to accomplish was blowing themselves up.

Apparently, engines are the only things that can survive an explosion of that calibre. In Lebanon in the 1970s, the photojourns were so jaded by all the car bombs, they turned it into a game to find the engines. Not that Mr. Muller was around then, but he describes the photo as a kind of tribute. This is the way his spiel runs every time he shows me his portfolio, like it's a recording and he just has to hit play. I think this is a side-effect of getting old.

The image is beautiful, almost black and white, although he shot in colour. It's the time of day and the way he's worked the light that washes it out. But it's the evocative simplicity of the context, of the meaning he's brought to a landscape that's impressive. It's easy to gut-wrench with people: Tiananmen Square or Kevin Carter's vulture baby or the Bangladesh Children's War, but investing an inanimate object with the same quality is an accomplishment.

If I was still at Michaelis, I would make this the focus of my thesis, but I walked out of classes when dad died and didn't go back to explain, and now my bursary is null and void. Jonathan keeps nagging at me to reapply, to plead extenuating family circumstances.

Actually, I wanted to use some of Mr. Muller's images, from the quarantine series in particular, as a juxtaposition for an exhibition. But when I told him about it, planning a contrast between the photos of crams of people fighting through the smoke from the burning tyre-barricades and the hack gas versus the shots I took of the stadium crowds at the Extraordinaries concert last year (on assignment for a PR company), he told me it was pretentious art school crap, that it was totally insensitive to what people in this country had endured, and thank God I'd dropped out of that awful place.

'So what's it today?' Mr. Muller asks. 'No, wait, let me guess. Portraits of street kids holding their only possessions. Reflections in rear-view mirrors. Close-ups of people's shoes on the underway.' He's always amused by my choice of subject matter, although the street kid idea is genius.

'You'll just have to wait and see, Mr. M. I think you'll like them, though. I've been pushing the film.'

'And how go your plans for the exhibition? All in order, I trust?'

'We did the final selection yesterday. It's looking good, although Jonathan's a bit freaked out by the format, too archaic, the repro ...'

'Yes, yes, you told me. It won't be perfect carbon copies.'

'Unless I scan them, which goes against the whole concept of non-digital.'

'You just stick with what you know. Ignore the whole bloody lot of them, especially that Jonathan. They're blowing smoke out their asses. You ready?'

We always do the developing together. I wish I could say it's a sacred rite of the alchemical process, a communion, but really it's because he doesn't quite trust me with his expensive chemicals. I'm also not allowed to address him as Dan or even Daniel. Just Mr. Muller, which is so retro.

I reach up to push aside the black plastic bags and he gently takes my arm, pushing up the sleeve. 'My goodness. What's this?' And suddenly I'm embarrassed.

He regards the glow logo seriously. 'When I was young, I wanted to get my grandfather's number from the prison camp tattooed on my arm. A sort of homage to suffering.'

'Why didn't you?'

'Jewish. It's not kosher. And it was in remarkably bad taste. I didn't realise that at the time.' He shrugs and takes another sip of ultra, gesturing to the darkroom. 'Shall we?'

Tendeka

Sent Messages Folder / --

17/09 23h09. Toby. Not answering UR phone. Did U get msg switching the meet? Damn SAPS. SIM denied entry @Don Pedros. Here it is again. RendezV @ 19 lwr main wdstock instead. Unimore Packing co warehouse. Call 4 directions if U need. No rush

17/09 23h29 Still waiting 4U. Still coming? Havent heard from U. Concerned?!?! Hour late now

17/9 23h51 Cant do it w/out our key guy! Dont want 2 rip the plug at this late. Get in touch!

17/9 24h12 Not cool Toby

17/9 24h17 WHERE U?!?!?!?!

17/9 24h23   FUCKER. FUCK YOU. YOU FUCK

'Little tense, bro?' Toby calls out, waltzing into the warehouse, and it's only because I don't want to set a bad example for Zuko, or scare off our new recruit, that I don't fucking slam him through a wall of crates.

The bastard actually laughs. 'Relax, china. I didn't realise this was a military operation here. So we're a little late. It's quieter on the highway now anyways.'

'Are you fucking high?' Which is a stupid question, considering his pupils are so dilated his eyes are black.

'Yeah,' he says, looking round, unconcerned. 'What is this place? Boxworld?'

'Jasmine used to work here. She kept the keys. And the alarm code,' Ashraf says, as if this conversational thread is a priority right now, as if I'm not going to see through him changing the subject.

Toby scopes her out with a leer. 'I don't think we've had the pleasure?' But before he can kiss her hand, I intervene.

'Oh, gosh. Where are my fucking manners? Let me introduce you. Jasmine. Toby. Jasmine's a political-economy student at UCT who's interested in joining the cause. Toby's a fuckhead.'

'Tendeka.'

'Sorry, Ash. But this is not cool. Toby, you cannot fucking come here fucked up and fucking think you can fuck this for us!'

'Ooh,' he says, pulling a face. 'Thanks, but not on the first date.'

'What?'

'All the fucking. Not on the first date. Sorry.' Zuko snickers, and this time not even Ash can stop me. I shove Toby, and he tumbles back into a stack of boxes, spraying the floor with packing material. He rebounds, like one of those punch-bag clowns, laughing.

'Jesus, what a rush. Do it again. C'mon. Once more. Hit me. For real this time. C'mon. Just not in the face, okay?' He bounces like a boxer, shaking out his hands. 'Wait. Wait. Okay, I'm ready.'

'Fuck you.'

'Yeah. Already said that. Moving on ... We gonna go wreak some havoc on capitalism or what?' Ash has a gentle restraining hand on my arm. But it's cool. I know the fucking score here. I shake him off.

'Is your friend ready, Toby? Because if she's not, you can just fucking go home.'

'Waiting on my beck.'

'Well, call her then.'

'I'll msg her when we're imminent. Not

before. She doesn't like prolonged chats. It raises her risk profile.'

I pull him aside, rougher than necessary, away from Jasmine, who is already looking nervous, and getting more so since Zuko started on a systematic sabotage half an hour ago, gutting boxes so they'll spill everything as soon as someone tries to lift them, switching labels. 'It's bad enough you come here fried when you know how I feel about that shit, but don't undermine me in front of my people, okay, Toby?'

'Okay, china, we're cool. I wouldn't want to affect your status with your people.'

'Are you fucking mocking me?'

'No, Ten. No. How can you think that? Look, I'm sorry. Let's just hit it, okay? Rewind. Press play. Back on schedule and everyone's happy!'

'All right. But this is serious. This is deep water.'

Toby looks confused.

'We're not playing in the shallow end.'

'Right. Got it.'

'Hey, Tendeka. Can he stop that?' Jasmine says, worrying at her thumbnail with her teeth. The girl's not going to last the night, I can tell. She's got heart, absolutely with the cause, but she doesn't have the nerves to endure the risk. It's the same for almost everyone who joins us. Either they're believers, or they're just along for the ride, but they never last. It's a complex operation and we've got a high turnover, to use the enemies' lingo.

'It's standard anti-corp, Jasmine. Don't sweat it. We can't limit the sentiment to the large-scale corporati. Every capitalist enterprise propagates the system that fucks people over, keeps the poor and the sick down and out of sight. Your boss has it coming.'

'Okay. It's just that my boss was, like, a decent guy, yeah?'

'How decent could he have been if he fired you?' Toby cuts in, getting a grateful look from Jasmine.

'All right, whatever. We're heading out. Now that everyone is finally here.'

As we pull up our hoodies, I can't help noticing that Toby has ignored the very specific instructions to wear all-black.

Outside, the humidity from the rain earlier sinks down on us together with that musky smell of wet tar. I'm already starting to sweat. At least it's deserted. The lofts above the warehouses are all lit up, but nobody bothers to look out the window. The loft dwellers are all locked away. All the stuff they need is inside, cafés and laundros and private gyms, so they go direct from garage to apartment, never venturing out on the street unless it's in the security of their cars.

We turn left into Roodebloem, stepping up the pace. Zuko is playing handlanger, carrying the ropes and the harness. It's a test run, his first major sabotage, and I have high expectations of him.

The rules are that the targets have to switch constantly. It's self-evident, but you'd be surprised at how many wannabes don't think that far ahead, and get bust when they hit the same board the third time round. It's great that kids are doing it, that they're actually getting out there, but they fucking have to think it through properly. It's not like we haven't made the information available.

Most of them do it for the thrill. And when it comes down too heavy, the first time they get crisped, say, then they're out. They'll still hang in the forums, they might make it down for a protest or a flash mob, but they won't go on a raid again. Zuko is going to be different, though. I can tell.

I turn to tell him this, but he's not behind me as I anticipated. Instead, he is tagging along with Jasmine, both hanging tight with Toby, who is spouting shit, dragging up the whole Hope Modise thing, as if Jasmine weren't nervy enough already.

'Twenty years' disconnect. And the kid was only fourteen. You seriously didn't hear about

this? It was, what, three years ago? There was
that whole ad campaign?'

Zuko trots up, obedient. 'Sorry, Ten. Toby was
telling us about–'

'Hope Modise, I heard. But he's got it wrong.
You got it wrong, Toby. She was thirteen. And
she didn't get twenty years. They remanded her
sentence.'

'Yeah, yeah, yeah, I was getting to that.'

'What do you mean, remanded?' Jasmine
says, too bouncy in her step by far, wired on
adrenalin.

'After she hacked Sonica Wireless's servers,
some dumb teenage crush thing, sending out
a worm that interrupted people's programs
with a message about how much she loved this
guy–'

'Her programming teacher,' Toby interrupts,
'who was way older, like 34, and she figured
this was the one way she could prove herself. It
was beautiful. Love made code. Cos she did it
all in binary, right? So you would be working
on your spreadsheet or your email or whatever,
and this thing would pop up, like an animation,
but all ones and zeros just flipping out all over
the screen. The general public didn't have a
clue. Thought it was a crash or a virus. Hit half
the world in four days. They estimated the loss
in productivity at something like 6.3 billion

while they tried to sort it out, and I'm talking dolleros, not rands. But here's the stupid thing, cos Hope had stamped it. I mean, how else was her teacher gonna know it was her unless she included his name? Disguised in the code, but they figured it out, traced it back to him, and then to her. He got off with a warning, I reckon due to turning her in, cos by then she'd realised this was some heavy shit, and had gone to ground. So no one was going to lure her out except him.'

'I think that's a little far-fetched.'

'No, come on, Tendeka. They could have nailed him on aiding and abetting; I mean, someone had to teach her how to code like that – that, or improper relations with a minor. So he lures her out into the open and he gets off absolute scot and Hope goes down for twenty. *Mal* Nollywood stuff. Unrequited love and betrayal.'

'Jesus,' Jazz breathes.

'S'okay. It didn't quite work out like that. So she's s'posed to get a disconnect. We're talking relegated to homeless, out of society, cut from the commerce loop, no phone–'

'I think we all know what it means, thanks, Professor. I'm on a temporary, remember?' I cut in, irritated at the way this has turned into The Toby Show.

'Oops. Yeah. Sorry about that.' I can tell he's not sorry at all.

'But what happened to Hope?' Jasmine whines.

'Sonica cut a deal. Three years' juvenile detention to take her up to sixteen and legal employable age, and then they scooped her up. She works for them in security, closing up loops and backdoors to stop the next gen of Hope Modises getting through. And then they turned it into a PR stunt. I can't believe you haven't seen the luscious ad campaign they did with her. You can download the video of the original msg, without the contagious aspect of the code. Now it's a fucking screensaver for your phone, a Valentine's download for geeks. Poor Hope,' but he's grinning.

'Subvertising. Like what Levi's did when those kids in Brazil hacked their storefronts. Turned it into a challenge, a hacksibition, appropriating the street culture for their own twisted purposes. Motherfuckers in advertising. Can't be bothered to do their own creative.'

'I dunno, Ten. Sounds like a pretty creative solution to me. Elegant. And aren't you trying to get sponsorship for your graffiti project?'

'Well, actually, Tendeka doesn't want to use corp financing–' Ashraf starts before I cut in. I wish he'd just leave things to me.

'It's against everything we're trying to do, which is to give the kids a voice, not the corporates. They have a voice. They have adboards and push media to your phone and into your fucking home. These kids have got nothing. They're totally disenfranchised. Our project's a creative outlet. They're making a mark on the city. It means a lot to them, right, Zuko?'

'Yeah. It's sharp.' I wait, but Zuko doesn't seem to have anything more to add.

'So how's that working out for ya?' Toby asks.

'We're on a break. We're raising more money. But we're not going to take fucking corporate funding!'

'Chill, bro. Didn't mean to diss your little art project.'

I can't believe I have to put up with this shit for brains. He wouldn't even be here if we didn't need his techster friend so badly. We've done it before on our own, but they keep upgrading the security. It's like a game. We make a move, they up the stakes. Used to be any kid with a decent connect and junior school programming could do this – hack the central server, fuck up all the adboards, and replace the video with your own stuff.

When culture-jamming society first figured it out, we used to have movie nights, staging screenings of whatever people were working on, animation or documentaries or home movies or whatever, broadcasting free to the whole city on the adboards. Ash and I met on one of those rooftop *jols*, sharing a blanket, drinking cheap beer, watching amateur shorts, something about a depressed clown. I wasn't paying too much attention at the time.

But the bastards caught on quick. They de-centralised, so now you can't just hack their broadcast server and interrupt the transmission. It's all independently managed, each company maintaining its boards via satellite downlink to transmitters embedded in the board. It's a one-way connection that's completely inaccessible remotely. But that doesn't mean there aren't other ways to fuck with them. If you can chip the satellite receiver, you can run interference, even if you can't upload your own content any-more.

It's getting to the satellite receivers that's the bitch, no matter what people say in the forums. I've read the postings. If anyone on my local crew's egos get too much, I drop 'em. If they want to do it on their own, that's their own ind-aba, but I'm not having people who put us at risk, especially if they're just in it for the kicks. And that includes Toby.

I hadn't even noticed the roar of the highway, like the ocean before they installed the tide drives that levelled it off and keep the hover-trains running. And six lanes across, in the central island, the N2 Communique-108x bill-board, playing out various aspirational vignettes featuring unobtainable crap. I am itching to take it down.

We duck off the main drag into Devonshire Street and down a side alley that runs between two of the houses, semi-detached Victorian farmhouses, from back when this was open land, to a wire mesh fence that is the only bar-rier between us and the highway. We scouted everything a couple of months ago. We're al-ways looking for access points. Due caution. Always.

Ashraf snags the fence with bolt-cutters and peels it open like a tin can, so we can climb through. He goes first; given my current status, it's wisest that he takes lead tonight, followed by Zuko and Toby, who winks at Jasmine and holds the wire open for her. She scuttles awk-wardly through the gap like one of those Screebot rat-catchers.

The adboard is facing the traffic coming from town. In four hours, it'll swing round to face the incoming commute, like a sunflower turning to-wards the light. In other words, it's gonna have a major impact. We'll get most of the morning rush before they can get maintenance out to fix it.

We can only see the back side, set like an easel on its giant pylon legs, but reflected light from the cast catches the damp patches of the highway, tinting them with hints of colour. The traffic is sparse, so hopefully by the time we get across, Toby's friend will have deactivated the smart barb wire that's coiled around the base. The wire is inspired by nature, some scraggly vine that senses motion and snarls you up.

Ashraf is going through the ritual equipment check. Torches, auto screwdriver, rope, harnesses, karabiners. He'd be on video duty as well if Toby weren't doing the honours tonight.

The adboard's security runs on the powergrid, which means it can be taken off the powergrid, making it look like just another blackout, another Eskom power shortage, while we do our thing. The only problem is that the adboard freezes for the duration. And if someone notices that the screen has gone blank and calls it in, we're done.

'You ready to talk to your friend now, Toby?'

'Already sent her a text,' he says, holding up what is clearly an illegit phone, the defuser circuitry ripped out of the back and shoddily patched up with duct tape. It's a brute hack-job, but effective – if you know what you're doing. If not, the thing might kill you. I can only hope.

Ashraf whistles. 'Toby. Where did you pick that piece of prime?'

'I got my means and ways. I can get you one, if you want … Cost you premium, though. Probably out of your league. Handles movie downloads too.'

'Seriously?' Zuko and Jasmine crowd in.

'Can I see?'

'Focus, for fuck's sake! What does your friend have to say?' I cut in. This is all taking way too long.

'She's good to go. Whenever you are. Security's going down in… oh, it's down now. We got eight minutes. As of ten seconds back.'

'Shit! She's done it already? What the hell – never mind, just go! Go! After this one.' A Renault cruises past, headlights slicing the night, and we all dash across the highway before the next batch of intermittent traffic comes through, scrambling up onto the island.

We step gingerly between the coils of wire, just in case Toby's friend has not lived up to her promises. I jump to catch hold of a beam and swing my legs up, to the left of the maintenance ladder, which is off-limits, unless you have an official SIM ID or a particular desire to get crisped.

'Tendeka! Your harness.' Ashraf hisses, displeased, clipping himself in and starting after

me, hand over hand up the rope, Toby right behind him. Jasmine and Zuko are supposed to
stay at the bottom to keep watch, but the kid
has other plans. He's clipping in too. I don't
have time to worry about him, though. Not
with the insane deadline we're on.

I pull myself up onto the catwalk that runs
behind the adboard and wedge the screwdriver
under the corner edge of the screen, prising it
away from the casing, cracking the plastech. But
there's no need to finesse it.

The great thing about smear is that the tech
is straight out of the box, compliments of my
friend in Amsterdam, so there aren't preventive
measures in place yet. Smear's not the technical
word, of course; it's a TSR-3 signal delay device
that interferes with data packet transfer, so the
image that gets displayed is garbled and incom-
plete like that painting with the melted clocks.
It was invented in America to try and shut
down streamcasters who were getting too vocal
in criticising the administration. It's nice to be
able to turn it around.

I click open the plastic container, disguised as
a flashdrive, in case of random searches in the
street, but I'm sweating so heavily, I nearly drop
the damn thing. Ash nudges his way in beside
me. 'Two and a half minutes,' Jazz calls from
below. Ashraf's jaw is tight with stress as he

takes the smear chip and binds it onto the motherboard with his pocket solder.

'Can you guys move it? Let me get a clear shot of this?' Toby tjunes, his abruptly added weight making the catwalk shudder.

'Fuck off, Toby, there's no time. You can't film this part of the operation. It's too sensitive.'

'Hey, fuck you, Tendeka. It's my connection. I get the footage I want. And you think they're not going to figure it out when they come to fix it tomorrow morning?'

And then Zuko swings up, so the walkway is dangerously overcrowded, when we should already be down and safely back across the highway.

'You're risking all of us, you asshole.'

But Toby is unmoved. 'Yeah, so are you. Just give me a clear view, and we can all go home.'

'Ninety-six seconds,' Jasmine calls from below.

'Shit, shit, shit. Everyone down. Now!'

Toby jostles in to get his shot and it's all I can do to stop myself shoving him against the railing, which is the perfect height to hit him behind the knees and tip him into the mesh of barbwire below. Even deactivated, it would do plenty damage.

'You're on your fucking own.' I swing out round the side and start the descent, not bothering to look back. Ash is already halfway down, but Zuko has stalled on the walkway, trying to get in the picture. 'Thirty-seven seconds.'

'Would you get down?' Ash snaps. 'There's no time!'

Zuko finally catches a wake-up and starts scrambling down.

Toby rolls over the railing, real dramatic, and I'm praying he clipped in incorrectly, that his harness is going to spill him the twenty-metre drop, but no such luck. The karabiner catches and he rappels down, easily overtaking Zuko.

'Six seconds. Come on!'

I touch down. Ashraf is struggling to unclip, and there really is no fucking time when we're ankle-deep in smart barbwire that is about to reactivate. I flick open my Spiderco, rip the blade through the reinforced webbing of his harness, and we vault over the wire, his hand locked in mine.

'Minus three.'

Toby kicks off hard from the support beams, still relatively high, so that he swings out over the highway, clear of the wire, and then the moron simply unclips, which means he tumbles two metres onto the tar. He lands hard. I hope he's broken something.

'Jesus fuck!' He stands up and starts hobbling across the highway, clutching his shoulder.

But right now I'm worried about Zuko, who is only halfway down. If he gets caught, and caves and links this back to me, it's going to be the end of more than just a promising junior soccer career.

'Minus sixteen,' Jasmine says, still watching her clock. 'I'm sorry, I must have messed up the timing. But it's going to kick in any second.'

'Jump, idiot!' I shout. And Zuko does, landing on his feet, barely, but his boot catches one of the barbs, so it shears through the leather and skin underneath, and then he's in my arms, almost sobbing with relief.

Except the barbwire is not twitching back to life. The screen is still frozen. There's no time to consider. I yank Zuko up and out of the coils at his feet and pelt across the highway, holding up a hand to the oncoming headlights that swerve round us, disappearing into the curve of Hospital Bend, horn bleating angrily.

Toby is waiting on the other side, sitting on the fence and rolling his shoulder. I hope it's fucking broken.

The adboard comes back up with a flicker. And I feel that hard kick of victory. Cos we've fucking done it. And now, with the TSR fraying the signal, all those too-beautiful clebs and models and realife™ virtua spokespersons frisking in the ocean or nodding into the latest cell or acting in the consumer mini-movies for LG or Lucky Strike or Premiere Recruiting will look somehow wrong.

And maybe it will take the commuters a second or two to figure it out. To pick up that the features of the bouncy beach babe or the cool hand smoker in the ads on this board are melting, running down their faces. Smeared. And it feels fucking great, even with Zuko sporting an injury that is going to be difficult to explain to casualty. Until Toby opens his mouth.

'Shit, that really hurt. Do not try this at home, kids. Oh, what. Don't be so panicky, Tendeka. I was kidding about the eight minutes. Lerato's real generous. She gave us twelve. I just thought you could do with added incentive, up the drama, you know?'

This time I do hit him. In the face. Full on.

Lerato

I get to work to discover that Mpho has turned stalker boy. There is an outrageous bouquet of flowers on my desk, complete with miniature butterflies, the kind gen-modded to stay within a hand's-length radius of the scent of the assigned homing flower and guaranteed to live seventy-two hours, if you believe the advertising. Until now, I've never met anyone cheesy enough to fall for it.

Seed has paired us on the MetroBabe Stroller audio job, designing an interface that works for both toddlers and parents. At the touch of a button, it has to be able to play back rockabyes, current hits packaged as instrumental lullabies for baby, or MetroBabe's private info station, simply jam-packed with useful information to help guide new parents through the very special hell they've signed up for. The things already come with two cup-holders, one for baby's

bottle, one for mom's moccachino or, more re-
alistically, mom's whisky flask.

I wave away the butterflies that are hovering
near my screen, attracted to the light, and
shove the bouquet to the edge of my desk,
which will hopefully limit the little bastards'
range. There's no sign of Mpho, which is savagely annoying.

There is a MetroBabe audio file in my jobs
folder, so I can get some idea of the content
we're dealing with. I ignore it and kill time waiting for Mpho by checking my mail, updating my
dating profile on Seed and prowling the responses. There're three pre-approved potential
matches, all within Communique or affiliated
companies (which means no lengthy mutual
nondisclosure contracts to sign before you can
move on to the sex), one civilian, which I delete
without even looking at (at least I admit I'm bi-
ased), and a man of real interest from a rival
corp, which Seed has tagged as questionable,
meaning a potential headhunter.

Considering how I got here, to this twenty-
third floor office, to this desk with its views of
the seaboard, you'd think the system might
trust me to spot one all on my own. Or maybe
they're letting me know that they know. Heads
up, girl, we're paying attention. Hopefully not
too closely.

The guy's profile looks sony, as Toby might say. Stefan Thuys. Forty-one, which is ten years older than my ideal, but hey, I'm open to trying new things. He's a development exec on game-soft, reasonably attractive apart from the craggy nose that looks as though it may have been broken at some stage, which is unreasonably hot. He claims an interesting selection of media, although his choices are suspiciously hip. But who doesn't paint themselves in a prettier light? And I've always been interested in development. I msg him. He msgs back, and we hook up a date for later in the week.

At last I'm prepared to get round to the MetroBabe audio file. I drag it into my player and crank up the volume. I'll be damned if I have to suffer through the incessant infant-stuff alone.

'...*surrogate breast milk is a risk, Noeleen, but it's a qualified risk if you go through the correct channels, and get a certified provider who can provide you with a full medical history. You can get cocktails specially made to order, get your provider to take vitamins and nutrients tailored to the very specific needs of your baby's gene map.*'

Across the office, a couple of people raise their heads. Genevieve mouths at me, 'Can you privacy that?' but I ignore her.

And finally Mpho materialises at my desk, pushing a stroller, the dull grey of the plastic marking it as a prototype fresh off the printer. 'Hey, L. Hope you haven't been waiting too long. I thought I'd get a demo model from product development so we can really nail this thing. Oops, nearly forgot!' He produces two lattes with a flourish from the cup-holders. 'Mamzelle.' In four days of getting room service together, you'd think he would have picked up that I take my coffee black.

'But couldn't you just add those to the content afterwards? Or, I don't know, give your baby supplements, Dr. Redelinghuys?'

'Thanks, babe.' I deliberately let the coffee slip through my fingers so it drops into the bin, spilling its contents en route. Someone else will clean it up. I probably should have done the same with the flowers, just swept them off the desk into the rubbish. Mpho looks shocked.

'So, M,' I emphasise the consonant, how it's really not a name. 'You ready to tackle this baby thing?'

'I'm sorry. Was there something wrong–?'

'I'm lactose-intolerant, Mpho. Thanks for asking.'

'Shit. I'm sorry. Let me get you another one.'

'Can we just do this?'

Mpho is insistent. 'Seriously, let me get you another one. I'll be right back.'

'No, honestly–' but he's already dashed off.

'That's a good question, Noeleen, but really I think we have to look at the way the body system processes nutrients, and how that's passed on to your baby. She really needs all this goodness in a way that's palatable to her still-developing immune system, that she can readily absorb, especially when it comes to HIV antibodies–'

I click it off. As if actually having a drooling, mewling, puking little troll weren't enough. If I had to listen to this shit all day, I'd kill myself.

There's a good reason I need to get this out of the way asap. I'm expecting a tech support call-out any minute to deal with a damaged adboard. I stayed up all night coding upgrades with some neat little added features of my own for the security software they're going to have to install today, and then covering my tracks to ensure it looks like they've always been there.

When the maintenance team head out, I need to monitor them remotely to ensure there aren't any unexpected surprises that might betray me when the software update goes live. But of course, I'm not supposed to know that an adboard has been hit. Not yet. So I wait.

Mpho finally gets back, balancing a filter ultra and a selection of every variety of sweetener and cinnamon/chocolate/mint additive possible, just in case. I drink it black just to spite him, not that he notices.

'What did you do to your hair?' he asks, in a little-boy-wounded way. He should have seen it before I had the Communique inhouse stylist tidy it up this morning. 'I liked it long.'

'I get bored easily.'

You'd think I would know better than to get involved with someone in my own department. But I'm really crap at resisting sexual tension. Oh, it's entertaining for a few weeks, the fuzzy sting that rushes down your vertebra to your groin when the eyes meet, the banter spiked with innuendo – then it becomes irritating, and you need to get it out of your system. Neutralise it by indulging it, which is fine, assuming you can both keep it tidy.

'You've had a listen, what do you reckon? The prototype isn't functioning 100%, but you can see the way it's structured is there's one big tactile button for baby right where he can get at it, and here, on the pushbar, full audio controls and screen for mommy...'

'I'm just the programmer,' I snarl, cutting him off. 'I'm only interested in the internal processes.'

'Whooo! Someone is *grumpy* this morning.'

'I was up most of the night,' I snip, too defensive. He's caught me off guard, and I've slipped up, which is a good indication that I haven't in fact had enough rest, but please let him not try and get into the why. Fortunately, his brain defaults automatically to the same strand of primitive code every time.

'You should have called me,' he leers. 'I could have come over. Helped you *sleep*.'

'The job?' I point at the screen, impatient.

'You didn't even say anything about the flowers.'

'They're stunning. Amazing. How did you ever think of such a meaningful and original gesture?'

'Wow. You are vicious.' He seems hurt, and because I need him to hurry up and get this out of the way, I kiss and make up.

'I'm sorry, Mpho. I'm ratty when I'm sleep-deprived. You should tell the product designers it should be a hanging mobile rather than a button. You want something the little shit will want to play with, something sparkly or dangly that he'll reach for anyway, and then it just happens to make a cute sound or play a lullaby or whatever.'

'Rockabye.'

'Yeah, okay. That too.'

'That's actually brilliant, Lerato.'

'I know.'

'You should be in design. You should be heading up design!'

'Oh, I know.'

It takes twenty minutes to work out the details of how the interface needs to work, and then I chase Mpho off so I can focus on the programming. I have an idea I can patch in a fair amount of the code I used in a previous job (the PlayPlay Pterodactyl Robot Friend), but it's still going to take me most of the morning, and I run into trouble with a finicky bit with the voice recognition, getting it to filter out baby's babblings. Of course, the real solution here would be to program it to recognise the different gooing and gurgling and translate it into English for mama. Didn't I read some pushmag thing on the theory of baby communications? If I could figure out baby's language code, that would be a product feature. Let's call it Radio Gaga.

Toby calls, just as I'm about to crack it. Okay, so I'm nowhere near cracking it, but I tell him it's his fault anyway. He's not sympathetic. 'Don't dump me with your dilemmas. I need serious work-related tech support.'

'Uh-huh?' I say, carefully neutral, surreptitiously activating privacy on my cubicle so the audio dampeners kick in, just in case he's stupid enough to make any passing reference to the adboard. There still hasn't been an official report. Not that I don't know that invoking privacy means that Seed automatically tags my conversation, all phone calls will be recorded for quality assurance purposes blah blah blah, but I've got misdirects in place. I have a mix of pre-recorded conversations, from the polite and cursory catch-ups with my sisters (when Zama can be bothered to call), to a variety of hot and heavy that gives the spyware controllers upstairs something to do with their hands. The only hassle is constantly updating them, so the monitoring boys don't get suspicious. I needn't have bothered on this one. Toby's 'dilemma' is almost a legitimate request. Easy enough. And fucking hilarious.

'Whenever you're ready, sweetness,' Toby says, put out, which only makes me laugh harder.

'That's a new record in lame, Toby.'

'Yeah, let's see how *you* handle getting cut off from your trustfundable by your motherbitch.'

'Oh nice, Toby. Real nice.' The only thing I ever got from my parents was a kickstart into corporate life.

'You know what I fucking mean. Don't get touchy.'

'Fine. But you owe me.'

'Rack it on my tab.'

'And you're still king lame.'

'Love ya, babe. Gotta run, got little kiddies to kill for fun and profit.'

It takes a minute and a half to reroute Toby's IP address so it looks like he's logging in from Melbourne rather than Cape Town, which should sort out his little problem.

And then, at last, the adboard call comes in. I'm not technically involved in the maintenance process, but I have access to the job sheets, and it's not unusual for coders at my level to monitor the execution. Yusuf and Petronella get the call as the closest technicians in the vicinity. I couldn't have calibrated it better myself. Yusuf is smart but lazy, and Petronella is just plain lazy. They'll be more worried about the damage Toby and his friends have done to the hardware than any inconsistencies in the software. Assuming my code holds, all will be well.

And it does. And it is.

There's a surplus of people who do what I do, to the extent that I'm surprised they don't consider culling. Good programmers are as easy to score as a blowjob on Lower Main Road, and just about as cheap. You really have to distinguish yourself if you're going to make any progress.

It was easy getting noticed at nineteen, but I'm getting on, and if you haven't cracked management by twenty-eight, your chances of doing so decrease exponentially for every year you add to your CV. I've still got a few years, but

I'm not ending up like Jane. Rather be a startling failure than a benign success.

I figure my options are pretty limited within Communique. But with the penalties for inter-corporate poaching running into hundreds of thousands, it's going to be difficult to persuade another corporate that they need me, when they can get fresher and younger talent straight out of the skills institutes for much, much less. Unless I have something to sweeten the deal. Like a backdoor, say, installed in their rival's security software on the adboards that allows you to access Communique's proprietary information, track the data and the response rates. Call it market research. 'Corporate espionage' is so over-dramatic.

A monarch alights on my keyboard, flexing its wings, flashing the striations of velvety orange and black. Strayed too far from the nest, little guy. They don't like that around here. I crush it delicately under my thumb.

Toby

Digging through my laundry to find something relatively fresh and suitable for public consumption, I happen upon Jasmine's scarf, which she left here after the raid last night. It smells like her, very faintly through the musty wool and the overwhelming notes of Fairtrade caramel butter, cos Jazz isn't the kind of girl to wear perfume, but she's not the great unwashed specimen of activist either, which I appreciate. I take a deep breath of that warm girly goodness, and then trash the thing. Hey, it's not like she's going to be coming back to get it.

I stagger over to my console, clip the Moxy chip into the game socket and, instantaneously, there are little blobby monsters bouncing around all over my projecta walls and *singing*. This, after all the sugar, and with the residue ache of being sucker-punched in the face, is a very bad thing, kids. My cheek has turned a bluish-yellow where that bastard Tendeka got me.

I reduce the display to just one wall, skip the jangle, choose the first character I'm offered (some furry blue thing with oversized paws – RomperStomp, special move the Shaker-Quake) and connect to the gameworld along with the 1,487,763 other players currently on-line, 99% of whom are in the eight-to-twelve demographic. The remainder are like me, gate-crashers cashing in on the system, or maybe paedophiles looking to hook up. I suspect the former group may be the more evil of the two.

The trip connects, and RomperStomp shimmers into existence in some cheesy-ass neo-classical archway in a candy-coloured jungle, swampy pools burping oily bubbles that pop to release weird little flittering manta rays, and, in the distance, weird looming rock things like you'd get in Vietnam or somewhere, craggy columns with a thatch of greenery on top and a path of floating step blocks leading away. It's vomitously cute.

I haven't made it two steps from the entry portal, let alone figured out the fucking buttons, when three furry blobs land on top of me, all claws and teeth.

'Shit! Wait!' The wall blanks suddenly and Moxy fills the screen. Cos Moxy is always

watching. He waves a stubby little paw in dis-
approval.

>>So sorry! You have been booted from
Kiwi Pop for bad behaviour! If you promise
to play nice and not swear any more, you
can play again for sure!

I'd forgotten the vocal interactions. I turn it
off, no sense betraying my age by my voice, and
click on the 'I promise to behave' button.

I respawn in the arch only to be immediately
ambushed by the little bastards, who are clearly
waiting for me.

>>Hi guys! Will you be my friend? says Romper
Stomp, one of the default pre-selects in case
you're too lazy to type or vocalise.

>>Die, newbie scum! yells the one called
Fluffoki in a little girl's voice brimming with
malice.

I hit back, punching and kicking, but they've
got more experience and there're three of them.
I've just got the hang of the Shaker-Quake,
knocking Fluffoki off her feet and doing some
serious damage when one of her little chums
takes me out with a blow to the head, KO-ing
me one time.

The screen blanks again.

>>So sorry! You have died. But at least you
tried! Would you like to try again? You've
still got nine lives out of ten.

This is Unathi's revenge for the chicks dig.

When I call her for help, Lerato is the antithe-
sis of sympathy, giggling so mega-hysterical, I'm
sure she's gonna pop a valve. Which would
serve her right. 'That's a new record in lame,
Toby,' she says, when she manages to breathe
again. But she cuts me some slack and saves my
ass.

It takes genius girl a full minute and a half to
circumvent the entrance portal where Fluffoki
and Co. are waiting for me in ambush, rerout-
ing home™'s IP address so it looks like I'm
logging in from Melbourne with a whole new
character. She's done this before on my home™
sys back when we ordered those medical-grade
biogen 'shrooms from Thailand. It took three
weeks to get the damn things with the bouncing
around to fake addresses, but it was so worth it.

We spent the day on Communique's private
beach in Clifton, fucked out of our brackets,
building sandcastles like little kids, having really
bizarre conversations with her co-workers and
giggling a lot in general. When I started freaking
out about the water catching on fire, though,
she hustled me out of there simunye, cos a

major scene could reflect badly on her prospects. I don't see why anyone would care. As long as it doesn't interfere with your job, what you do in your recreational is entirely up to you. Not that I'm unappreciative of getting a backstage pass to the corporati highlife.

Anyway, thing is, spawning is random the first time you play, but once you touch down in the special hell that is Moxyland, whichever portal you emerge out of becomes your home base. You die, you go back there again and again and again, and if some psycho bratlings are waiting to maul you every time, it gets Sisyphean quick-quick.

I re-surface as an all-new character, a Popling Ludo, special move the Reverb Roar, in an all-new home base, this one pseudo-Halloween with creepy husks of trees and lumo moss that hangs off the branches like beards, miles away from that little bitch Fluffoki and her crew.

This time, I'm prepared for any juve delinquents who even think of jumping me. I ditch the greets and wade in bloody as soon as any new character makes an entrance, despite the shaky finger and more trite couplets from Moxy.

>>On your scorecard, here's a blot, for playing mean; that sucks a lot.

Who writes this *shit*? And worse, gets financial remuneration for it? I need to get in on that game.

It takes four and a half hours to battle it out to level six, get to the sacred Maori hideout in the Waitomo caves and beat the pulp out of the guardian spirit, which resembles a giant cuddly platypus, until he surrenders the purple BlinkaStinka.

Trophy in paw, I invest another hour twenty backtracking to find my original spawn-in spot, and reduce Fluffoki and her little friendlings to so much dead flesh, although sorry to say, it being a kids' game, they die in splatters of sparks rather than bloody gibs. Fluffoki does break out some very bad words, not entirely appropriate for an eight year-old girl.

And as a finishing touch, I put in a special request to Lerato to trace the little bastards' user names and get them banned from the gamespace for violating protocol. The pretext for locking them out is killer.

Overage players.

Tendeka

We arrive at the Green Point market, to find that Emmie is AWOL. Ashraf tries to convince me we've got the wrong row, but I know exactly where her stall is supposed to be, wedged between the downloads booth and the over-pierced goth girl with her radical handmade fashion, all velvet, lace and PVC with complicated lacings, now also available in Pluslife, according to a sign in dayglo purple highlighting.

I know we're in the right place, only instead of Emmie with her plastic chickens and wire jewellery, there is an aggro Kenyan punting kangas and cowrie bracelets, and for all I know dodgy defuser interference devices under the counter, who starts screaming at me when I ask why the fuck he's working the stall registered to my wife, Emmie Chinyaka? Especially when Ash paid the full month's rental in advance two days ago.

'You should look better after your *wife*, hey?' the Kenyan cracks smugly.

I drop Ashraf's hand abruptly. I would wipe that smirk off his face if it didn't mean I'd have to deal with the cops.

We cause enough of a fracas that the market manager, who introduces himself as Mr. Hartley, no first name provided, materialises and takes us to his office stadium-side.

It seems Emmie terminated her contract yesterday, and took a refund on the rent, no problem for management with so many clamouring to fill the space. Only 50% of the eight thousand though, due to last-minute notice clauses. She sold off her wares and her shadecloth to some of the other traders, packed up the scant remains, and left. No, unfortunately, terribly sorry, he doesn't know where she went or why.

'Have you tried the hospital?' Mr. Hartley says with sugary concern, like we wouldn't have thought of that already. She's not due to pop for another month, unless it's a miscarriage or a premature, both eventualities Ash obsesses about constantly. We don't have a clue who the father is, whether it was some border guard demanding a toll, or a militia rape. Emmie won't talk about it. But Ashraf and I have discussed it, and we believe the kid shouldn't have to carry the karma. This is the chance to make something good out of the worst possible scenario. And soon he'll have two dads. We're going to name him for Ash's father.

'I'm sure she's at home,' Ash smoothes. 'Thanks for all your help. I'm sorry if there was any misunderstanding.' I hate it when he apologises for me.

It takes an hour to get to Delft by train with the strikes. Of course, these don't affect the corporate lines.

It's a 2k walk to the temporary residential hostel where Emmie's been staying; a severe three-storey block, identical to the hundred other severe blocks surrounding it, a warren of concrete bunkers. We've given Emmie an open invitation to come and stay with us, at least until she has the baby, but she always refuses, which makes Ashraf crazy with worry.

'Temporary' residential is a hideous joke, of course. The two girls she shares a room with have been there for three and a half years, and still no word on when their assigned RDP housing is going to come through. It's another perfect example of the system's egregious failings. There's a backlog of 1,190,000 or something, and that's just counting the legal applicants, not the African refugees or the rurals coming in under the radar, the ones who can't afford to wait around for the proper health clearances.

A man, scrawny and dark, not local, opens the door to the dank stairway. 'What do you want?'

'Is Emmie here? We were supposed to meet her at the market–' Ashraf starts.

'She's not here.' He tries to close the door on us, but I lean on it with my full weight, so he's forced backwards.

'Emmie! You here? You all right?' I'm aware of Ashraf and the guy following in my wake as I pound up the stairs, three at a time. A kid with snot crusted down his lips peers down, blankly disinterested. A woman in the communal kitchen looks up startled from the *Daily Voice* with its screaming headline 'DYING FOR A CURE? MUTI MURDERS MULTIPLY'.

'Emmie?'

Her door is wide open, casting a rectangle of light into the corridor, but just before I get there, the security gate clangs hastily shut and a fumble of keys locks it tight.

'Emmie. What are you doing? We spent hours looking for you. We had a meeting, remember? For Home Affairs?'

Her hands curl round the bars of the security gate, real Pollsmoor. I feel that familiar knot at how painfully young she is, how naïve and far out of her comfort zone. She doesn't look up at me, staring down at the bulge of her belly. 'Go away. I can't see you today.'

Behind her, there's nothing as obvious as a half-packed suitcase lying open on her bed, but something has changed in her room, with its scant possessions, the three beds barely a foot apart, with bedsheets hanging from the ceiling like dividers, the paraffin safestove, the broken-down Fifties kitchen cabinet that might be worth something restored, on which a small TV is balanced precariously among a clutter of cheap cosmetics. A piece of cardboard, an advert for a Sunlight Soap competition, is taped to the window to cover a broken pane, advertising a prize of one million clams, all those zeros clamouring for attention, insultingly unreachable, above the face of a grinning little white girl in pigtails.

We've drawn spectators: the snotty kid and the reader, whom I recognise now as one of Emmie's roommates, and door guy, who is plucking insistently at my arm. 'You must go.'

'Fuck off, bro! Emmie, listen to me. This is majorly important. I don't care what you did with the rent money from the stall. We'll get you another spot, more stock. Whatever. But you can't pull this disappearing act. If Home Affairs suspects this isn't makoya, you'll be deported.'

'I'm not staying.'

'Don't be mental. Where are you going to go?'

'You must leave, please.'

I shrug door guy's hand off my shoulder. 'Emmie. Be reasonable. You have a job here. You have a real possibility of a life. What about the baby?'

'You have to go. You must get out.' Door guy is trying to tug me away.

'Jesus Christ! Will you get off!' I shove him against the wall, Emmie gasps, and only then do I click the fucking obvious that's been staring me in the face all along. The bedsheet with its pathetically faded floral print has been pulled closed around her bed for privacy. And among the coconut butter and hand cream and mascara is a man's deodorant, a man's brand shaving cream.

'Ah, fuck, Emmie. Is this–?' But of course it is. Door guy blinks hard when I round on him, but then draws himself up, resilient, and why not? Compared to what he must have gone through getting here, who the fuck am I that he should be afraid of me?

'Emmie. Why didn't you just tell me? Do you realise–? Fuck! I could go to fucking jail, Emmie. They could disconnect me for this. Permanently.'

I shake the security gate, so hard that it

judders, and Emmie cowers back, automatically putting one hand to the bump that has turned her bellybutton into a protruding jellytot. Babydaddy puts his hand over her fingers clutching the bars, reassuring. But where the fuck was he two months ago, when she was begging on the street corner, filthy and gaunt around the swell of her stomach?

'What about your baby, Emmie? What are you going to say to your baby when you're all fucking starving to death in some under-resourced camp in Lilongwe? Huh, Emmie?'

'Tendeka.' Ashraf finally speaks.

'I don't fucking care. You still have to do the interview. You are not going to put me at risk. And you are not getting our child – your child – deported. It's three years, Emmie, three years that we have to stay married before your residency is safe. You're not going anywhere until then, Emmie. You hear me?'

'We need more money,' she says quietly, meeting my eyes for the first time, drawing strength from babydaddy, closing me out.

'Fine. Of course. Whatever you want. How much?'

'Eight thousand. Mr. Hartley only gave me half–'

'Yeah, you should have thought that one through.'

'C'mon, Tendeka.'

'Cut it out, Ashraf. She can have it after the fucking interview. You hear me, you manipulative lying cow? After.'

Ash wants to talk about it, all the way home. 'It doesn't mean it's over. She probably just wants to have the baby and be done with it. Take off with her boyfriend, start a new life somewhere. We could even help them. They could disappear.'

'And what's Home Affairs going to say? Refugee wife just ditches her kid with us and runs off, and they're not going to investigate? No, fuck that. We signed up for the full deal here, Ash. Our kid is not gonna get taken away from us just because babydaddy's back in the picture. And they're not running off and getting deported to cause all kinds of shit for us. They're just gonna have to see it through.'

'Ten, don't be stubborn, please. Think about it. It's three years we'll have to keep this up. And what if she changes her mind? Runs away with him?'

'No way. Forget it. This is my stand against the bullshit of artificially imposed borders and bureaucracies. And if Emmie and her pop-up babydaddy don't understand the implications, then I'm just going to have to hold her hand through it all. She's sticking it out. And she's not going back on our agreement.'

'But this is not a moral stand, Ten. This is our lives.'

After the horrendous day, it's a shock logging into Avalon. My enviro-friendly house and the three houses surrounding it have been replaced with loxion shelters, the tinshacks appallingly incongruous among the mansions and mani-cured lawns.

I'm already on the backfoot when skyward* walks out of the corrugated door, his avatar grinning idiotically wide and extending her arms with a little twirl, like a Miss Mzansi con-testant.

>> skyward*: tada! what do you think? do you like it?
>> 10: What the fuck? I didn't authorise this. u can't just hack my dwell
>> skyward*: it's a new direction. we're abandoning the subtle approach.
>> 10: It's DEFINITELY not subtle
>> skyward*: should it be? does subtlety cut it? how was your green house working out for ya?
>> 10: It's an idealisation, it's setting an example, showing people an alternative to what a perfect world might be

>> skyward: is it enough to set a good
example? how much of an impact have you
really made here? and what the fuck does
that matter anyway? it's not real.
>> 10: I don't understand. I do REAL shit
realworld
>> skyward: you have Struggle
connections in your family, right?

The part of me that is not still reeling from the
surprise of finding my house transmogrified into
shack chic is impressed that he remembers this
from the conversation we had when we first
met through the future*renovate site last year.
But I may have overemphasised the connection.
It was a second cousin by marriage whose
grandmother helped shelter Ruth First, a Com-
munist journalist blown up by a letter bomb in
the 1980s. They had to scrape bits of her off the
walls. Not a nice way to go.

>> 10: Yeah. And?
>> skyward*: you ask that cousin about
the effectiveness of politely asking for
change, of peaceful demonstrations, the
total pointlessness of street theatre or civil
disobedience. or democracy.
>> 10: She's dead. She died last year of a
heart attack. We flew up to Port Elizabeth

for the funeral.

>> skyward*: whatever. it's time to radicalise, 10. assuming you're ready for more ambitious work? but maybe i've misjudged you? based on how upset you are by such a minor adjustment? it's just a virtual house, after all.

>> 10: No, you just, you caught me by surprise. I wasn't expec

>> skyward*: best time to catch someone, wouldn't you agree? unprepared. is your protege fully recovered from his scratch, btw?

>>10: What?

>> skyward*: your soccer boy. the one who was injured?

>> 10: Oh. Yeah. Mostly. He's taking some downtime. The meds patched him up. He spun them a story about falling off a roof, doing stunts, trying to impress a girl.

>> skyward*: i posted the video from your friend's jacket cameras to the net, by the way. it's doing the rounds of the jam circuit. already spilling into the mainstream viral content. a colleague in new york sent it to me via her phone, didn't have the faintest idea of my involvement. she thought it was cool.

>> 10: But we haven't modded it yet. You can see all our faces. That was strictly for

your personal viewing.

>> skyward*: don't worry, it's all taken care of. we edited it beautifully, distorted your voices, smeared your faces. it's untraceable, trust me. we rerouted it via an anonyma server in trinidad.

>> 10: Are you sure? Jesus

>> skyward*: it's all taken care of.

>> 10: No, it's just. I've got a lot of shit going down right now. I mean Emmie and Home Affairs and the disconnect and trying to raise funding for Streets Back.

>> skyward*: do what you have to do. and stop fucking around with the art project. you need money to make it happen. just take the corporate cash.

>> 10: But

>> skyward*: what do you care?

>> 10: It's tainted. It's against all our principles. I mean, you talk about making a real impact, what's the point if you're doing it dirty, breeding more misery? It's like terrorists dealing heroin for the cause. It's a cycle of darkness.

>> skyward*: terrorists? drugs? come now, are you saying we're on the same level? i expected more of you. what we have here is a world that is more apathetic and more violent than ever. the newscasts are so

filtered to individual tastes, people only
ever hear what they want to hear. and the
genocide in malawi, once the model of
peaceful african democracies, not only
doesn't make the front page of the news
sites, it barely ranks a mention. and you
can't solve it by marrying a refugee.

>> 10: Actually

>> skyward: i'm not finished. call it mass-
scale compassion fatigue or selfish genes or
the obvious conclusion capitalism has
always been headed for, but the reality is
people don't give a flying fuck. they've seen
all the old strategies before. they're tired
and worse, they're boring. and if there's
one thing our culture doesn't stand for, 10,
it's boredom. you know that. we have to jolt
them, surprise them, it has to be
spectacular. we're competing with media
and advertising and promotions and
pluslives, all helping people to avoid
confronting reality.

>> 10: Okay, okay, I see where you're
headed

>> skyward*: do you? let me put it to you
this way. does anything you've done
compare to what the corporates have done?

>> 10: What do you mean?

>> skyward*: corrupting govts with their

own agendas, politicians on their payroll,
exacerbating the economic gaps. building
social controls and access passes and
electroshock pacifiers into the very
technology we need to function day to
day, so you've no choice but to accept the
defuser in your phone or being barred
from certain parts of the city because you
don't have clearance. you tell me how
that compares to you hacking an
adboard.

>> 10: So, we're not doing enough.

>> skyward*: hallelujah! yes. nowhere
near enough. we need to jar people from
their apathy. we need spectacle. we need
to fight the corporates on their own terms.
Counter-exploitative.

>> 10: Using their money.

>> skyward*: what better way to subvert
them? it's not just perfect, it's beautiful.

>> 10: I guess.

>> skyward*: you _guess_? there's no
space for hedging. if you're not up for the
serious work, i can find someone else. it'll
take time, but you're not irreplaceable, 10.
don't you want to be part of something
bigger than you?

>> 10: Yes.

>> skyward*: yes what?

>> 10: Yes, I want to be part of something bigger. I want to rearrange the world for real. Okay? Is that fucking good enough for you? I'm totally fucking committed to whatever needs to be done. Whatever that means. All right?

>> skyward*: you see what i'm saying? trust me, 10, what we have on the horizon is going to be massive. the ripples are going to be felt globally. and we couldn't do it without you. so, what are you doing thursday night?

>> 10: Sounds like a bad pick-up line

>> skyward*: ha. it's going to be better than sex, 10. it's going to be beautiful. the city is a communication system. we're going to be teaching it a new language.

Kendra

Dr. Precious makes a note in her file and snaps it closed.

'You can step off the scale now. You'll be pleased to know everything's fine. The nano has taken hold.'

'You make it sound like I'm possessed.'

Andile laughs. 'Taken hold, babes. Like it's happy in there. Your immune system is convinced the tech is friendly. No more trying to shoot it down. No more sniffly noses or itches. No problems.'

'No meltdown?'

'Tsk.' Dr. Precious really doesn't like my jokes. She doesn't think I'm an appropriate choice for 'The Project'. I know this because I overheard her saying so to Andile as I stepped from the lift. He replied, 'What are you going to do? Flakiness comes with creativity.' Which I kind of resent.

Andile claps his hands together with decisive enthusiasm. 'Well, now that we've got the icky check-up stuff out of the way, we need five more minutes of your very precious time for the doccie. Making history, babes.' Andile ushers me out of his office, down the elevator to the second floor and through the configuration of desks in the agency proper.

It's open-plan, the desks partitioned by gauzy white curtains hung floor-to-ceiling, audio dampeners woven into the fabric for privacy. There are interested looks, a couple of heads popping up like meerkats.

'Just ignore them,' Andile says. 'It's not often they get to see *real* talent.' There is a snort of disgust from behind a console. 'Back to work, you graft-dodging slacker reprobates!' Andile shouts cheerfully.

The lounge is weighted against the view, suede couches incongruously lumped together with an assortment of beanbags shaped like liquorice candy, pieces I recognise from a design magazine. Slumped on a plump foam sandwich of pink and black candy is a boy, bored, good-looking and intent on studying the floorboards.

He looks up when we come in, dark hair spiked and swept over his forehead in defiance of the thinning at his temples. Brown pinstripe jacket. White tie. I recognise him from somewhere, maybe from a glimpse of his file on Andile's desk.

Andile seems surprised. 'Damian, china! You haven't interviewed?'

'No. The camera-chick said, like, ten more minutes?' The boy slits his eyes at me, wary-friendly, like a cat.

'Cool, cool. Can I offer you guys some coffee? Tea? Tequila? No, just kidding! Nothing? Okay! Just hang tight, shouldn't be too much longer. Be cool. You're ambassadors now. First generation! I'll just go see how she's coming along.'

I take a seat opposite the boy, Damian. I've realised he's from a new spectro band, Kitten Kill or Killer Kittens, or some other configuration playing off violent acts towards baby animals. The point is that they're bigtime.

Maybe he picks up on it, because the first thing he says to me is, 'So, how'd you get with the program?' As in, you don't look the type.

I play it down. 'I'm a photographer. Fine arts.'

'Oh yeah?' he says, not really interested. 'The rest of the guys are pretty peeved,' he goes on, just assuming I'll know who he's talking about. Unfortunately, I do. 'That they only wanted me, y'know? It's *swak*, hey. I mean, don't get me wrong, it's awesome, but end of the day, I gotta get up on stage with the rest of the band and perform.'

I smile and nod. He is the obvious choice for the next evolutionary.

'So, you in for the creative exchange? Ah, man, I'm so stoked about getting to play Seoul. I had to look it up on the map. I mean, yeah, okay, New Korea, but where is that actually?'

A woman in chunky jewellery and stiletto boots over her jeans scissors into the lounge, holding a microcam. 'Damian? You're up. I hope you've been thinking up devastatingly smart and interesting things to say. Oh, don't look so nervous. Just be yourself. Recite some lyrics or something.' She winks at me. 'Don't think I'll be too long with this one.' She leads him away between the maze of curtained cubicles, already recording.

'So, what is it that moves you, Dame? What's the one thing about music that grabs you, that hits you right in your gut?'

I slip my Zion out of my bag, having already snuck it past the receptionist, and surreptitiously snap a photograph of the indentation Damian has left on the liquorice beanbag, the crease like a smile down the middle. Because things are only real if they are documented, if there is visual evidence.

I mention this to camera-chick when she comes clipping back in. 'Oh yeah,' she says, 'absolutely!' and hustles me out onto the balcony, buffered with sliding glass panels to keep the wind at bay.

The red bead of the camera winks steadily, for the record, recording, recording. 'So, is that why you became a photographer? To capture *life*? Do you feel like you don't have a hold on it otherwise?'

'I'm not exactly a professional.'

'Don't be humble, honey. And can you do me a favour? Can you start your sentences with "I became a photographer because blah blah blah…" Otherwise it's a nightmare in the edit. Fragmented sentences. You've no idea. So what do you like about photography? What about it moves you, that…'

'Hits me in the gut?'

She's unapologetic. 'Yeah.'

'The immediacy. Sorry, sorry. What resonates with me about photography is the sense of immediacy. Catching the transitive before it slips away.'

'So why'd you get into it?'

'Easier than real art?'

'That's great. That's funny. Self-deprecating is good. Now, can you do it again in a whole sentence?'

'I became a photographer because it seemed easier than real art. And I can't draw.'

But really, it was because I'm terrified of losing anything.

I get off at Salt River Station to pick up printing paper at an arts store at the Neighbourhood market that imports small orders specially for me. I'm about to cross Sir Lowry Road, when I'm distracted by a commotion outside the bottle store. It shouldn't be a bigtime deal, a woman having a seizure on the pavement, and normally, I wouldn't pay much attention to a defuse, but it's like something is pulling me over to gawk. I'm not the only one. An Aito is loping up and down on the kerb beside her, whining impatiently and yipping in excitement. There's no sign of his operator.

'What? Never seen a robbery in progress, honey?' the liquor-store owner snaps at me, watching from his door, arms folded. I haven't actually, although I've seen plenty of defusings, but that's not why I stopped. Maybe it's a leftover I'm still dealing with from the pool hall, but it's like I'm compelled to be here.

'Move along, chicklet. This is nothing to do with you.'

'Okay,' I say, but I don't move. The woman's ravaged face and clothes mark her as street. She's as scrawny as a sparrow. Harmless, surely?

The defuse seems to be tailing off. The manic tempo of her dirty bare feet drumming the concrete is slowing down, and this seems to calm the Aito a little. It stands quivering in excitement, shoulders hunched, ears pricked forward, intent on her. More like cat than dog. Although who knows what goes on in that re-engineered brain?

More people have gathered to rubberneck, passing shoppers and a crew of street kids.

'Nothing to see. Move along. Get going! You want I should have you crisped too?' The shoppers shuffle off indignantly, but the street kids stick around, just far away enough that they're out of the Aito's immediate reach, but not far enough for the shoppie, who flaps his arms at them in disgust.

The defuse tails off and the woman lies there gasping, her eyes scrunched up. The Aito raises a proprietary paw and puts it on her chest, lightly, just enough to claim her. Despite myself, I step forward. The Aito raises its head, instantly alert, and its snout twitches as if to peel back its black lips in a snarl. But then it meets my eyes, gives a dismissive little whuff, and turns its full attention back to the woman.

'You and this doggie got something going on, lady?' drawls the shoppie, to the delight of the street kids, who howl with laughter and catcall,

slapping their thighs as if to call the dog – or me
– over. I sink down next to the woman on the
street, ignoring the filth. There is a Chappies gum
wrapper crumpled in the gutter, and some
unidentifiable mulch, food waste or other organic. I don't look too closely. She lies completely
rigid as the Aito noses round her body, sniffing
for drugs, under the shock-sharp rankness of her.
It's like the rat that died in our ceiling in Durban
and lay there for three weeks before my brother
finally climbed up there, swearing at my dad for
using the cheap poison – the kind that doesn't
auto-dissolve the bodies. But there's another
smell here, ozony cold and chemical.

The woman is making horrible little whiny
sounds, her eyes still squeezed shut, while the
Aito shoves its snout into the saggy folds of her
over-sized tracksuit, as if she'd been liposuc-
tioned fresh that morning. Her fingers flop and
twitch reflexively on the pavement, but she
knows enough to keep her arms by her side,
hands down, while it snuffles around her.

'You a cop? You with the guy inside?' the
shoppie says, bending his knees to talk to me
confidentially. 'Cos it was legitimate, okay?
Bitch started pulling down the merchandise,
falling around. *Dronkie*. She's been in here
before, causing shit. Stealing shit. And how long
is your friend gonna be in there anyway?'

Behind him, out of range, the street kids are
capering and strutting, waving their arms,
imitating him.

Her forehead, when I lay a palm on it, is
clammy. But what else was I expecting? I don't
quite know what I'm doing or why I can't leave
the situation alone. At my touch, her eyes flare
open. She stares at me, frantic, her lips popping
bubbles of spit as if she's about to say something, but then the Aito rumbles warningly and
she squinches her eyelids shut again, clamps her
lips as if she could suppress the tight squeaks escaping her throat.

'You check my records, okay? You'll see. Always, every week, some bergie or skollies
causing trouble for me. What are my customers
supposed to do?'

I raise a placatory hand, keeping the other on
her forehead. The Aito lifts its paw off her chest,
now totally disinterested. It swipes its head up
and down the street, scanning, and then starts
digging into its flank with the edge of its teeth.
I guess fleas are a problem when you come into
regular close contact with the homeless and
criminals.

'I'm logging one crisp every coupla days. And
now I gotta pay extra cos I'm over the limit? It's
not fair. It's not my fault you can't take care of
this rubbish. Now I gotta do your job?'

The woman opens one wary eye, and blinks it, comically. And then the other.

'I wasn't…' she starts in a voice so little and pathetic, I have to lean in to hear her. Her breath is ripe with cheap *papsak*.

'Hey, you even listening to me?' the shoppie snaps.

And suddenly, the Aito lunges forward, leaping over the woman's body, shouldering me aside, and grabs one of the street kids who has gotten too close, fastening its mouth like a bear trap on his arm and crashing him down to the street in one movement. There is a branch-crack of bone, followed by the inevitable screaming.

The other kids scatter. Gone before the Aito looks up, like roaches skittering away into the city's dark places. Without thinking about it, I already have my Zion out, snapping the dog-hybrid standing hunched over the child, growling, the boy's left arm twisted underneath his body. The shoppie is sprawled on the pavement where he'd tumbled over backwards with surprise. And I know this is illegit, that you're not supposed to photograph police procedurals without a media permit, but I don't care.

Behind me the woman sees her opening, scrambles to her feet and takes off down the street. The Aito cocks its head at me with what I swear is disbelief. It snaps at the boy, closing its teeth with a sharp clack a hair's breadth from his face, and then bounds after the woman, almost playfully.

And then – it's gone. The feeling, the compulsion, whatever it was, has vanished. I snatch my bag from where I was kneeling – was that what the kid was after? – and stow my camera deep inside.

A citicop emerges from the liquor store, doing up his belt, relief apparent on his face, but his face drops when he sees the scene and the kid screaming and writhing.

The shoppie turns on him. 'Finally! Look what your dog has done while you were dicking around in the toilet!'

'Excuse me? You can't talk to an officer like that.'

'Look at this! This is scaring away my customers!'

'You want I should fine you for verbal abuse? Hey, you, girlie, get away from that kid. You don't want to interfere.'

'His arm is broken.'

'I can see that, lady. But this is police business.' He softens this with a sugary smirk. 'Don't worry your little head, sweetness, he'll get the medical attention he needs.'

'Hey, she was taking photos!' The shoppie, seeing his opportunity to worm out of the hot spot, flings an accusatory finger. All the attention is now diverted to me, no one is paying the slightest heed to the kid sobbing through his teeth.

'Was she now?' The cop saunters over, so I can smell his sweat and the cinnamon of his gum, the pink chewed lump lurking in the back of his mouth. 'I'm sure she didn't mean anything by it. Né, cherie?'

'I'll delete them. I'm sorry.' I'm furious with myself for apologising, for the instant wave of guilt.

'What's with this hair? One colour not good enough?' He moves to touch my hair and I twitch away, which makes him laugh. 'What's your name, *meisiekind*?'

'Kendra.'

'Ag, don't worry, *Kendra*. I'm not going to take your camera or even put in a log on your unauthorised activity. This time. But I'll be watching out for you.' For an awful moment, by the way he's leaning in, I think he's going to ask me for a kiss. 'Now shoo, we're busy here.'

I turn on my heel, burning with humiliation, in the opposite direction to the Aito, which is standing guard over the once-again subdued homeless woman. I walk briskly away from the howling child and the burly cop and the snickering shoppie. And into the first spaza I can find, for a Ghost.

Lerato

Zama calls. And it's not even my birthday. Of all of us, Siphokazi is the only one who cares enough to try to hold the family together, and naturally, that's what Zama's calling about.

'You've forgotten, haven't you?' says my sister, her tone dripping accusation.

'No,' I say, 'of course not.' But I have. Who has time to keep track of these things? And it's morbid, dredging it up year after year. The past only holds you back. It's like a drift net. The kind you get tangled in and drown.

'It's important to her.'

'Yeah, yeah, I know. Which day is it again?'

We tried to do a pilgrimage a few years ago, at Sipho's behest, to visit the clinic where they died, because we don't have a clue where the graves are. But two days before we were set to leave, government inc. announced a new round of quarantines, which made travelling into the

Ciskei impossible. When Zama and I pulled out, she tried to go anyway, on her own, without a car, with some of her Buddhist buddies tagging along. You can guess how far she got. Turned around at the first checkpoint.

She nagged for a year after that, but there was always an excellent excuse not to go, and I didn't fabricate all of them either. I've been doing a lot of travelling lately. For the moment, she's content to settle for the memorial ceremony, but I live in dread of her suggesting another attempt at our own personal hajj.

Zama gives me the day and the time we're going to meet at Cape Point for the 'ceremony'. She guilt-trips me into agreeing to host dinner as well, although she's horrified when I suggest using Communique's chefs.

'We have to cook a meal together, it's traditional.'

'I don't cook.'

'Fine. Sipho and I will cook. You do have a kitchen, right?' I have to think about that one, about when last we used the hob. I manage to convince her we should just go to a restaurant, maybe the one at Cape Point, because if Sipho cooks, we'll be eating some vegan lentil glob that you have to chew for ages. This is my idea of family, actually, a sticky morass you can't chew your way out of. We wrap up, but I try and spin the conversation out a little. I can tell Zama is secretly pleased and flattered, but it's only because I need extra material for my pre-records to throw off the spyware.

Zama likes to play the family historian. She's a font of all these great stories about our parents, but the Eskom orphanage – let's not cop to the PC term of 'trade school', even if they are cultivating proprietary workforces – has always been more vivid in my head than my idea of home, which is a patchwork of broadcast images. Green hills and sky and a threadbare chicken with long scrawny legs scratching through dust that would never yield a juicy maggot, let alone mielies. It's all cliché, a communal sepia-toned memory that all us Aidsbabies have in common.

I was only seven at the time. The baby of the family after Zama and Siphokazi, and Tebogo, who succumbed even before our parents. I just have to accept whatever Zama says, the stories polished and brittle from so much repetition.

I think I remember a clinic with walls painted a sickly avocado green, and playing Darth Vader in the sterilmask until I got a smack. In my memory it's Zama who hit me, but I suppose it could just as easily have been a nurse.

She says we used to walk miles along the railway tracks, picking some raggy weed, cosmos I think, to give to our mother. Predictably, the nurses confiscated it all when we got there for fear that we might contaminate our parents. We weren't even allowed to touch them.

I remember rows of beds crammed together and sour metal smells and a man, limbs as spindly and sharp as a locust, who terrified me. It's going to sound harsh, but I'm glad I never had to go back there, never had to deal with the reality of Thomokazi and Sam Mazwai, which is all I have of them, their names on my birth certificate. And the legacy of two sisters, one turned hippie-vegan-Buddhist-dropout, the other fermenting in her dead-end job at Eskom, never having graduated beyond our first parent company.

It may be partially my fault Zamajobe never made it out of Eskom. I probably had some kind of familial obligation to tell them when I realised that only the brightest and most productive get out – to better companies that pay a premium for the privilege. But they were older. They should have been guiding me. And besides, I didn't need the competition.

Within a year, I'd been handpicked to go over to Pfizer SA Primary in Cape Town, and suddenly the story sums in class were focused on medication doses rather than wattage, and the school didn't have the same level of desperation. There weren't girls selling themselves at the side of the road to truck drivers for tuck money.

At fourteen, I had my pick of bursaries at secondary institutions run by Telkom, Cisco, Wesizwe and New Mutua. I knew I wanted to get into media, and by then I knew how to negotiate, how to play the system. No more fucking around in squalid dorms with the hordes. When I took up New Mutua's scholarship, I demanded a private room, and it was great for two years.

Communique got me through a Pluslife chat room. In those days it was music sharing and flirting, before the record labels started imposing criminal sentences and meshing their crippleware with defusers. I met my first handful of boyfriends through the chats. But then one of my online friends made me a proposition of a different nature.

By the end of the day, New Mutua knew all about it and I was being forcibly evicted, marched out by security guards with Aitos, not even allowed to go back for my phone. Looking back, it's obvious that my new friend ratted me out to make sure I didn't change my mind. I never learned his real name. Headhunters are only as effective as their anonymity.

Technically, I still had another four years of training to go before officially entering the workforce, but Communique was willing to let me skip two, provided I waive the gap year that all skills institute grads are legally entitled to. But I've been here six years, almost seven, and that's starting to feel like a very, very long time.

When I get off the phone, with a whole half-hour's worth of filler for the spyware boys, I find a summons to Lesley Rathebe's office. My stomach clamps with a momentary dread, because there is always the possibility that someone has picked up the minuscule drop in bandwidth of the data being siphoned off the adboards through my newly installed backdoor.

But the meeting with Rathebe is not a disciplinary. It's about the report on the MetroBabe Strollers, and how very much she liked my out-of-the-box Radio Gaga suggestion, and how very wasted she thinks I am in core coding. There's a position that's just opened up in strategic, developing new tool sets for existing technologies, and she'd be happy to back me if I were 'gutsy' enough to apply for it.

I could bring Mpho Gumede with me if I like, she says. We seem to work well together. I decline, politely. Regrettably, I tell her, and only under duress, he's too volatile. No imagination. He nearly jeopardised the Bula Metalo job.

I know, I know, it's heartless. But if I'm stuck in Communique for the duration, I can't afford

to be coupled with someone who might hold
me back.

Toby

In the fourth corridor, kids, I finally find something potentially useful. It's a mural, giant-scale and kif skilful, of a Nguni cow in profile, the kind you only ever see now emaciated in the background of the politsoc broadcasts about how fucked up the Rural is.

This pastoral beast, by comparison, is plump as the motherbitch's credit rating. But I catch on quickly that it's not just paint rendered ultra-realistically, it's actual hide (dark speckled brown on a dirty cream) cut to shape and mounted up fresco on the wall, which is creepy as hell. Not an obvious clue, but disregard at your peril, kids, when you got nada to go on after thirty-nine abandoned rooms, that *noise* getting closer, and still no sign of anything resembling the Redux Core, which is the last, best, only hope for the Nemesis star system.

Under the sound of the dripping, like Chinese

water torture in the reverb, and the skrawk of rusted pipes, apparently susceptible to shifts and groans, and the machinery clanking off-kilter on twisted gears, is a distinctly kitchen sound. And if that doesn't sound particularly frightening, I'd like you to imagine the gurgling of a drain remixed with the metal screech of the garbage disposal, only more organic – as if it were coming from something's larynx. Something big. And alien. And very fucking scary. Let's just say it's not encouraging, kids, especially when I can't tell if it's getting closer with all the ambient noise.

Okay, but I gotta focus on the cow, or bull, if the fuck-off sharp and long horns are anything to go by. The local flavour is a nice touch – a little extra the developers threw in to mod the experience to whatever part of the world you're logging in from – like water buffalo in Indonesia. Whatever, the moo is almost a storey high, reaching nearly all the way up the factory wall to the narrow row of filthy windows (too small to climb out, too high to get to, thanks for the suggestion, I've already tried). Where they're broken, light comes in so bright and sharp it slices the gloom into thin geometric slits, swirling with dust. I've been avoiding them. It's superstitious, like not standing on the cracks, but also I don't want to be exposing myself in a bright blast of sunlight to whatever is making that noise.

And cos it seems the obvious – although it wouldn't in realworld – I collect some of the crates scattered oh-so-conveniently in the near vicinity and push 'em over to the wall in a tee-tering pile to get a better look at the damn thing.

There's something odd about it. The beady eye is a dissected marble, the kind with a green cat's eye twist in the centre, so it looks really fake. And the hooves and the horns are espe-cially weird, cos they'd be the bits it would be easy to get, just stick the bones right up there. But they're made up of big oval sequins, mis-shapen and discoloured and overlaid on each other like scales.

On closer inspection, the hide is patchwork; no cow big enough to cover this mural on its own, but well done – you can barely see the seams. When I run my hand over the bristly texture of the hide, against the grain, dust stirs up. And there it is. I'm *seriously* disappointed. Could they have been more obvious? A key-hole. Now if only I had a key. I must have missed it on level fifteen. Fuck.

There is a scritching sound. I feel like it's been going on a while, subconsciously, and I'm only just clicking on to it – too involved in the god-damn moo. Or maybe it's only just started. I turn very quickly, in case it's the tick of claws on the concrete behind me, yanking out the Luger from the back of my jeans. There's only one shot, and that's if it doesn't jam.

But there is only the clank and creak and dripping. The factory floor is empty, as far as I can see into the dark recesses on the other side. The slices of light coming in from outside make it harder to see, but I've already freaked myself out too many times straining to detect movement in the shadows. And anything could be lurking among the carnage of decrepit machinery and tumbled crates and the stacks of packaging. (Styrofoam. Already cut one open, spilled out the spongy S curls onto the floor – was using them like a trail of breadcrumbs until I twigged that it would lead other things to me as much as leading me back.)

The scritching comes again and I realise, only now that it's been absent for a second, how close it is. Right here. I bring the Luger up real slow, watching for the hide to stretch and distend cos I know, I just fucking know, something grotesque is scratching patiently on the inside, like a dog at the door.

There is the faintest hint of movement and it takes me a second to pinpoint it. Light shifts on the hooves and I ease the Luger up, please fuck let it not lock up now, placing one hand against the hide for balance, which is warm now and moving steady cos the fucking cow is breathing, and the sequins aren't sequins at all, but nails, fingernails bruised black and stained, and I can tell this because there are rotten fingertips emerging behind them, scraping out and over the other nails, so that there are six layers of intertwined wilted hands tearing their way out from the wall.

As I throw myself back, pulling up the gun to fire, two things happen simultaneously. The Luger clicks, cold. And my sudden shift topples the pyramid of crates. The air opens up behind me, so I'm looking up, falling back, as the things seethe out like gas – murky, taloned things, clawing past each other to get at me, making a rustling like rice paper. And what hits me as I strike my head on the concrete is that it wasn't even the gurgler that took me out.

>> GAME OVER

I toss the plug-in to one side in disgust and wedge myself out of the gamewomb and into the barcade, lit cosily dim so that pulling out into realworld isn't so jarring. I stumble over to the bar and get distracted by a girl with relaxed curls and a mole above her mouth, old-Hollywood-style, sitting alone in one of the perspex booths. The only game she's playing is voyeur on everyone else's, multiple screens projecting the action.

'You buying?' I say, pulling in next to her.

'Excuse me?' she says, all cold surprise, like she's never been hit on before.

'C'mon. I'll get the next one. You can make it expensive. But you buy this round. I just got fragged one time and I need a commiseratory drink.'

'Oh right. You're the one who just got torn limbless by the Dark.'

'That's me. Toby. And you are?'

'Julia.'

We sit in silence for a long moment. She's waiting for me to get uncomfortable and leave. But I'm not shifting a millimetre and eventually she can't resist, if only to drive home her superiority.

'You need the BFG automatic. It's in the substation behind the geysers.'

'I looked there.'

'It's up, not down, wedged behind the pipes. And you missed the key.'

'So, if you're the resident expert, how come you aren't playing?'

'How do you know I'm not?'

I tap the tabletop to pull up the drinks menu, skim it, but it's same old. 'Tequila?'

'You are incredibly forward.'

'Do you play? Or do you just like to watch?'

She stares at me, unbelieving.

'Cos I didn't use to. I reckoned it was all time wastage, you know?' And this is true, kids. I was big-time ambition once, Masters in literature, novel ambitions, before the cast, before the sugar, before the girls. 'When I was a kid, I only ever used the educationals.'

This riles her. 'You can't simplify like that. It's all blurred now, the lines between education and entertainment.' And I've hooked her.

'What, like the kids' games? That Moxyland shit? Murder and mayhem. Training them to be savage, don't you think? It's not about making friends with kids all over the world, it's about getting ahead, getting one over.'

'But don't you think it's appropriate? Considering.'

'The world, you mean? That's a tad harsh. Is that it? Won't they learn that shit later?'

'All right. So, what should they be learning?'

'Compassion? Empathy? How to get along? Life skills?'

'You're an idealist.'

I shrug, all modest coy, as if she's bust me. I look down at my drink, cos the tequila has arrived on the conveyor that runs between the terminals, so the players won't be distracted by comings and goings, so they'll stay longer, spend more money.

'To compassion.' She grins with a sardonic twist to her mouth, taking the tequila.

'To beautiful women with a mean sarcastic streak,' I toast back.

Later, Julia comes back to the swivel with me. They always do.

Lerato

The date goes much better than I'd anticipated, but for all the wrong reasons. Stefan is as craggily beautiful as his profile photograph, and smart and lucid and engaging and funny and refined – and gay as a rainbow bumper-sticker.

'I fucking knew it,' I say, sipping on a papaya mojito, which he's taken the liberty of ordering for both of us because it's Gravity's speciality. Gravity isn't my first choice of afterhours, but in its favour, entry is strictly corporate pass, so you don't have to deal with pleb civilians. And it's set on the 44th floor of the Vodacom building on a revolving floor, so the view rotates around you at a gentle clip, mountain-city-sea, ideal for those with a short attention span for the spectacular.

'I'm sorry?' he says, slightly taken aback. Normally, I enjoy the deft manoeuvring around what can't be said, the subtle, skilful politicking of negotiations. I had an Iranian friend, Sha-heema, who taught me the finer tactics of never saying what you mean, when she came out on exchange to Communique from the Emirates office. It's as useful in the secular corporate en-vironment as in Persian culture. Which is not to say I'm prepared to abandon subtlety altogether when monitoring is a real concern. I lean for-ward, exposing maximum cleavage, and touch his arm.

'We're both adults, Stefan. We both know why we're here. Why don't you and I just skip straight to the main course.'

'Uh – I thought perhaps we could just have a quiet drink, get to know each other.'

'We could go back to my place. But I have a roommate, which might make it tricky, if we're to make all the noise we want. What about yours?'

He's utterly confused, the poor thing, but then his eyes crinkle and he half suppresses a smile, shaking his head. 'I thought you were se-rious. I have an audio interference, if that's what you're worried about.' He clicks the silver pen lying on the table beside his notebook. 'We can make all the noise we like. No spyware's going to pick it up.'

I toy with the glass, keeping up the flirtatious masquerade for the sake of anyone watching.

'And how do I know you're not with…'

'Internal investigations? That this isn't a set-up?'

'I do have a history, Mr. Thuys.'

'Don't we all, Ms. Mazwai. I'm afraid I don't have anything to offer to allay your fears. You'll just have to trust me.'

'Give me a secret. One that I can verify.'

'Why?'

'Leverage.'

'I'm not in the habit of trading secrets with beautiful women, especially not so they can blackmail me.'

'Only beautiful boys?' I've managed to get under that buffed and exfoliated and mois-turised skin. He unfolds and refolds his legs.

'You know, if I was from your current em-ployer's internal investigations, you would already have incriminated yourself.'

'I really don't know what you mean. I was in the middle of asking you if this was another one of Genevieve's half-baked romantic set-ups. You interrupted, rudely, before I could finish my sentence. It's hardly my fault if you want to jump to wild conclusions.'

He slaps his leg and laughs loudly enough to disturb the suits on the couch across from us, who glance over briefly. Unfortunately, audio interference only works on electronics.

'You really are something. So, what would it take to – uh, get you into bed?'

'I'm not a whore, Stefan. But if you're asking me about my ambitions, my dreams? The kind of things we might discuss on a date? I want to live up to my potential. You know I was raised in a skills institute? Eskom Energy Kids.'

'I saw it on your CV.'

'Compared to scrabbling for opportunities with three thousand other Aidsbabies, believe me – corporate life is a breeze.'

'Good wine does depend on its terroir. So what are your dreams, Lerato?'

'The things any girl wants. A pony. True love. A diamond ring. A generous car allowance. A sea view, a space to call my own, that's really my own, sans roommate. Work that is meaningful, you know, where I can make a real and valuable contribution to society, although I'd settle for challenging and remarkably well-paid with international firstworld opportunities. Maybe one day.'

'Maybe soon.'

'I'll toast to that.'

Toby

Unathi is still wearing the same leopard-print vest. I study it carefully to make sure, but even the stains look identical.

'What is with you? Stop staring at my tits, man!' He hands me a gamechip. 'Congratulations, you made the big league. Realspace, and you don't even have to go elf. Or vampire. Personally, I don't think you're qualified for this, but some chick did a recommend on you. Julia Thambo? Know her?'

I shrug, non-committal. Fucked if I know. Which is probably exactly what happened.

'Said she saw you play in the barcade up St. John's Wood way? She's quite the cherry. You better not have slept with her, you twat.'

Again I shrug, which winds him up more than a straight confession.

'Asshole. Anyway. Their clan has a last-minute casualty. They need a replacement.

Don't go thinking this means you get to play with the grown-ups regularly.'

'So what's the game?'

'Load up the chip, asshole, and see.'

I slot the card into the gameport on my phone. The screen goes that particular cyan that quickens any realspace gamer's pulse, cos it's all happening now, kids, connecting to Playnet.

FallenCity^{tm} Scorpions Elite
>>Welcome agent BUZZKILL

'Great call sign, you've preselected for me, Unathi, thanks.'

'Thought you'd appreciate it.'

'How do I change it?'

'You're stuck with it. The account is all paid up. That's your call sign.'

'You are such a bitchmonkey.'

'Just read the assignment, asshole.'

>>You have a new mission briefing…
BRIEF DATE: Wednesday 20 September
OPERATION: Rosa Parks
TYPE: Realworld
LOCATION: Adderley Station Deck, Adderley Street, Cape Town City
RISK LEVEL: 4+
MISSION OBJECTIVES: Find and subdue

terrorists on the underway and recover
and disarm dirty 'suitcase' bomb. This is a
multi-operative mission.
EXECUTION: 20h05, Saturday 23 September

DETAILED BRIEFING: Scorpion Elite's
intelligence agents have uncovered a
terrorist plot by militant mercenary group
MaVimbi, to plant a 'suitcase' nuclear bomb
on the M-line train with the intention of
detonating it once the train reaches
Robben Island Memorial Industrial Park.
Fallout will affect the entire East City
coastline. Projected casualties are 16,000
on Robben Island alone.

The carrier is believed to be the
terrorist known as UNITY. No further
information is available, but s/he will
certainly be disguised as a corporate and
will likely have fake identification. S/he may
have additional terrorists travelling with
him/her as protection and cover.

Your mission is to infiltrate and take
over the corporate coaches on the M-line
underway at Adderley Street station,
subdue all passengers, prevent the train
from departing the station, identify and
subdue the terrorist/s, and find and disarm

the suitcase bomb. (Scorpions Elite Bomb
Squad operatives only.)

   Because of the scale of the operation,
mass action is required. You will be required
to co-ordinate your action with one or more
teams. Mission control can assign you to a
team should you not already have one.

ADVISORY: This mission will take you into
civilian territory. Discretion is advised.*
All operatives must tag their SIMs with
PlayNet FallenCity™ chips to identify them
as players.

DISCLAIMER: FallenCity™ is not real.
FallenCity™ does not have any real-world
affiliations with the Scorpions or the
criminal   underworld   or   terrorist
organisations. InGame agents are actors
employed by Inkubate Inc. to validate and
enhance the player's experience in
realworld play and advance the game.

LEGAL: FallenCity™ and add-on packs,
FallenCity™ Scorpions Elite, FallenCity™
Underworld,   FallenCity™   Wire,   and
FallenCity™ Apocalypse are registered
trademarks of Inkubate Inc. FallenCity™

players are not formally affiliated with Inkubate Inc. and the corporation cannot be held legally responsible for any actions by FallenCity^{tm} players during the course of play, whether virtual or physical.

By entering into game time, FallenCity^{tm} players agree to the terms and conditions of play and acknowledge that they are fully aware that FallenCity^{tm} is only a game.

Players are solely responsible for their actions in realworld play and any repercussions thereof.

By registering on the system, players acknowledge that they are of sound mind and not on stimulants, legal or criminal, which might impede their judgement, and that they are fully able to distinguish between gameplay and reality.

Players who enter realworld play without chipping their SIMs with FallenCity^{tm} identifiers, or who create a public disturbance or interfere with non-player civilians will be suspended from gameplay for the period of one month. Repeat offenders will be disbarred from the game. Players who break the law in the course of play or enact physical violence on any persons (players, InGame agents, or civilians) will be barred from FallenCity[tm] and all other Inkubate Inc.'s titles. If necessary, their files will be uploaded to the SAPS.

*All passengers in the corporate coaches on M-line are InGame agents. Please do not interfere with other passengers on any other lines or in the station.

>> Do you wish to accept the mission, BUZZKILL?
--Yes

>> You are registered temporary affiliate with Scorpions Elite CLAN STINGER. Would you like to maintain this affiliation?
--Yes

>> Operative status confirmed. T-minus three days to execution. Further details will be uploaded to your FallenCity[tm] chip. Proceed with caution, BUZZKILL.
--Log out.

Tendeka

Zuko rattles the can of spray-paint far longer than he needs to, but he's working the crowd, both the kids he's teaching and the passers-by, which makes for a considerable crowd on a Wednesday morning on the Parade. It strikes me that this must be one of the only occasions that the kids are drawing positive attention from the public. Zuko takes to the showman role brilliantly, demonstrating how to hold the nozzle so you get a smooth flow without collateral spillage on your clothes, and why you have to wear the fumemask.

The kids who live on the street make their own agenda, and if you try to force them into yours, you're just going to lose them. We're not overly worried if they don't rock up first thing or if they leave before four p.m. They can come and go as they please, the only rule is they can't be fucked up or get fucked up while they're

working with us. If we catch anyone huffing
paint, it's an instant red card.

I've got no illusions. I know exactly where
they go when they peel off at two or three, after
lunch, because that's the deal, four hours' work
and you earn a decent meal; and I know they
won't be coming back till tomorrow, once
they've slept it off. The thing is to respect them
and how they run their lives. We can't force
them to be here, but we can offer an attractive
alternate to rummaging in the garbage or begging for food. We're building a conversation, not
handing down a lecture on high. Respect is re-
ciprocal.

It's remarkable how fast Ash pulled it together, once he got over his shock that I had
changed my mind about the sponsor thing.
Fast-tracked by his corporate buddy boy at
Chase Standard Bank's CSI program, which
makes me think he's got something going on for
Ash. Of course, Ashraf thinks that's hilarious.

Chase Standard insisted that we didn't use
straight chipped flyers or posters, that they had
to have an opt-in function, so that you have to
physically stop and interact with the poster, but
the kids are overloaded with all the slick club-
vertising on Long Street, there's no way they
would have paid them any attention. So we
saved the cash on the posters and hit all the

shelters instead, speaking to the kids personally, and getting the social workers onside.

It's disgusting how much of a difference real sponsorship makes. Instead of badly printed tees, the kids have navy overalls, with the logo stitched tastefully over the heart. The stitching on the back boasts 'Investing In Our Youth'. Instead of cold potjie stewed at home with whatever ingredients Ash can find, we have nutritionally enhanced hamburgers delivered promptly at quarter past twelve from the kitchens of Chase Standard's head office, two blocks over.

Unfortunately, we have to take the overalls from the kids at day's end. We tell them it's because we need to wash off the paint, but it's at Chase Standard's insistence, so they don't go off and get vrot and harass people, still wearing the logo. Likewise, no one's allowed to leave with paint, in case they tag with it or, worse, inhale.

Practising is all designated within this specific zone, although all the kids get branded sketchbooks and a box of pencil crayons (because you can huff koki) to take back with them. It's an inspired gesture, which could have only come down from a corporate social investment dick who doesn't have a clue about streetside reality, where kids get mugged for anything vaguely precious or personal.

We've pulled together some seventeen kids, itching to get their hands on the paint, but this is not just tagging shit. There are techniques to be mastered. The kids with no artistic ability get to do the manual fill jobs, but even that requires a measure of skill, using tight little circles, or precision strokes to make sure the paint doesn't run.

The LEDs, on the other hand, are plug and play. Tiny bulbs the size of the head of a drawing pin, imported specially from Amsterdam. We're using magnetic paint, so it's just a matter of positioning and slapping them on. It was what sold Chase Standard on the project – that we could embed lights in the shape of their logo, which would blink all night for all the incoming traffic to see. You can pre-program patterns to add dimension or words. 'Peace'. 'Love'. 'Ubuntu'. 'Revolution'.

It's easy to embed other things in magnetic paint too. Totally stable, skyward* assures me. I wouldn't expose the kids to unnecessary risk.

We're doing up all three of the panels on the side of the ex-library, up there with the logos and adboards and videomercials beaming down. All in the name of a Good Cause, the street kids channelling their frustration into something useful, something beautiful. Something the public can feel good about.

Watching Zuko workshopping the rapt crowd, spraying up an outline of letters, 'LOVE', the style somewhere between the fat curves of Sixties' hippie typo and the jagged tangle of Eighties New York subway bombing-style, I don't know why we didn't do this earlier.

I tell Ashraf as much when he comes back from giving the tour to the bunch of Chase Standard employees on their lunch break, and that I'm proud of him. He practically glows, which makes it harder to come clean about all the extra-mural we've got planned.

Oh, he knows about the animal rights thing, that's his baby anyway. He's always been a rabid defender of our furry friends. He was hectic PETA before we got into working with kids. And the station protest has been a long time coming. But he's not in on the picture on the optional extras, the stuff that is gonna make the news.

The point is that the kids are homeless already. As long as we don't get caught, they have nothing to lose. They can't be disconnected because they don't have phones. The disenfranchised will get their moment of glory.

I've discussed it at length with Zuko and some of the other boys, Ibrahim and S'bu, not with all the details, but they're up for it. The only worry is the dogs, but there are ways, skyward* says, of dealing with gen-mod animals.

And making headlines at the same time.

Kendra

There is already spillage out of the doors by the time I get to Propeller, which can only be a good sign when it's just gone six-thirty. I feel fractal with nerves, or maybe it's that I'm on my fourth Ghost in under an hour.

'You're late.' Jonathan latches onto my arm at the door and swishes me inside through the crowd. I can't believe how many people there are, crowded into the gallery. There is a queue up the stairs to see Johannes Michael's atom mobile, but the major throng is in the main room, and not, I regret to say, for my retro print photos.

They're here to see Khanyi Nkosi's sound installation, freshly returned from her São Paulo show and all the resulting controversy. She only installed it this afternoon, snuck in undercover with security, so it's the first time I've seen it in the flesh. It's gruesome, red and meaty, like something dead turned inside out and mangled, half-collapsed in on itself with spines and ridges and fleshy strings and some kind of built-in speakers, which makes the name even more disturbing: '*Woof & Tweet*'.

I don't understand how it works, but it's to do with reverb and built-in resonator-speakers. It's culling sounds from around us, remixing ambient audio, conversation, footsteps, glasses clinking, rustling clothing, through the systems of its body, disjointed parts of it inflating, like it's breathing, spines quivering.

It's hard to hear it over the hubbub, but sometimes it's like words, almost recognisable. But mostly it's just noise, a fractured music undercut with jarring sounds that seem to come randomly. Sometimes it sounds like pain. It is an animal. Or alive at any rate. Some lab-manufactured plastech bio-breed with just enough brainstem hard-wired to respond to input in different ways, so it's unpredictable – but not enough to hurt, apparently, if you believe the info blurb on the work.

'It's gratuitous. She could have done it any other way. It could have been beautiful.'

'Like something you'd put in your lounge, Kendra? It's supposed to be revolting. It's that whole Tokyo tech-grotesque thing. Actually, it's so derivative, I can't stand it. Can we move along?'

I run my hand along one of the ridges and

the thing quivers, but I can't determine any noticeable difference in the sounds. 'Do you think it gets traumatised?'

'It's just noise, okay? You're as bad as that nutjob who threw blood at Khanyi at the Jozi exhibition. It doesn't have nerve endings. Or no, wait, sorry, it does have nerve endings, but it doesn't have pain receptors.'

'I meant, do you think it gets upset? By all the attention? I mean, isn't it supposed to be able to pick up moods, reflect the vibe?'

'I think that's all bullshit, but you could ask the artist. She's over there schmoozing with the money, like you should be.'

Woof & Tweet suddenly kicks out a looped fragment of a woman's laugh that startles me and half the room, before it slides down the scale into a fuzzy electronica.

'See, it likes you.'

'Don't be a jerk, Jonathan.'

'There's some streamcast journalist who wants to interview you, by the way. And he's pretty cute.'

My stomach spasms. This is another thing Jonathan does to keep me in my place – as in, we're not together.

'Great, thanks. I need a drink.'

'I'll get it. Just go talk to Sanjay. What do you want?'

'Anything.' It's unlikely that the gallery bar would have Ghost on hand.

Jonathan propels me in the direction of Sanjay, who is standing in a cluster of people, in deep conversation. The one is clearly money, some corporati culture patron or art buyer; the other, I realise, is Khanyi Nkosi. I recognise her from an interview I saw, but she is so warmly energetic, waving her hands in the air to make a point and grinning, that I can't match her to her work. And the third, I realise with a shock, is Andile. It shouldn't be a surprise that he should be here, considering he picked me on the basis of my work, but I still haven't come clean with Jonathan about the branding, and this doesn't strike me as the time.

I can't deal with this right now. I push through the queue, detouring back towards the entrance and the open air – only to skewer someone's foot with the '40s-style blue velvet heels I bought for the occasion.

'Hey! Easy!'

'Oh god, I'm sorry.' Shit, I really, really, really need a Ghost. I wonder if I can make it to the spaza down the road and back before Jonathan notices.

'No worries. Art is what the artist does, right? So technically, my bruised toes could be worth something?'

I didn't even realise it was Toby whose foot I had crushed.

'So you must be the famous artist, then?'

'I'm the less famous artist. I mean, I'm not; the thing, it's not mine. But you know that.' I laugh self-consciously, still thinking about how to get a Ghost, my mind chanting a little litany of need, wondering if they serve them at the bar.

'Is now a good time to get an interview?'

'You're the journalist?'

'Ouch!' He mock-staggers back, clutching his heart. 'Yeah. I brought my own phone mic and everything.'

'I'm sorry. That's not what I... Oh God. Can we just start again?'

'Sure. No prob.'

He turns away, clears his throat, and then does a little twirl, one hand raised in fabulous salute, hamming it up like he's on the red carpet.

'Hello. I'm Toby. I'll be your journo for the evening.' And I can't help but laugh. 'Do you have a drink?'

'No, thanks. Someone's getting me one.'

'Rocking.' He suddenly turns serious. 'Okay, now listen, Special K, if you want, we can talk later. I know it's your opening and you've got things to do, people to schmooze. I will totally understand if now is not the most opportune moment.'

'Actually, do you want to get out of here?'

'What?'

'Just for a sec. I need some fresh air. And a drink.'

'I thought someone was getting you one.'

'A non-alcoholic.'

'Ooooooh. Right.' He winks.

'You want to come?'

'Sure. Can my mic come too?'

We're not the only people hanging outside. We have to push through a crowd, including an astonishingly gorgeous blonde, with fucked-up hair, who makes me feel conservative. We get halfway down the block before I take off my heels in disgust. 'That doesn't make it into the copy, okay?'

He holds up his hands. 'Do you see me making notes?' We walk in silence for another block, stepping over a bergie passed out in the street. And I'm relieved not to feel any sense of an urgent compulsion to touch him. And no Aitos in sight, either.

At the spaza, Toby opens the fridge at the back. 'Ghost, I'm assuming?' he says, putting it on his phone. It's cold and crisp and clean and it hurts my teeth and I realise my hands have been shaking all this while – or maybe my

whole body. And this can't be good, but it does-
n't feel bad.

'Mind if I join you?' Toby cracks the seal on
another can. 'Wow. You really are an addict
deluxe,' he says, a little too admiringly.

'Hey, did you check my coat tonight?

'Yeah?'

His BabyStrange is black, which is a relief
after the goreporn he was projecting last time I
saw him.

'It's my little shout out to *Self-Portrait*.'

'Cute. So, do you want to do this?'

'Am I allowed to take notes now?'

'Yeah, yeah.' I wave my hand impatiently.

He hooks a mic into his phone and points it
at me. 'So. What's with the oldschool?'

'Didn't you read the press release?'

'Let's say I didn't.'

I quote it from memory. 'Adams's use of non-
digital format is inspired by her fascination with
the capacity for error…'

'Okay. Let's skip the press release.'

'Ah, it's just – film is more interesting than
digital. There's a possibility of flaw inherent in
the material. It's not readily available, so I
have to get it over the Net, and some of it has
rotted or it's been exposed even before I load
it in the camera, but I don't know that until I
develop it.'

'Like *Self-Portrait*?'

'And it's not just the film. It's working without the automatic functions. The operator can fuck up too.'

'Did you fuck up?'

'Ha! That's the great thing about working with damaged materials. You'll never know.'

'It's the same in audio, you know. Digital was too clean when it first came out, almost antiseptic. The fidelity was too clear. You lost the background noise, the sounds you don't even pick up, but it's dead without the context. The audio techs had to adapt the digital to synth the effects of analogue. How insane is that? It's contentious, though – now they're saying it's been bullshit all along, just nostalgics missing the hiss of the recording equipment.'

'That's exactly it. You can do the same thing in photography. Apply effects, lock-out the autofocus, click up for exposure, all to re-create the manual.'

'And you're looking for the background noise.'

'Yeah. Or something like it.' I set my empty can neatly down beside my shoes. 'Got enough?'

'Yeah. I'm good. You give good soundbite,' he says admiringly, so that another Ghost down, we're still sitting on the pavement, just talking, away from the madding, when a dark-haired boy I recognise as the guy from the band, from Andile's office, comes walking down towards us.

'Hey, photographer girl,' he says, friendlier than last time. 'Damian, remember? From Kill Kitten?'

'Hey, Dame,' says Toby. 'How's the band-scene? Did you catch the cast from your gig?'

'Yeah, man, it was killer. Shot. We really appreciate the exposure.'

'It was all you. I just filmed what I experienced. You guys were tight.'

'Well, it was *great*, man, thanks. We're playing next Saturday, if you want on the guest list.'

'Thanks. So, how do you know our star rising over here?' Toby asks, nodding at me. We are both still sitting, sprawled on the kerb, so Damian is looking down at us. There is a drawn-out silence.

'Ho-kay,' Toby shrugs in mock defeat. 'There's obviously some deep unspoken going on here, and I do not need to know the gruesome details.'

'It's nothing like that. We're...' I look to Damian for approval, but he doesn't seem concerned. 'We're both branded.'

'How come you're not chugging Ghosts, then?'

'Are you kidding me?' Damian laughs. 'I've had three already tonight.' He drops to sit on the pavement beside us.

'How much do you drink in a day?' I ask, trying to make it sound throwaway.

'Six, seven? Somewhere around there. My girlfriend keeps tabs on me.' I don't say anything. I'm doing nine to twelve. This is my seventh since four thirty.

'It's lucky you're both the same brand,' Toby says, and is that envy in his voice?

'What if you were competitive? There must be a clause about that. "*Section 31c. Thou shalt not fraternise with the enemy.*"'

'Yeah, can you imagine?' Damian says. 'Coke wars for real.'

'No rival soft-drink friends for you!'

'I don't think that's going to be an issue anytime soon,' I interrupt their banter. 'Andile said they're not doing this with other brands just yet. Ghost has the proprietary licence for three months.'

'Yeah, but we're only first gen. They'll be popping out sponsorbabies like toast.'

'I hate that word.'

'Toast?' chirps Toby, trying to find a way in.

'And what happened to it being exclusive?'

'You'll be able to buy your way in. Got enough cash, enough cool, you're representing. Just like the cosmetics.'

'So we'll be outmoded already.'

'Bleeding edge no more.'

'So, Dame, where's yours? Can I see?'

'Toby!' I'm scandalised, but Damian shrugs it off.

'S'cool. I don't mind. I signed up for the freakshow.' He turns his back to us and yanks down the collar of his shirt to reveal the faint radiance of the glowlogo between his shoulderblades.

'That doesn't seem exactly high vis,' Toby says.

'Not now, but I have a tendency to take my shirt off on stage. I get hot, okay? It's not like some sex-appeal thing. Hey, are you recording this?'

'Sorry, bad habit. I'm a junkie for collecting vid. I can delete it if you want.'

'No, it's cool. Shouldn't we be heading back, anyway? Aren't there supposed to be speeches and shit? And I know Andile wanted to say what's up.'

'You go ahead, we'll catch up,' Toby says, laconic, and this suddenly strikes me as a very Jonathan thing to do.

'I think I'll go with Dame. We've been gone a while.'

The gallery seems even more oppressive, but I'm less freaked now, even when I see Andile talking to Jonathan. Luckily I get side-tracked by Mr. Muller.

'Congratulations. It's wonderful. Wonderful. Although I'm not sure about this messy animal thing. It's very Damien Hirst. Cheap shock-treatment stuff. Yours is infinitely superior. And people will see that, take my word for it.'

I'm still basking in the afterglow, when I overhear some over-groomed loft dwellers giggling into their wine. 'And this. I'm so tired of Statement! Like she's the only angst child ever to embrace the distorted body image.'

'Oh Emily. I quite like the undeveloped. Because she is. You know, still young, coming into herself. The artist in flux, emergent.'

'Well, precisely. It's so *young*. You can't even tell if it's technically good or not, it's all so... damaged.'

'Don't let the heathen savages get to you.' Toby has popped up again, speaking loud enough for the woman to hear, but I'm more amused than insulted. I'm about to point out that under the black of *Self-Portrait* is a photograph of a photograph, clutched in my fingers, captured in the mirror with a reflected flash of light. That it's all meant to be damaged. But then I realise I don't have to. I don't have to make my motives transparent.

Damian appears at my shoulder with the astonishing blonde, who he introduces as his girlfriend, Vix, a fashion designer for her own small label. Vix distracts Toby, the two of them heading off to the bar to lay in supplies for all of us, leaving me with a convenient gap to ask Damian if he's experienced any weird side-effects. He seems puzzled.

'Like what? I had really *mif* flu for about four days. Sinuses and sweats, but it worked its way out.'

I try and tell him about the thing with the Aito, but it comes out all garbled.

'It doesn't sound that freaky,' says Damian. 'You felt sorry for her. You stopped to help. That's pretty awesome.'

I'm miserable that he doesn't get it. 'It wasn't empathy or altruism or anything. It was like I had to, like a real compulsion.'

The same way we're compelled to drink Ghost, I think but don't say. Damian isn't paying attention. He's watching his girlfriend across the room, trying to get through to the bar while Toby clowns around, making her laugh.

It makes me feel desperately alone. There are all these people circling, like Johannes Michael's swirl of paper atoms upstairs, but the connections to me are only tenuous.

'You know the dogs also function on nano?'

Damian says, ripping his eyes from Vix. 'Maybe you got crossed lines,' he jokes.

'Maybe.'

We're cut short by a flurry of activity at the door. I've been aware of a low peripheral clamour, but now it erupts. There are people shoving, wine spilling from glasses and yelps of dismay.

'This is a private function!' Jonathan of all people yells, spouting clichés at the rush of people in black pushing in through the crowd, their faces blurred like they're anonymous informants in documentary footage. It is so disturbing, that it takes me a second to catch on that they're wearing smear masks. Another to realise that they're carrying pangas and a prog-saw.

A few people scream, sending out a reverb chorus from *Woof & Tweet*. The crowd presses backwards. But then the big guy in front yells, 'Death to corporate art!' and Emily, the woman who dissed my work, laughs scornfully and really loudly. 'Oh god! Performance art. How gauche.' There are murmurs of relief and snickers, and the living organism that is the crowd reverses direction, now pressing in again to see.

Damian grabs my arm and pulls me back out of the front line, because I haven't moved, just as one of the men (women?), towering over the others, grabs Emily by her hair and drags her forward, forcing her to her knees, spitting with contempt, 'Don't you dare make me complicit in your garbage!'

The terrorist raises the panga, pulling back Emily's head by the roots of her hair, exposing her throat. She raises a hand to her mouth, pretends to stifle a yawn.

'Are you going to chop me into little itty-bitty pieces now? This is so melodramatic.'

And it is. The crowd is riveted. But I didn't think this kind of promotional stunt would be Sanjay's thing.

From the bar, Toby catches my eye and mimes mock applause to the spectacle. Vix has her hands clamped tight round his arm, looking shocked and excited at the same time. And that seems to be the prevailing mood. Not outrage or fear, but excitement. People are grinning, nodding, eyes overbright, which makes it seem all the more horrific.

But what frightens me most is the reaction of one of the men in smear. When the protagonist yanks Emily's head further back, the other guy moves forward, as if frightened himself. 'What are you–?' he starts, but the one with Emily's hair twisted round his wrist gives an impatient jerk of his head, and his hesitant friend backs off. Bowing his legs, he raises the arm with the panga as if to slice across her throat, only at the last instant – so late that she winces back involuntarily – he deflects the blow to a side-swipe, aimed not at her, but at *Woof & Tweet*, which is directly in front of them.

The thing emits a lean crackle of white noise. The audience is rapt, camera phones clicking. There is a scattershot of applause, and laughter, as the others move in, four of them, with one guarding the door, to start laying into it. It's only when the artist starts wailing that it becomes apparent that this was not part of the program. And only then do the smiles drop from mouths, like glasses breaking.

Mr. Hesitant hangs back as the others step in, pangas tearing through the thin flesh and ribs of Khanyi Nkosi's thing with a noise like someone attacking a bicycle with an axe. The machine responds with a high-hat backbeat for the melody assembled from the screams and skitters of nervous laughter. It doesn't die quietly, transmuting the ruckus, the frantic calls to the SAPS, and Khanyi wailing, clawing, held back by a throng of people. It's like it's screaming through our voices, the background noise, the context.

The bright sprays of blood make it real, spattering the walls, people's faces, my prints, as the blades thwack down again and again. The police sirens in the distance are echoed and distorted

as *Woof & Tweet* finally collapses in on itself, rat-
tling with wet smacking sounds.

They disappear into the streets as quickly as
they came, shaking the machetes at us, threatening don't follow, whooping like kids. With the
sirens closing in, the big guy spits on the mangled corpse. Then, before he ducks out the door
and into the night, he glances up once, quickly,
at the ceiling. No one else seems to notice, but I
follow his gaze up to the security cams, getting
every angle.

I'm sick with adrenalin. The woman who was
taken hostage is screaming in brittle, hyperven-
tilating gasps. Her friend is trying to wipe the
blood off her face, using the hem of her dress,
unaware that she has lifted it so high that she is
flashing her lacy briefs. Khanyi is kneeling next
to the gobs of her animal construct, trying to re-
assemble it, smearing herself with the bloody
lumps of flesh.

There is a man trying to comfort one of the
drinksgirls, but he is the one weeping, laid
waste by the shock. Toby is clambering down
from the bar, why I don't know, Mr. Muller is
sitting slumped on the staircase, hugging the
banister like a friend. Vix fumbles with lighting
a cigarette, her hands shaking, until Damian
materialises by her side, takes her hands in his,
and holds the lighter steady. She folds into him

like a collapsible paper lantern. And even from here, I can see him mouth her name. I hadn't even realised he was gone.

There is still a prevailing undercurrent of thrill, a rush from the violence – no one was hurt, apart from Khanyi Nkosi's thing. Everyone is on their phones, taking pictures, talking.

Toby is shouting above the ruckus, into his mic, like he's reporting live. There are even more people trying to wedge into the space, so that the cops, who have finally arrived, have to shove their way inside.

Self-Portrait is covered in a mist of blood. I move to wipe it clean, although I'm scared the blood will smear, will stain the paper, but just then Jonathan wraps his arms around me and kisses my neck. And now it's my turn to collapse against him.

'It's okay, sweetheart, everything's going to be okay.'

Tendeka

If there's one thing street kids know, it's how to vanish effectively. Ashraf is still shaking by the time we get to our refuge, a garage in a neighbouring apartment block. skyward* sent me a basic key SIM, that jimmies a signal to get in doors that aren't coded high security. It's a blunt hack job, but it works.

All the protests I've been involved in till now have been phone-based. Text msgs are the quickest, cheapest, most convenient way of co-ordinating and relaying information instantly. 'Someone arrested.' 'New rendezvous.' 'Take Strand Street, cops are waiting on Riebeeck.' But tonight there are no phones. No way of passing on msgs or warnings – or being tracked down.

'This is what we should be campaigning for.' I try to explain to Ashraf how we need to create an alternate economy that doesn't rely on SIM

218

IDs and credit rates. We should all live like Emmie and our street-kid army collaborative. But he is too furious to listen.

'You told me the knives were just for show.'

'It's not about show. Not anymore.'

'Oh, cut the big talk. They're children, Tendeka.'

'They're disenfranchised. Society's dropouts, the lost generation. We're giving them a purpose.'

'Anyone can give a kid purpose! You can twist them whichever way suits you. Especially if you're letting them vent their aggression. You can't just put a leash on that afterwards.'

He scrapes his hands through his hair. 'I just don't know what you were thinking. This wasn't the plan, was it? This Lord of the Flies number you just pulled? Please tell me that.'

For once, his frustration leaves me unmoved. There are bigger things at stake than Ashraf's inhibitions.

'I don't need your stubbornness right now, Ten. God, you make me crazy. This fucks everything we've done. You want to talk violation? This – fuck, this is the moral opposite of everything we believe in. This is going to make the news in Tibet!'

'That's what I'm counting on.'

'You really don't get it. I mean, you really, really don't. Did you see the fucking cams in the gallery? Do you know the licence you've given them to crack down?'

'Looked right at 'em. That was the point. skyward* said we needed to make global news, to force their hand.'

'You don't even know who skyward* is. He's an avatar. A fucking online persona whose orders you blithely follow, like a lapdog. Roll over. Play dead. Drag a bunch of kids into what's going to be classified as terrorist action. You don't know anything about him.'

'I know he sends us first-class tech. Shit we'd never get our hands on. Shit so new they haven't even drawn up countermeasures on paper, let alone implemented them. The smear, the LEDs for the graffiti project.' I've let slip too much, but Ashraf is so angry, he doesn't even notice.

'So fucking what? How does he get access to it? You don't know who he is. What his motivations are. If it's even a he.'

'I understand his motivations better than yours. At least he's committed to a revolution–'

'Don't be like this.'

'–not just play-play in amateur hour.'

His shoulders slump, but I can't afford sympathy. He has to face up to his erroneous thinking. He nearly fucked up the whole gig with his interruption. It's not like I was going to hurt her. It was only intended to scare. Part of

the act. I was in control at all times. It's not like
it felt good.

'You need to get over yourself, Ash.'

'Really? I need to get over myself. I'm the
play-play amateur? At least I'm not nice
middle-class boy pretending at hardcore
revolutionary.'

'Fuck off.'

'You know what the difference is between
us? When all this goes bad, you can go running
back to the family homestead in leafy Houghton
– and the rest of us fucking can't.'

'I would never.'

'I'm afraid for you, Ten,' he says, something
in his face caving.

I'm not made of vibracrete. I pull him to my
chest and we just stand like that for long minutes. Until he murmurs, 'We have to call off the
pass protest.'

I pull back, the better to gauge if he means it.
'We can't. It's all fucking arranged. We've been
planning it for months.' And we have. If I think
about the effort involved... to abandon it now?
It's impossible.

It's going to be the ultimate, to demonstrate
the divides in our society between the Emmies
and the Zukos and the corporati with their gold-
plated all-access passes and the things they do
to keep us in our place.

'We can't, Ash. I'm sorry. The gamehack has already gone into effect. All those FallenCity players won't know what hit them. It's going to happen no matter what, now, and if we're not at the forefront, then someone else will be, and they will fuck it up. You think you can stop those kids going? Zuko will lead it personally if we don't. Do you know what the end result of that would look like? Those kids running rampant with the players?'

'I can't. Tendeka. You shouldn't. I'm tired. It's too much.'

'One more, okay, baby? Just one more. Then we can lie low, I swear. This is massive. This is the culmination of everything. You can't let this *incident* throw you off. I'm sorry. I fucked up. I admit. It got away from me. I won't let it happen again.'

'No more putting the kids at risk. No more violence.'

'Not from us.'

'Because if there is…'

Toby

The footage from the security cams in the gallery is playlisted on all the newscasts, animal rights activists gone seriously mental, and there's all kinds of uproar, from the Minister of Safety and Security swearing to step up measures against terrorism to arts critics alternately decrying it as a tacky publicity stunt or lauding it as bold political theatre that outstrips any performance art done previously. Or, to put it another way, kids, it's huge, and my exclusive eyewitness is piggybacking off it beautifully.

It's not that there weren't plenty of people with cams and chamo clothing, but I was the only one with the smarts to jump up on the bar to lock down the best angle.

My report went out this morning – the edited version with extra commentary. I've already had an offer to syndicate Diary of Cunt from a producer on MTV.

But maybe you want to watch that again? I can do it easily, you know. Just hit 'replay'.

KENDRA ADAMS'S SHOW is a sell-out. Her shockingly intimate portraits taken on old photographic stock interplay light and texture like a Dutch Master. The effect of using disintegrating film means the work is inherently flawed, inherently damaged. Her first exhibition has been an unprecedented success, every work snapped up in a bidding scrum that forced the prices up to eight times the sticker. Not bad going for a girl who dropped out of Michaelis Art College six months ago.

No insult to the artist or the striking technical mastery demonstrated in Unspoken – a woman's jawline arching out of shot, delineated against a twist of stairwell and the arc of city lights, or the harsh reality of a homeless woman being defused, or the witty statement of *Self-Portrait*, a 2 x 3.5 m print that is entirely black, but her skill is not the reason her work is suddenly so popular. It's because her photographs are newly flawed that she's flooring the critics and the art-buying public, hungry to claim a whiff of scandal, a bloody scrap of current events.

Those fourteen portraits all carry the mark of violation from the invasion of Thursday evening, when animal-rights actives hacked apart enfant terrible Khanyi Nkosi's controversial and grotesque biomod creature, *Woof & Tweet*.

Nkosi commented:

[insert Nkosi soundbite]

'It's revolting that anyone would try to profit off my loss. This is an atrocity. It's up there with blood diamonds and wartech corps racking up their cash registers over the stink of corpses!'

Prices for her work have already skyrocketed, especially on her other almost-animals like *Sweetheart Sputnik*, an oversized heart riddled with receivers, that quickens or slows its rhythm according to incoming text messages from the audience. And the corpse of *Woof & Tweet*, stinking or not, has already been sold to a Dubai businesswoman, who paid, it's rumoured, in the region of R1.7 million for the bloody gibs, together with the video footage and one panga that was left behind, unused.

The 22 year-old Adams was unavailable

for comment, recovering from the
fraught of the eve, although her man-
ager-elect, Jonathan Rider, said:

[insert art bitchmonkey soundbite
here]

'We hope to assure Khanyi Nkosi that
no one is trying to undermine the agony
of what she must be going through. I
don't want to suggest that it's egotistical
to believe that the only reason Kendra's
photographs have sold so well is that
they have some residue of blood from her
piece's awful preemptive disassembly,
but I believe Ms Nkosi is quite undone by
the grief. It's very unfortunate that she's
demanded a share of the profits on
Kendra's sales, considering her stature
internationally in the art world, while
Kendra is an aspirant up-and-coming
young artist, fresh to the scene. Kendra's
work speaks for itself and it obviously
speaks to its audience. And that's really
all there is to it. We've also offered to
have the prints professionally cleaned
and restored, removing any traces of
organic matter, for those buyers who
request it.'

So far, none have.
<follow up story
Monday 25 September>

It's enough to spike interest, a calling-card to the world that's helped drive up a more generous price on the candid interview with Kendra and Damian talking about their all-new injectable tech.

I've edited together a teaser – you might have seen it already, it's the one that starts:

> KENDRA ADAMS SOLD out her first exhibition a couple of days ago, but now it seems that she's sold out in another way entirely, as one of Ghost's controversial sponsor babies.

And now I'm just kicking back, waiting for the offers to start spinning in.

In the interim, Unathi is not letting me squirm out of the FallenCity mission. It's not so bad. I can kill some waiting time and blow off steam by fragging a few people in realspace.

And hey, it'll be good to see Julia again, seeing as how Kendra is not speaking to me at the moment.

Lerato

'What are you doing?'

Mpho raises his head from his arms to look up at me. It's fairly obvious he's been crying. It's bad enough I have the whole family memorial ceremony ahead, but finding him here, camped outside my apartment door, just upped the ante on a day already heading straight for shitty territory.

'Waiting for you,' he says, getting to his feet.

'Well, I'm here now. Sooooo, I guess you can go.'

'Can I come in?'

'I don't think that's a good idea. I mean, what's the point?'

'We could–'

'Talk? That would be based on the assumption we have anything to talk about.'

'I don't understand.'

'That's because you don't listen. I told you it was a one-time deal. I'm not up for a serious affair. It was just fun, Mpho. Good times. And now the good times are done. Excuse me, you're kinda blocking the door.'

'Jesus. Do you have to be so hard?'

'Yeah. Sorry.' I start to move around him, but he takes me by the elbows.

'Yeah, me too. You obviously care. Otherwise you wouldn't be such a bitch about it. It's really sad, Lerato.'

'Not as sad as this, this last-stand psycho-analysis thing you're doing. Nice try, Mpho. But you, what we had? I don't give a shit. For really really real. I'm already seeing someone else. And he knows how to get me going.' I run the tip of my tongue over parted lips. 'If you know what I'm saying. Now get out of my way.'

He lets go of me and steps aside, his face tilted to the floor, not even looking at me. I swish past him into the apartment and he turns to make the long slow walk back to the elevators.

Before the door slides closed, he calls back bitterly, not looking round, 'Congrats on the promotion.'

Jane pokes her head out of her room, looking disapproving and happily scandalised at the same time. 'You really can pick them. He's been sitting outside for two and a half hours.'

'He'll get over it. What he needs is someone as sweet and dull as he is.'

'I was about to take pity and let him in.'

'You should have. You two might have hit it off.'

'Oh thanks, Lerato.'

'Come on, you know that's not what I meant.' That's exactly what I meant, but I don't want to upset the peace. It's only a couple more weeks max that I'll have to put up with Jane's fustiness.

'It was more like, you know, when was the last time you had a date?'

'Thanks for the vote of confidence. I've got one tonight, for your information.'

'Oh yeah? Me too. Unfortunately, it's dinner with my sisters. Obligotainment.' I open the fridge to see if there's anything to snack on in the interim. It's another hour and a half before I'm supposed to meet them at Simon's Town station.

Jane gives in. 'All right, mine too. I'm meeting my boss.'

'Oh really? You got something going on?'

She flushes, the swathe of pink swallowing up her freckles. 'No, I'm handing over some files. We're talking career prospects. You know, where to go from here.'

'Mmm-hmmm.' There's nothing in the fridge. Unless I feel like eating a wodge of butter.

'And you?' she asks.

'And me what?'

'I heard you're getting bumped up.'

'It's not a big deal. More of a step sideways than up.'

'Lead software designer, though. You're young to take that on. Twenty-three?'

'And three-quarters.'

'What?'

'Sorry, you know how little kids say that. Puffing themselves up. Always looking forward to the next year.'

'Well, it sounds like it's going to be a good one for you.'

'I think it'll be all right. Hey, do you want to get baked?'

'Really?'

'Yeah, you know, I could do with something to take the edge off. You do smoke, right?'

'The legal stuff.' She snickers. 'Mostly. You know, you've never asked me before.'

'I thought you were too stuck-up.'

'And I thought you were a ruthless bitch.'

'Now you're saying I'm not? Nice. Insult me in my own home.'

'What did you think about the terrorist thing?' she asks, while I roll a neat joint of corp-issue Dormor, sprinkled with a touch of sugar, which is decidedly not pre-approved.

'The gallery? I saw Toby's cast. It was pretty retarded. Not the cast, I mean; the attack.' Jane is quiet and then she says, 'It frightened me. That they could be so bold, you know? So arrogant.'

'It was supposed to, Jane. It's a big splashy press release. They want you to think that your happy little status quo isn't as safe and cosy as you assume. Of course, there are better ways to do it.'

'What do you mean?' I take a toke and hand her the joint.

'I'm saying if I was a terrorist, I'd up the stakes. Billboard smears? Art galleries? Retarded. They're not terrorists. They're idiots. You give them way too much credit.'

Kendra

Jonathan prises apart the carcass of another prawn, a real one, with curled scratches of legs, not the gen-mod easy-peels – which makes it expensive. So expensive, there are conspicuous intimidating blanks on the menu where prices would normally appear. It's a species removed from the café fare and readymeals I'm used to, or even the upmarket where Jonathan has taken me before – and a whole genus away from my cooking. But I'm secretly disappointed, and somehow that's more satisfying than if it had lived up to my expectations.

Despite it being my first time, despite the ultraglam pink Black Coffee dress Jonathan sent over by courier to the house this afternoon, and the industria minimalism of the décor, fit for any of the style mags with its bare-stripped walls and sharp white scatterlights like an interrogation room, it's not what I'd imagined. Even

Naledi Nxumalo, sitting at a table opposite us, where she's pointedly not talking to the rugby captain whose name eludes me, is strangely inadequate in person, like she's a watercolour version of the woman in the soap, somehow diluted by the assertions of the purposely dilapidated interior.

The waiter greets Jonathan by name, which tells me he's a regular. I'm still feeling frayed and stunned from the newscasts and Toby's extra report, but I ask anyway, 'Why haven't you ever brought me here before?'

'Why haven't you, sweetheart?' He's intent on his dismemberment, deftly cracking the carapace open and scraping out the meat.

'I couldn't even get into this place as a waitress. I don't think I could afford the breadsticks.'

'I didn't want to spoil you.' His oversize fingers scrabble in the remains. 'But you know,' he pecks at his mouth with the linen napkin, 'now that you're famous, I expect you to keep me in the manner to which I'm accustomed.'

'So I get to keep you?' This comes out more clingy than I intended, but Jonathan takes it in his stride.

'It's a little-known fact that you can determine the appropriate time to introduce philosophy into the conversation by using the number of glasses of wine already imbibed as a measurement. And Kendra, my love, we are still at least three glasses shy of being anywhere near that mark. Not least because you are not drinking. Or not anything alcoholic, at least.'

'I think you're covering for both of us.'

'I don't think I have ever been in a situation where I've been forced to pay corkage on a soft drink. We may never be able to return here. So take it all in! While you can.'

'You know I'll pay for it. Don't be patronising.' If I sound defensive, it's because I am. Even if the maitre d' hadn't handled it with excruciating courtesy that was more telling than a smirk or arched eyebrow.

'I wouldn't dream of it. Not when you already have a patron encouraging your dreadful habit.'

I raise my glass in mock salute and take a long slow sip of Ghost to irritate him. 'At least it's not heroin.'

'I don't know. I believe heroin can be very stimulating, creatively. And very credible with that whole artist culture thing. You know, we need to cash in on your cachet. We can only coast so far on the scandal. Maybe a lesbian affair with Nkosi, in the wake of her devastation.'

'You're a mean drunk. You should stop. '

'Someone has to. Or would you rather I switched to your beverage of choice?' He leans across and takes my glass. 'Does it have any effect on us mortals?'

'No. It's just a soft drink. It's how it interacts with the nano. Didn't Andile tell you?'

I don't know why I entertained the concept for one instant that there was something I could accomplish on my own. I'm furious for not guessing this was Jonathan's doing from the start, for not recognising the mark of his blunt fingers.

Of course he was the one who recommended me to Andile, old colleagues from when he used to shoot the Nokia Fash Week catalogues. It could just as easily have been any other young up-and-coming. I've tried to explain how he's undermined me, but Jonathan just laughs and trudges out hackneyed clichés about how it's who you know.

'Or,' I snap, 'who you're sleeping with.' Not that we've slept together since I had the procedure done.

He tells me I'm too tense, and I am. The articles are freaking me out, but this is something I can't forgive him, because, dammit, this was supposed to be mine.

He takes a sip. 'Ugh. That's nasty. The lime-vanilla's quite nice, but the aftertaste. It's so chemical.' He thrusts it back at me. 'I suppose you're right, though. The lesbian affair is very passé. Right up there with the heroin thing, and you're a new breed. My little art star.' He leans over the table to kiss me, awkward.

'You mean, your meal-ticket.'

'Same thing. So, how are we going to build on your first success? What's next? You said something about street kids and their pitiful possessions? Oh, Kendra. Don't cry.' He is more impatient than sympathetic.

'I'm not crying,' but denying it only makes my face slip more.

'You're being way too sensitive. You shouldn't take it personally.'

'It's my work, Jonathan.' I'm desperately aware of people in the restaurant looking. Naledi Nxumalo leans in to the rugby player with the exact gossipy gleam in her eyes that's her trademark in Bright City.

'And your work is very, very good, baby.'

'I feel hung out in limbo. I want to sledge-hammer my cameras. I want to set the film stock alight.'

'Not a bad idea for a performance piece. Okay, I'm sorry. Don't look like that. I'm sorry.'

'I wish you would take me seriously.'

'Kendra,' he says, taking my hands across the table. 'This is the best thing that could have happened to you, career-wise. You couldn't have planned it.'

There is something in his voice, a wink, a pride that tips me off.

And I realise something that's been simmering in the back of my brain since I first saw the newscasts.

'The security footage had audio.'

Jonathan grins. 'Don't be so naïve, my darling, of course it did. We had it specially installed.'

I drop my fork with a clatter and shove the chair back from the table so that Naledi Nxumalo and the rugby captain and half a dozen others perk up with interest.

'Don't be so dramatic.' Why is it that half of what he says to me always starts with 'Don't'?

'Come on Kendra, there aren't even any press here. It's a wasted effort. Sit down, please.' And despite my best intentions to defy him, I do.

'You're a rational animal, Kendra. You know what this means for you as an artist.'

In my head, I am fashioning scathing putdowns, like I wouldn't expect someone who never graduated from photographing fashion shoots – even if it is for the likes of Vanity Fair – to be capable of comprehending artistic integrity, but somehow these don't make it out of my mouth. Because I am afraid. That he's right. That without him, I am a nonentity. Girl in limbo. Ghost girl.

Jonathan orders me another one, unasked for, which I know the waiter will have to run down to the corner café to get, and I realise this is the end of something. Maybe not limbo so much as the falling space, like the moment after you've thrown yourself backwards off the boat, your hand on your regulator to stop it jerking free, but before you hit the water. Poised between.

Tomorrow I will spend the day apartment hunting. I will find a place to stay, no matter how much of a hovel, that is mine. As in, nothing to do with Jonathan. In the evening, I will take the underway down to Replica. Maybe hook up with Damian and Vix. Make new friends. I still have Toby's comp.

That e-vite suddenly feels like a passport to somewhere other than here. And maybe tomorrow, everything will be different.

Lerato

So here we are, three mismatched women holding a meaningless memorial to three people I don't remember. It's bad enough I have to endure my sisters – Zama looking positively plump and matronly in a white kaftan and Xhosa-styled headscarf, her attempt to dress up nice for the ancestors; Sipho in jeans and an orange t-shirt, with a shaven head that makes her look like a chemo survivor – but the gale-force wind is something else. We have to lean into it to get to the edge of the cliff overlooking Cape Point, and the herbs Sipho throws into the air get whipped straight back at us. There is a small cluster of foreign tourists who have braved the baboons and the wind to get up here, and who are utterly charmed by the proceedings, cameras clicking.

The reason we're doing it here, at the craggy tip of the peninsula, rather than somewhere less exposed to the southeaster (like Clifton corporate, say) is because Sipho says we have to throw our prayers out to the wind and sea to carry them to our loved ones. It would be touching, if it weren't so Hallmark, if we hadn't done it all before. As remembrance rituals go, it's an empty gesture, Sipho chanting some Buddhist shit and tossing around more bits of crushed leaf, just adding to the flotsam already whirling in the wind.

'If we were following tradition, we would kill a goat,' says Zama sagely, as if she hasn't offered some variation on this insight every year. This makes me lose my patience.

'As if we would get a licence to kill a goat in public. As if our Buddhist vegan over here would stand for it. But okay, Zama, assuming we could get that all worked out, then we could all have a big party, just like tradition specifies, eat our goat, drink mqombothi which you would have brewed up as the eldest, and each of us would get a bit of bloody sinew and hide tied onto our wrists to dry out. Because nothing says thanks to your ancestors like a bracelet made of smelly goat's flesh.'

Zama is pissed. 'I think it sucks that you don't have any respect for your culture.'

'I think it sucks that you're deluding yourself that you have some deep spiritual connection, like you didn't just read it on Wikipedia. There's a difference between tradition and culture, Zama. The only fucking culture we got was growing up in a corporate skills school.'

Fighting instantly reduces us to being nine and six all over again, with Sipho trying to play peacekeeper in the middle, spinning her hippie crap about the moment and how we're ruining it.

'Please guys. Look!' Sipho pulls a bundle of red elastic bands from her pocket.

'Stealing stationery from the monks again?'

'Lerato!' Zama snaps, scandalised, as if she doesn't agree with my diagnosis that Sipho's a nutjob.

'No, look. It's not goat. But it's something.'

Zama's eyes go all glassy. 'This is really… Did you bring this along specially?'

'No. It was what you were saying.' She is so sweet, so much a naïf, you can't really be mean to her. I wonder if she'd be tougher, smarter, if she wasn't always trying to balance us out.

I snap the elastic onto Zama's wrist, stretching it out, so that it'll hurt on the rebound. 'Uh, yeah, but isn't this more Kabbalah than Buddhist? Now *there's* a tradition.'

They both glare at me.

Family are the people who irritate you the most and the most effortlessly. If it were anyone else, I wouldn't give a damn and it bugs me a lot that I let them get to me, Zama's more-spiritual-than-you bullshit and Sipho's little-girl-lost act. Not for the first time, I swear this is the last time. That I'm not coming out here again. I will stop returning phone calls and emails. I will cut conversations short. I will forget birthdays and not be able to make anniversaries. I will let this drift, like continents, slowly, imperceptibly. Or fuck it, just put one between us. My exit plan is my faux-goat red elastic, my backdoor embedded in the adboards, sending me secrets worth money to the right eye. If Stefan doesn't come through, it's all I have to hang onto.

We sit in awkward silence inside the restaurant, protected from the wind but not the uncrossable distances between us. The only part of family 'tradition' we get right is the getting drunk, so that when I get home, I pass out and miss everything.

Toby

The underway is so jammed I have to loop and thread between the press of commuters. No worries for a boy on the skinny, nipping the gaps. But I am worried (not much, but they're only paying me the second instalment after mission accomplished) about the rest of Clan Stinger in my wake. Doyenne especially. That girl is built sumo. But a backwards glance reveals that she's just ploughing that construction worker bulk through, the crowd sensibly parting for her, while Ibis (aka Julia from the barcade) slipstreams in her wake. I've lost view of Twitch, but I'm sure the little shit can take care of himself.

In realworld, Doyenne is a taxi driver in her mid-40s – maybe a tad decrepit for fun and games, but who am I to thwart her recreational? Cos that's what it's about, right? Re-creations of lives you could never live.

We're all civilian. Specs were undercover, although I'm not going anywhere without my BabyStrange, that's for you, kids, for your enjoyment. It's switched to live-feed from my splinter-new phone, no delay on the uplink. It's also perfect for hiding the telltale bulge of the .44 riding on my hip.

On the escalator, standing behind me, Ibis aka Julia checks her lipgloss in my coat. You gotta admire a girl who has the presence of mind to touch up her prettifiers pre-combat. She's been relatively cold to me since we were reintroduced. But then, I didn't call. But then, I never do.

'You activated?' she murmurs behind me, so soft only I can hear, cos we're playing strangers for the moment, until such time as Doyenne decides we're good to make our play. As soon as Twitch has scoped out the lie of the land.

I don't bother to answer. As if I would have forgotten in the heat. My phone is already blinking blue, logged onto Playnet and legit with the relevant authorities – although unlike my crime-busting colleagues over here, I'm registered under a fake name. It's not necessary, but let's say I've developed a taste for anonymity, for taking on an artificial ID (like Diary isn't an exaggerated persona already). I'm sure it's all going to get terribly confusing. Try to keep up.

I grab hold of the rails with both hands and swing over the top steps, my coat flaring behind. Julia pushes past me, just another underway annoyance, her boots making sharp cicada clicks on the vibracrete as she vanishes into the cram. I swivel on my heel and prowl over to the newsstand to buy a bottle of water. No sense going into this dehydrated. It's still lank early. Fourteen minutes ahead of schedule. We've got time to kill.

Doyenne's strict on the punctuality, Twitch told me while we were sitting in the taxi waiting for her to come back from the petrol station loo, cos she has a spastic colon. He was switching through the motions on his rifle, checking the mechanics until the constant clack got to me, and I grabbed his hand to stop him doing it.

'Leave him alone. It chills him out.' Ibis aka Julia spoke from the front of the car, not even looking round.

'Well, it's riding me one time.'

'He needs it. He's OCD.'

'For fuck's sake. Can't he take meds? Or a hit of sugar?' My luck to latch up with a crew with sufficient medical ailments to fill a doctor's waiting room. And that's not even counting the guy I'm replacing, who broke his collarbone moving a fridge.

'Nah. Meds blunt his focus. And Doyenne

doesn't shine to drugs, so don't talk about whatever you're on now, okay?' She cocked her
head over her shoulder, presenting a shadow of
profile, just enough so I could see the dark mole
at the corner of her lip that makes her mouth
look faintly misshapen. 'And besides, he's fourteen. So lay off, okay?'

'Okay. Kit Kat!' I lifted my hand off his, and
the kid went right back into the damn clicking,
sliding the ammo clip out, slamming it back in.
'Do your parents know where you're at tonight,
Twitch?'

He looked puzzled, although at least he
stopped with the damn clicking for an instant,
and then launched straight back into it, not looking up. 'For your information, fuckwit, my mom
was the one who hooked me up with Stinger.'

From the front, Ibis aka Julia snickered.

I take a sip of water and flip casually through
the racks, sneaking previews on some of the
pushmags, but being particular in not *skeeming*
the gaming titles, cos you don't want to be too
obvious. Keep it tight.

'You gonna buy that?' The shop chick, a
bovine dumpy blonde, eyes dulled by one too
many soapcasts, picks at her teeth with a
fingernail, intent on the blurbvert playing on
the screen above the till.

'Me? Hmm. No. I don't think so.'

'Well then, skip it.'

'Hey, I already bought the water. Doesn't that entitle me to browsing rights?'

'You gotta buy.'

'Fine.'

I skim the shelves and grab a dark porn push, way up top, hand it to her to scan and flash my phone at the till. And then I crack the seal and start paging through it in front of her, pausing to show her a grotesque special on page six, cranking the volume up. She grimaces, managing to look even stupider and uglier, and leans back on her stool, pumping up the sound on her soap to try and drown me out.

I'm enjoying this now. I flick through to find another disturbing combo – oh, don't sweat it, it's all digital re-creations, they wouldn't really force a hyena to mount a nubile teenager.

Her repulsed reaction, the way I'm playing her, kicks up my rush. It's a sugar–bliss combo, if you were wondering, just enough to remix my experience of the world a little.

I glance round to check on the mission status. There's no sign of the little OCD monster. Doyenne is standing peering at the map but really scouting out the junction, looking through the screen to the platforms below; Ibis/Julia is sitting primly on a bench, reading a book, her posture straight as an arrow.

Someone in the crowd jostles me harder than is politely acceptable, so I nearly drop the pushmag. Often, I get off on the tight; walking so close you can feel the swerve of the air currents between you and the people coming in the opposite direction. And it's always fun to infringe on people's personal space. But the crush is even thicker now, like fucking rush hour or like there's a soccer game on. Last time Orlando Pirates played the city stadium, eight people were fatally squished in this very station.

I catch a glimpse of a sludge hoodie bobbing away, carried by the surge, and recognise it as Twitch's signature style, or rather signature lack of style. Which means either that he's fucking with me, or that it's time.

I glance over at the team's positions. The bench is vacant. No visual on Ibis/Julia. Doyenne is heading down the stairs at an easy amble. Nice of them to let me know. I sneak a peek at my phone, which is thrumming insistently with an in-game msg and an attachment of ID images.

>> *SECURITY ALERT. #SD-17* Scan cams identified four (4) known terrorists in immediate vicinity.

I dump the pushmag in my pocket, saving it
for later, and let the throng sweep me towards
the lifts, as per our blueprint. It's basic stuff.
Ibis/Julia and Doyenne will take either end of
the train, working their way down towards
each looking for the terrorist called Unity, the
one with the dirty bomb, while I cover the
platform – and the little shit keeps a bead on
all of us from some disused maintenance cube
lodged in the ceiling. They got access to a
maintenance cube through sheer fluke. Took
them eighteen hours solid gamespace play to
crack a drug-bust mission, and when they'd
fragged every junkie in sight, they found all
kinds of useful goodies tucked among their
stash, including an access card that unlocks
certain gameplaces realworld.

I click open the folder, flip through the images, supposedly uploaded fresh from the
station security cams. Not actually, sorry to
disappoint you. It's all pre-scanned. As lucrative as play is, and trust me, Inkubate Inc. is
paying Metro bigtime for the rights to play in
the underway and set up gameplaces like
Twitch's maintenance cube; they're still not allowed to interfere with actual realworld
goings on in the public domain, which includes linking to the security cams for our
gaming pleasure.

The photo-IDs are, in order:

A heavy in a gold vinyl tracksuit rubbed shiny with wear or maybe distressed on purpose, with tightly wound blond curls and a jaw designed to shatter all the bones in your fist.

A shaven-headed girl, around my age, done up all pantsula in pinstripes and carrying a black steel case, which is so blatantly obvious, I dismiss her as a decoy.

Another macho, business-slick in a suit with a gym bag slung casually over his shoulder, but it's clearly heavy, which is a tad more promising.

And. Hey, there.

I reverse direction, grinning. Of course, I'm contractually obliged to let one of the fulltime members of Clan Stinger take the glory, but is it my fault I'm intuitive? If I've encountered the target previously? I send a msg to the crew, but who knows how long they'll take to get back up here. It might be too late by then.

The people behind me don't take too kindly to me switching against the flow. Some of them have their phones held up at arm's length, beaming laser slogans in all caps above their heads: 'ALL ACCESS' and 'PASSES FOR THE PEOPLE'. Some of the protesters don't smell too fresh, and there's a higher content of street kid per capita than usual.

And I finally twig why it's so packjammed down here. The protest. Great fucking timing, although maybe that's the point – to make it more challenging.

I shove through the press of bodies back towards the kiosk where the podgy girl is attending to a protester with springy little dreads and a leather bandolier strung with audio chips instead of cartridges that are broadcasting slogans at decibel in most of the official languages.

'I'm sorry, did I leave my phone here?' I have to shout over the chips, pushing rudely in front of the protester, who *skeefs* me with a dirty look, to get to the counter.

The apparently not-so-dullard cow ignores me. And what choice do I have, kids? Really? The .44 is already in my hand, it's only a thirty degree flex of my arm to pull it free of the holster and swing it up so it's level with the bridge of her rather neat little nose. 'I'd suggest you surrender the merchandise.'

The protester squawks and leaps backwards, knocking over a rack of mags, but the resulting crash is drowned out by the electronic chatter of the chips and the protesters shouting and the ambient crowd sounds.

The cow whimpers. She's gone all pasty, which throws her zits into relief. Cunning bitch.

Gotta admire the acting talent. You'd think she was the real deal.

'I don't have time. Just give it over.'

She opens her mouth as if to say something useful, but then goldfishes soundlessly.

'Oh for fuck's sake.' I press the gun against her forehead. 'Three, two...' And sudden she finds her voice.

'I don't got nothing! Please!'

'The package?'

'Take it! Take it!' But she fails to hand anything over, covering her eyes and quivering instead. I'm aware that a space has cleared around me, and my phone is vibrating frantically in my pocket.

'Just give me the package and I won't have to shoot you,' I say, real slow, so she can't misunderstand. Maybe I got it wrong and it's the hip gangster girl or one of the heavies after all. In which case, I might have blown the whole fucking mission, exposed us too early. Fuck. And now I'm not so sure I looked at the picture properly in the first place. Maybe it was some other ugly fat girl plus wishful thinking on my part. Or maybe she's an unwitting mule.

I vault over the counter. She shrieks and wedges herself into the corner, weeping now. I pull her down, so that we're out of the limelight, crouched behind the desk. 'Everything's sony, honey, just chill. Stay right there. Don't you move.' I keep the gun on her, hunting around. 'Where's your bag? Where's your fucking bag!'

She points wordlessly at a turquoise tote on a shelf. I press it into her hands, even though she doesn't want to take it.

'Open it.'

'I don't got nothing. I don't.'

'Did anyone ask you to hold something for them? Or give you something? A present?'

She's scrabbling in her bag, spilling prettifiers onto the carpet, sobbing so hard her words hitch. 'My... my... boyfriend.'

'Yeah? What did he give you? Where is it?'

'Th-this.' She yanks off a plastech keyring attached to the bag's handle – a mini-figurine of Anika, the virtua pop star.

'Be careful! Shit.' It's not inconceivable that the bomb would fit inside a keyring. I take it from her gingerly and stow it in an inside pocket.

'Now close your eyes.'

'Why?'

'Cos I've been wanting to do this ever since I met you.'

She shakes her head vigorously, sobbing hard. I shrug. She should have known what she was letting herself in for when she took on the assignment.

I pull the trigger.

The .44 kicks in my hand with a sharp metallic roar. Which should have been the end of her, only the blobby cow is still shrieking, clawing at the wet gobs splattered across her face. She squeals even louder when her hands come away sticky with sheen. I am way pissed now, kids.

'What are you doing? You're analogue, baby. You're out. Fucking go down.'

She holds her hands out to me, all shaky disbelief, and catches me left-field by starting to cry, little pathetic mewlings.

'Oh. Hey. Everything's sony, okay? It's not… Look.' I'm about to wipe her forehead to show her, but I don't want to get the dye on my BabyStrange, so I grab her by the wrist instead. 'It's purple, see?' Inexplicably, she starts crying harder. 'It's not blood. You don't gush purple. It's just a game. It's icy. Okay?' But she's sobbing so uncontrollably, I don't think I'm getting through.

I holster the gun and start sliding away from the blubbering girl, making sure I still have the keyring. The hippie with the audio-chip bandolier barges in. 'Bro, that was so uncool.'

'Hey! She was registered gameplay. It's not my fault she's a rookie.'

'Oh yeah?' He bends down, comes back with her handbag and dumps out the phone, turns it over to show me. It hasn't been chipped for in-game. It's so outmoded, it wouldn't even support the tech. Shit.

I hightail it through the crowd, ignoring dreadlock boy's recriminations shouted after me. The protest is going off, it's too thick to move without worming between the bodies, and the amplified chatter is deaf-making. I duck down besides a motobin that's been stopped in its circuit by the human traffic, humming quietly to itself, and check my phone. My msgs display various riffs on 'where the hell are you?' from all three of my clan mates.

Surprisingly, Ibis/Julia is the most graphic of all of them, threatening my mother with violence if I don't get my skinny ass down there immediately. Maybe I'll take her up on it later.

But right now I have bigger pilchard to pan-fry. I skip the rest of the msgs and reload the target list, flipping through the visuals to saggy cow, who is indeed the girl I just fragged in the face, down to the last inflamed zit. This is all seriously dubious.

>> Weird stuff going on. Think the mission has been compromised. Could we have got bad intelligence? Considering mission abort? Confirm?

I sit tight and wait for an answer. The motobin is a little slow, only now detecting my proximity. It swivels on its axis and gapes its flap at me hopefully, waiting for a deposit. No one gets back to me, not even Twitchy, who is supposed to be holed up at high altitude.

Fuckit. What else to do? I throw myself back into the fray, all bargey elbows to get through the toyi-toyi, because the protesters seem to be holding fast to their positions. If they hoped to stop the station functioning today, they're doing well.

From the plastech pedestrian tunnel that crosses over the junction, I can see it's mal chaos below. On the platform, only heads are visible in the mesh of people, like coloured pixels, shoving in different directions. The trains are at a standstill, but there are bursts of flash-fire going off inside the compartments, six or seven while I'm watching. I skeem I'm not the only player here today with corrupt data.

A ripple of quiet spreads out from one side of the station as the audio chips suddenly fade out, as if they've been dampened. The protesters' voices sound hollow without them, too warm, too varied without their mechanical accompaniment, and even the voices are starting to falter. I can't see shit, but I can anticipate what's coming.

'*This is the South African Police Services,*' the announcement blasts over the PA as the protesters and the civilians all fall respectfully, no, fearfully, silent, so now we can hear the shouts from the platforms below. The toyi-toyi-ing wavers and stops as people turn expectantly to the entrance, where uniforms flanked by Aitos are descending the stairs in perfect formation.

'*This is an unlawful, unlicensed gathering. You are advised to disband immediately.*' It's pre-recorded. Legislation bars the cops from opening their mouths unnecessarily. There's too much room for human error, which means ammunition for the human rights groups – for all the teeth they've got.

It's the same reason the cops are indistinguishable behind their flicker visors – on purpose, kids, so you can't lay an assault charge if they beat you into submission too vigorously.

'*Repeat: You are advised to disband immediately. You are in violation of section 14(ii) of the Transport Authority Code, as well as section 11.2(vi) of the Commerce Protection Act.*'

I start edging towards the lift. I've no intention of sticking around to see the standard spiel play all the way through.

'*Warning: If you choose not to disband immediately, it will be assumed under the Tacit Liability Act that you are fully aware of the potential repercussions of your unlawful actions and that you waive your right to seek any kind of legal recourse or financial compensation for any injuries or damages incurred in the course of law enforcement response.'*

The uniforms have stopped, arranged in an invert V down the main stairwell, while the Aitos spread out through the crowd, yipping in excitement. It's enough to inspire some of the people to disperse, mostly nervous commuters.

'This is your last warning.'

The tension dies unexpectedly, like a battery running out of juice. It's like the crowd collectively shrug all at once, and start disassembling peacefully and in an orderly fashion so as not to piss off the cops or, more importantly, the dogs.

But then the lift doors open and it becomes obvious the msg hasn't reached the lower floors. Doyenne bursts out, splattered with dye, but not enough to take her out of the game, grinning like a berserker, rabid with battle lust. I'm close enough to see the purple smear over her mouth, as if she's wiped the back of her hand across it. She grins wider and launches into the painfully over-quoted line from *Sleepers Phoenix* – 'Hi-de-ho, neighbours! I regret to inform you it's time to die!' before opening random fire on the crowd.

Chaos breaks out in shockwaves from the nucleus of the lifts. People drop to the ground,

screaming, unaware that it's a game, cos they're
idiots, cos you'd never mistake the sting of a dye
pellet for a bullet. Others, caught in the panic,
surge towards the exits. And then in one convulsive move, *everyone* drops to the ground,
twitching, phones crackling as the defusers kick
in.

Unfortunately, mine *doesn't* go off, which is
plenty worrying if the uniforms notice that I'm
packing an illegal mod. I drop too, bit of a de-
layed reaction there, kids, but pay it no heed,
and try to avoid the thrashing limbs all around
me as I start inch-worming across the floor towards the nearest exit.

I'm not the only one unaffected. Almost none
of the protesters are KFC. There are about forty
of them, standing defiant in the epileptic human
sea jerking around their feet.

'And what are you going to fucking do now?'
shouts one of the protesters. The sound is amplified, distorted, but the voice sounds very
familiar in its puffed-up wankery.

'Your weapons are useless. We defy your at-
tempts to regulate society. We're voluntarily
disconnected! Voluntarily disenfranchised! You
cannot control us!' He holds up the remains of
a smashed phone, then drops it to the ground.

I catch on. It's Tendeka and his BF sur-
rounded by all manner of ragtag humanity;

MOXYLAND   261

bergies and skollies and street kids who all have
one thing in common – they're homeless and
phoneless. Which only means that when they
call the dogs in, they're going to be more savage
than usual.

Already the cops are switching over to canister guns. It's all strict by-the-book procedure.
Verbal warning. Defuse. Dogs. It never takes
more. Even the most defiant bloody-minded
idiot tends to shut up and give up when facing
down those teeth. Well, except for Doyenne.

By the lift, Doyenne has two Aitos attached to
her, one worrying at the sleeve of her jacket, the
other tugging her jeans, but she's still laughing,
still pumping slugs into the crowd and swearing
soldier, clubbing alternately at the dogs' heads
with her free hand. Two pellets explode across
the second dog's flank, the trajectory coming
from somewhere up high – like a ceiling hidey-
hole. Fuck, Twitchy. That's a disconnect offence.
I duck my head, smirking, as an Aito bounds
across the spasming flesh, its paws coming down
heedlessly on groins and heads.

One of the cops fires a chem cap into the
thicket of the protesters, hitting Ashraf solidly
in the chest, the impact knocking him back into
the mass of bodies writhing on the floor.

By now, the Aitos have pulled Doyenne
down, but now they look up, ears pricked

forward as they pick up the telltale chem scent, and abandon their victim to bound towards the protesters.

The next bit is mess. Tendeka and his ragtag regiment yank out pangas. The first dog to reach them goes down with a meaty thwack more robust than the art thing, which goes to prove, kids, that the attack at the gallery wasn't in aid of animal rights at all. I file this for reference. Ten's bunnyhugger boyfriend would surely disapprove – if he wasn't a little preoccupied drowning in a sea of thrashing limbs.

The Aito howls, but comes straight back up, its lip hanging off its jaw, exposing the teeth. The kids shriek, more horror than rage, lashing out as much to keep it at bay as anything else.

It goes down under a torrent of blows, real Rwanda.

On the stairs, one of the cops raises her baton and then lowers it again, uncertainly. Several of the others are locked in a screaming match, because this shit is way outside the bounds of procedure. People aren't supposed to attack the dogs.

A sharp keening buzz undercuts the noise, a subsonic signal to the Aitos, which all lose interest at the same time. Together, they raise their heads, then bound back to the cops, to the tune of their master's audio, abandoning their targets.

It's only temporary. Trust me on this. There's gonna be a bloodrush for sure, and it's only going to get uglier. I'm preparing to scram, shifting my weight onto my knees so I can launch towards the exits, when something unexpected happens.

The cops wait for the dogs to reach them and then turn sharply and tromp up the stairs, withdrawing.

It's apparent no one knows what the fuck this means. There's a wailing from the other side of the hall, like someone has figured this can only signify heavy shit to come, but minutes pass. There's no indication that the cops are coming back.

People scramble to their feet, helping each other up, laughing in relief, or bleating. The civilians don't know what hit them. Even some of the gamers are displaying classic shock. Couldn't cut it in realworld after all.

I'm already up, halfway to the exits, when runt boy peels out from behind a pillar, and tedious deluxe, sticks his gun in my gut.

'Oh fuck off, Twitchy, the game's over.'

'We're gonna go find Ibis. And Doyenne,' he says, all steely determination, despite his hand shaking so hard he has to steady the barrel of his gun against my navel.

'You fragged a police dog, Twitchy. You think they can't trace your bullets?' They can't, but

I'm not gonna tell him that.

'Only with dye! I thought it was–' His left hand is switching the safety on and off relentlessly.

'Part of the game? Got carried away? Like that's going to stand you in civil rehab. It's still an attack on police property. If you're lucky, they might downgrade the charge to defacing police property.'

His eyes are bugging out, but he won't let up on that damn safety catch. On/off/on/off, not unlike his brain malfunction.

'But what about Ibis?' he whines.

'I'm sure *Julia* will be fine.' He winces at her real name, and the implication that I might know her on more intimate terms. Someone's crushing on their clan mate badly. 'Doyenne, though, she's gonna need a whole lot of patching up, thanks to you. You really peeved those dogs. If I were you, Twitchy, I'd bail before they come looking for you.'

I shove the gun away – a pellet that close would leave a nasty bruise – and just for spite, ruffle his hair. But just as I'm about to make a graceful exit, dumping the kid and the whole bad situation, the sprinklers embedded in the ceiling open up.

Twitch looks up, holding out a hand, like a kid catching snowflakes. 'Wha–?'

'Shit, don't let it touch you!' I pull up the hood on my coat and tuck my hands under my armpits, but it's too late, there's already a fine mist on my exposed skin.

'Why? What is it? What's the matter?'

People are looking up, raising their faces to the spray; others, the sensible ones, are running for the doors, pulling their clothing over their heads. Some crusty chick in beads is dancing in it, kicking out her legs, like it's a rave.

'Chem marking. So the Aitos can follow you, whee, whee, whee, all the way home.'

A feminine voice crackles over the intercom – the SAPS's virtua spokesperson, who manages to sound warm and impersonal and regretful all at the same time, like a beautiful chiding mother from a Fifties sitcom.

'Important message. Brought to you by the South African Police Services. We regret to inform you that due to an attempted insurrection by terrorists using banned technology, the SAPS have had no alternative but to make use of statute 41b, Extreme Measures, of the National Security Act,' says the voice, sweet as high-fructose corn syrup.

'In accordance with this statute, activated for your protection, you have all been exposed to the M7N1 virus, a lab-coded variation of the Marburg strain. Do not panic.'

This has the opposite effect. A shock of people

rush for the exits. Against my better judgement, I yank Twitchy out of the way, so that we're both wedged tightly behind the pillar while the crush surges past.

'Repeat. Do not be alarmed. The M7N1 Marburg variation is only fatal if you do NOT report to an immunity centre for treatment within 48 hours. Repeat. It is NOT fatal if you present yourself promptly for vaccination treatment. Vaccination is 100% effective within three hours with minimal lasting side-effects. Vaccination treatment is a free service offered by the South African Police Services.

'Be advised, that if you choose NOT to report for vaccination, you can expect the following symptoms. Within three hours, your throat will become sore and inflamed. Your mucous membranes will become irritated. Within six hours, you will experience coughing and sneezing. Within 12 hours, your eyesight will become blurry. You will present with flu-like symptoms. Within 18 hours, your muscles will ache and you will experience prolonged coughing fits. Within twenty-four hours, you will feel weak, and you may notice traces of blood in your mucus and your urine. This is an indication that the virus is taking hold and beginning to break down your soft cell structures. After 48 hours, your organs will start to liquefy and collapse. You will be coughing blood uncontrollably, and you may be unable to breathe. Within 50 to 60 hours, your stomach acids

will reach your heart and lungs. The virus has lim-
ited capacity and is not contagious.

'*South African Police Services strongly advises cit-*
izens exposed to the M7N1 Marburg variation for
their protection to report to an immunity centre im-
mediately. Should you be too weak to report to an
immunity centre, please call the South African Police
Services and we will dispatch a mobile service to col-
lect you. Again, this service is free, provided in the
interests of public health and safety. The South
African Police Services are dedicated to serve. How
can we help you?'

Pressed against my chest, Twitch starts to cry.
It seems the appropriate response. Talk about a
come-down.

We coop up in the kid's sniper hidey-hole to
wait it out. Just because we have to turn ourselves in doesn't mean the fuckers aren't going
to be waiting for us with a little encouragement.
I'm not going to meekly tramp out with the
herd and see what happens. I need some time
to think, some time to suss out exactly what this
means.

The hidey-hole's normal purpose in life is as
a maintenance cluster, where the VIMbots go to
recharge, happy and humming. We have to
boot some of them out to make space for us –
it's not like they don't have work to do with the

mess outside – and even then, we're both sitting hunched with our knees up.

When it gets too cramped and boring, I send Twitch (real name Eddie, he tells me) out to scout, half hoping he won't come back. But he crawls back in a few minutes later, so I have to fold my knees up again to accommodate him. Just when the pins and needles were wearing off.

'Well?'

'I didn't. I was–' The little shit can't even look at me.

'You're hopeless, Eddie.' I scoot past him on my butt, only to have a VIMbot zoom in the flapdoor and ram full-throttle into my shin. 'Fuck!'

I chuck the VIMbot out of the cluster and drop down out after it into one of the toilet stalls, nudging the door open cautiously with my boot. The bot is already fully recovered. By the time I nip a glance around the edge of the men's room door, it's already skittered away.

The station is deserted, although there is a droning coming from somewhere near the entrance. There are no trains running, at least not here, but there's a dull sound that could be rumbling in tunnels further away. The space is eerie without people. Déjà vu city. I'm almost expecting to hear a rusty gurgle.

The surfaces are coated with a damp beaded film, like the walls have been sweating. I know I'm already infected, but can you blame me for not wanting to touch anything or prolong the exposure?

There is a human bundle collapsed on the stairs, which I have every intention of ignoring. I touch my hand to my gun, even though it's only loaded with chemdye. I'm still trying to figure out whether it's better to head down to the tunnels, try and find a service exit or just, fuck it, go out the front, when there is the squeal of tackies on wet marble behind me. I tighten my grip on the .44, but it's only Twitch/Eddie, looking even paler and scared, oblivious to the squelch of his sneakers. I flap my hand at him and he gets it. He shifts to his toes, so that the rubber doesn't squeak so much.

He points at the bundle and whispers, cos speaking would be too loud in all this space, even if we were absolutely fucking totally positive that no one else was around. 'What's that?'

'Don't worry about it. It's nothing. Leave it.'

'Is she… dead?'

'How the fuck should I know? Just fucking leave it.'

'But what if it's–'

'It's not.'

'Oh.'

'C'mon.' And he pads after me, obedient as a puppy, up the far side of the stairs, far as possible from the bundle.

The murmuring is getting louder. *'Please be advised…'*

'Hey, Buzzkill?' I cringe at the pre-assigned call sign.

'It's Toby. Okay? Just–'

'Toby?'

'I said, don't look. Ignore it.'

'Toby. She's moving.'

'I don't care.' But I look despite myself. And I don't know what I'm expecting, her face to be caved in, insides leaking out, even though they say this fucker doesn't work that fast. But who knows? Could be three hours or three months. They could have released the wrong fucking bug. For all I know, it could be the fucking flu and it's all a big psych. I look long enough to see that the pink sheen pooled underneath her body is not her liquefying interior but part of a slinky dress, long enough to see that it's not Ibis/Julia. 'Niks to do with us.'

'… is closed.'

'But–'

'Just shut the fuck up and just fucking leave it, okay!'

But it's like the gun all over again, the misfire in his brain.

'Toby?'

'I'll leave you here. I swear.' He shuts up for at least five seconds.

'More info?'

Then he says, sullenly, 'Your coat is still on.'

'Taxis are wait–'

'Thanks.' But as I touch the seam that deactivates the image capture, there's a snatch of green and silver reflected in my sleeve.

'Shit.'

'… transport you to Junction.'

Kendra-sweet is limp and unyielding when I yank her to her feet, my arm around her waist, ignoring the gloppy strands of puke clinging to her hair and streaked down the front of the pink dress, like she's been on a particularly heroic binge. 'Dammit. Help me!' But Eddie is hesitant.

'Please be advised…'

'What's wrong with her arm? What if–?'

'It's not.'

'… to terrorist action.'

'But how do you know?'

'More info?'

I pull the gun on him. Precarious, cos I'm holding up K, still unconscious and leaden against my hip. Eddie blinks at it stupidly. 'You're not allowed to shoot a clan mate.'

'Try me.'

We load her up between us, though the little shit is careful not to touch her or the spillage on her dress. She gags like she's going to kotch again, and Eddie nearly drops her. I cuff him with the back of my hand, the one that's not holding her up, so I knock his hoodie back off his head with the muzzle of the gun. He whimpers.

At the entrance, there is a row of lumo orange infocones in a row as sharp as soldiers, effectively cordoning off the area.

'This station is closed. Taxis are available on the concourse to transport you to Junction. Please be advised. This station is closed. More info?'

Kendra

'Don't.'

I try to break away, but they won't let go. I can't stand the proximity, the heat of their bodies is too close, too tight; it makes me feel nauseous. Until I was about three, I couldn't handle anyone touching me, I'd scream if they tried. It's common with premature babies, my parents said, but maybe they got it wrong, maybe it was my brother or another baby entirely. Maybe I never felt anything like this before.

They ignore me, and it's easier to go along with them, because the stairs abruptly seem too steep, laborious, like someone overtilted the axis into an Escher painting.

The emergency exit doors start howling an alarm as we push through them and into the night. It's drizzling. The wind is as cold as teeth. I don't know what I've done with my bag. I try to look back for it over my shoulder.

One of them, the smaller one, yelps, 'Hey! She's going to kotch again.'

I feel vaguely insulted, but then I'm distracted by swathes of blue light strobing the side of the building. The lights seem warm. I'm drawn to them, but we go in the opposite direction instead, and then there is a car, and I am leaning with my head out the window and a hand on my back and cold air and rain stinging against my mouth and I'm getting wet, but they won't let me back inside. And then there is shouting and we're all bundled out and the car screeches away and we have to walk.

And then I wake up.

'Well hello, sunshine.'

I close my eyes again as fast as I can. But it's too late, I've already let in the light and, with it, sparking dazzles of pain.

'Hey? Hell-o? Eugh. Shit, Eddie. Didn't I tell you to clean this up?'

There is a moist dabbing at my chest and I open my eyes, to see Toby – who else would it be? – working at the front of my dress with a dishcloth. It smells distinctly of vomit. The couch I'm lying on is damp with sweat. And I would feel miserably humiliated if the pain didn't override everything.

'Easy, tiger,' Toby says. 'Take it you're feeling better?'

I touch my face, feel a sullen welt on my jaw, where the cop got me with his baton. He would have got me again if his partner hadn't intervened, so his second blow was only a glancing lash across the kidneys as I scrambled past him.

Toby gives me the cloth. 'What were you doing, baby girl?'

'Going to Rep...' I say it again, because the first time it comes out as a malformed croak. 'Going to Replica. For the party? I was meeting friends for a sundowner.' Realisation hits. 'Oh God, they must think I stood them up. Where's my phone, I have to call...'

'It's almost three in the a.m., sweet.'

'Up and about?' An overweight man with a shaven head pokes his face into the negative space between the door and the wall. 'Good. Okay. Then you need to get out.'

'Would you just chill, Unathi?'

'Oh no. No, no, no, no, no. You said till she's conscious. And now she is. You have to *vamos*. *Andelay*.'

'I want to go home,' someone whines, and I notice, now that I'm able to focus, that the *sshh-ssshhs* sound in the background is a kid with bad posture and a worse haircut, ensconced in the depths of a beanbag, rubbing his palms down his corduroy thighs, over and over.

'At least let me upload my video,' says Toby.

'Forget it, china. They're not tracing that shit back to me.'

'Can I use your bathroom?' I sway slightly when I stand up, or rather the world does, taking an unnerving dip that forces me to blink, hard, to get it to realign. The lights are way too bright, flattening out everything into planes of colour. Or maybe it's just me.

'No. No ways.'

'I have to pee.'

'You'll just have to wait.'

'Dude.' Toby chips in, reproachful.

'Is it through here?'

'No, you can't. You have to leave. Right now.'

'Or I could pee on your rug.'

I push open the door into a dingy room overloaded with consoles and projectas playing unique content on every wall. Games, I think, and a vid chat sesh going, with dozens of little faces squawking at each other. I pick my way over empty boxes of instant tofu meals bleeding what I can only hope is miso into the carpet, and stagger into the bathroom.

There's no lock, or at least, no key, so I shove the laundry bin against the door. I wash my face without looking at it, avoiding my eyes in the mirror. My mouth is fucking sore. The bastard split my lip, where the edge of the baton caught me.

I shrug off my dress, step into the bath and turn on the shower full blast without waiting for the temperature to adjust. The pressure is stinging and the cold comes so brutal, it snaps something in my chest, but I refuse to cry. Not here. I lean my head against my arms and let the water surge over me until it turns hot.

'Hey, K. You okay?' Toby raps on the door.

'Is she coming out?'

'Yeah, she's coming out. Just relax.'

'I didn't say she could use the shower, man.' The door shifts but jams against the laundry bin. 'Just chuck her out. Shit.'

'I'll pay for the fucking water,' I shout. There's no shampoo, not surprising for a bald guy, so I use the sludgy bar of green anti-bacterial soap on my hair. I scoop the dress from the floor and try to deal with the stain. The bile and blood are too thoroughly bonded with it, though, and there is a faintly chemical odour too, reminding me of the overwhelming hysteria that came over me at the station, when the dogs surged forward. I couldn't help it. I had to go with them. I scrub and scrub at the stain, but all I'm doing is rubbing it in.

I dry off with a musty blue towel, the only one I can find. Scratching around in the hamper, I find a green t-shirt that isn't too stained. I wring out the dress and roll it down around my hips, tucking in the wet spots as best as I can, and pull the tee over it. It has a decal that says Ecco-5, which I think is a game. Or maybe a band. I avoid the mirror.

'Finally!' says jittery bald guy as I slide open the door. He pauses; the gears in his brain pop and grind. 'Hey, that's my shirt.'

'Are we going to get out of here?'

'I dunno.' Toby is suddenly nervous. 'Maybe it's not a good idea. After, well.'

'Hey. You absolutely cannot stay here. I am not kidding.'

'I mean, have you thought about it?' Toby asks.

'What?'

He laughs, but it's forced. 'Whether we should go or not. Or wait. To see, you know?'

'No, bullshit! You guys need to get to one of those vaccine places soon as.'

'Oh, I'm sorry, are we in your way, Unathi?'

'This isn't my problem, Tobias. You shouldn't have come here.'

'You were the one who hooked me up with the fucking mission! It's exactly your problem.'

Their fighting is making the pain in my head worse. It's like a flash-bulb popping, like the veins in my temples are threads of filament burning out.

'Do you have any Ghost?' The questions shuts them both up.

Baldy – Unathi – whatever, smirks. 'There's a spaza. On the corner. On the way out.'

The kid with the bad hair – I still don't know his name – tramps sulkily after us through two sets of security doors, which buzz open in succession to let us out through an alley that backs onto the delivery entrance of the spaza, which is closed.

'Tighter than a nun's–' Toby starts to say.

'Okay. Just. I'm sure there's another one.'

'Not in this neighbourhood.'

We're not exactly residential. It seems to be mainly warehouses and stacks of metal containers, which must mean we're near the old docks, not too far removed from the station. It's desolate, apart from a rat, loathsomely huge, perched on a mound of rotten tarpaulins. It stops to look at us, incuriously, and then resumes cleaning its face in little circular motions with both paws.

'We're never going to get a taxi now.'

'Couldn't pay for it anyway,' Toby says.

'What?'

I glance at my phone to check the time, but the screen is unnervingly blank. I hit the power, but the screen doesn't light up reassuringly, my signature tune doesn't kick in. I pop the battery, click it back in and thumb it again. But there's nothing.

'Yeah, they amped up the juice when the de-fusers weren't working.'

'Fried everything one time,' the kid says with genuine admiration.

'Even my illegit handset got toasted,' Toby says. 'How do you think we ended up here?'

'What do you mean?'

'No phone. No cash. The last taxi kicked us out.'

'Does this mean I'm disconnect?' It's too much. I sink down heavily on the kerb, not even worried about the rat. 'I don't know. We'll have to see.'

'My mom's going to butcher me if I'm discon-nect,' the kid says glumly, flicking a stompie at the rat, which only twitches its ropy tail and goes back to cleaning itself.

'Hey, come on, baby girl. Don't cry.'

'I'm not fucking crying.'

The kid looks away embarrassed. Toby checks his watch. 'Look, it's 3.18. My place is nearby. Well, relatively nearby. It's about six kays, we can walk it. And we'll just go chill out until morning, maybe email some people. Persuade someone to make a call on our behalf.'

'I'm going to an immunisation centre,' blurts the kid. 'You can't stop me. Don't even try and stop me.' He's holding a gun, his hand shaking.

'That's fine, Eddie. I don't give a fuck what you do. All the better. Means you're out of my fucking hair,' Toby says.

'There's nothing you can do. I'm going.'

'So fucking go already!'

The kid stands there trembling, his eyes wild, and then, with a little bounce on the balls of his feet, he turns and bolts away down the alley.

Toby shouts after him. 'Oh, and Eddie! The guns aren't real, remember? Fucking moron.'

It occurs to me that he's terribly young to be alone and disconnect in this neighbourhood at night. But then it occurs to me, so are we.

'So what happens after that, Toby?'

He yanks me to my feet. 'We talk to my corporate friend. She might be able to sort us out. Or we go get ourselves a vaccine and we deal with whatever comes up along the way.'

Toby's apartment is surprisingly immaculate. I know that was an unfair assumption. But when I comment on it, feeling awkward and sweaty after the walk, he laughs and drops a crumpled piece of paper onto the floor. Instantly, a VIM-bot shoots out from under the couch, scoops it up, and then darts for cover.

'My secret sharer,' he says, collapsing onto the couch and sliding off his boots with his heels. After the tense silence of the long walk for endless kays, surely more than six, to get here, and the mission at the entrance to convince the doorwatcher to let us in without the benefit of Toby's SIM, it's a relief to be inside, to be safe. Although safety is relative.

'Is that a reference to something? Am I supposed to get that?'

'Oh god, how pretentious. Sorry. It's Conrad. I'm still registered for a literature degree. At least as far as my folks are concerned. Don't ask me to recommend him, though. The book was boring as fuck, but all his stuff is. Total wank.'

'I didn't take you for the literati type.'

'Well, between that and bioscience...' he shrugs.

'Or the studying type.'

'There's no reason to be rude. My darling mother's probably stopped paying the tuition along with everything else. He shrugs, one-shouldered, 'Hey, what was I going to do with a Master's in lit, anyway? You want some sugar?'

'Got any Ghost?'

'You really don't let up on that shit. Have some sugar, it'll chill you out.'

'No, I really don't—'

'Whatever you want to do, sweetness. Doesn't affect me in the slightest.'

He stands up and disappears barefoot into the kitchen. A cupboard door bangs harder than necessary. I sit down on a folder chair at the dining-desk, so that he can't sit next to me.

'Maybe it's not a good idea to take drugs on top of whatever we've been infected with.' The desk is stacked with neat piles of epaper, the edges perfectly aligned.

'Best time,' he shouts back. Another bang disproportionate to whatever the hell he's doing.

I start flipping through the pages, careful not to mar that perfectly aligned edge, even though I know he's not the one who stacked it so anally in the first place. It looks like legal documents, contracts. A broadcast agreement. When I see my name near the head of a page, I drop it, burnt.

He stalks back in, carrying a silver cocktail shaker.

'Hey, cut it out. Do I come to your domestic and go through your shit?' He sits down in another folder chair, pulling it up so he's right next to me, and unscrews the shaker, knocking a fair quantity of sticky white powder onto the surface of the desk.

'You didn't have to be so mean.'

'In the streamcast? I wasn't mean. To Khanyi, maybe, not you.'

I shove the chair back, stand up, and prowl to the other side of the room, checking his bookshelf while he sifts the powder for clumps.

'Shouldn't we contact your friend?'

'When I've had a joint, okay? Besides. You may not have noticed, with all that beauty sleep you got in, but it's really late.'

'I said thanks.'

'Don't need your appreciation, baby girl.' He sweeps the powder into a tidy line with a pencil and wraps it up with two short twists of Rizla.

'Well, I appreciate it anyway.'

'Noted duly.' He seals the joint with the edge of his thumb.

'Look, should I just go? If I'm an inconvenience to you? I was so stupid to come here. Shit.' I'm ready to leave, walk another eight kays across town in this oversize shirt and my ruined dress and my broken heel, but I can't find my damn bag.

'Would you just sit down?'

And then I remember that it's still at the station. With my camera. Jesus. I wonder if it's still there, if anyone's taken it, if the pumped-up defuser has fritzed the Zion. But then I start thinking about what's on the memchip, what I've lost, what I can try and duplicate.

'Hey.' Toby takes my shoulders and presses me down into the couch. 'Sit down and have some sugar with me. All right? And then we can do whatever the fuck you want. Get hold of

Lerato or your dad or the cops or your boyfriend or whoever. Okay?'

'I've left my camera behind.'

'Least of our worries, sweet K. We could be dead in forty-eight.'

'And he's not my boyfriend. We broke up. Although it's not like we were really together before, I mean–' I'm rambling. 'He was a prick.'

'How are you feeling?'

'Not thinking about it.'

'I have a headache.'

'Me too. Sugar will chase it. Here.'

He hands me the joint and squeezes in next to me.

'I'm not supposed to. The nano. It was in the contract.' On page sixteen, a list of non-standard chems and supplements that are absolutely prohibited, accompanied by dire warnings, long-term damage potential, unpredictable results, permanent health risk, possible heart failure.

'Don't fret it. They're just covering their asses. They know all about you creative types. They would have tested it. They just don't want some supersmack freak ODing and making bad publicity noises. What did you think they were going to say, "mix it up"?'

'I haven't done–'

'I know. It's cool. Hold it like this.'

He lights it for me, putting his arm around me to cup the flame. I take a deep breath, and instantly the room spins and the air takes on a puffy consistency, like we're the centre of a candyfloss vortex.

Toby takes the joint from my mouth, his fingers brushing against my swollen lip, so that I flinch away. But I've already chosen what comes next, even before the air goes shimmery. Even though I know it's only because we're both afraid.

Toby

Sweet K is unexpectedly bold. She pulls into me even before I'm anticipating reaching for her. It's a little annoying, kids, cos where's the fun in that? I think about blocking her, but reconsider and kiss her back, hard, devouring, so that she winces from the wound on her mouth. I don't care.

By the time we make it to the bedroom, her legs are pretzelled round my waist and she's whimpering for the want of it. The third time, I don't even get to the condoms. 'It's coke,' she whispers, looking at me with those pale, pale green eyes. 'The nano'll kill anything you got.'

'Did it say so in the contract?' She laughs and bites my neck and we fuck until I'm raw and aching and glazed from the exertion. Or that could be the virus kicking in. I'm woken by K's fingers gripping my shoulder in a vice.

'They found us,' she hisses.

'Mmmggh.' I try to shrug her free and roll over, cos I'm still mostly unconscious, but she won't let go 'The chem spray. They tracked us.' She's breathing in small rabbity panicky breaths.

'Go back to sleep. You're just paranoid.'

'They're right outside. Toby!'

'It's the sugar. You're not used to it.'

Only then there's a noise, a scratch at the door.

She makes a small choked-off sound.

'It's just the VIM, baby.' I pry her fingers loose from my shoulder. 'You need to drink something.' I feel around for the glass of water I keep by the bed, but it's not there, cos my little cleaning friend is too particular in its habits. Grudgingly, I peel back the covers, which are sticky with an alchemy of juices. How did I end up in the wet spot?

As soon as I stand up, though, inky spots swarm in my head and a jazz beat of pain kicks off behind my eye sockets. I stagger, mostly blind, in the general direction of the kitchen. Credit to the girl, she comes after me, naked and armed with a book off my bedside – the collected works of Curtis Malebi, whose prose is dense enough to kill anyone, or at least cause a concussion, if your aim was good. I haven't opened it in months, but the high-gloss cover makes for a perfect rolling surface.

While I'm focused on getting to the kitchen and a glass of water, she sneaks towards the front door, trading the book for a steel vase, which holds the calcified remains of a chrono-orchid. Not as unkillable as the product blurb would have you believe.

'Hey. Do you want to get your own water? Cos I was quite happy in bed.'

She shoots me a look so tortured, I almost laugh.

'Baby. It's okay. It's just the drugs. There's nothing out there.'

She's so sweetly lost, I can't resist her. I go over and wrap my arms around her, and she's shaking, wired on the adrenalin. But also very soft and curvy, which stirs something up all over again. Feebly, admittedly, but it does stir.

'I can tell, Toby. I can feel it,' she whispers.

'Shhh. It's okay.' I keep my voice as low as hers. 'Come back to bed.'

I lure her back into the warmth, but she's not up for anything else. And the truth is, kids, sorry to say, neither am I.

Tendeka

It's over.

Ashraf is gone.

Taken S'bu and Ibrahim with him, along with any of the other kids he found en route. Gone belly-up, slinking off to the nearest vaccine centre, and then to find Emmie, make sure she's okay. Always the responsible one. Too impatient to wait it out, to call their bluff. He couldn't see this is exactly what we've been working towards. Pushing the corporates and the cops so far over the line there's no coming back for them.

skyward* says not to stress. There was a box waiting for me, on our bed, when I got eventually got home last night. Inside was a new Nokia. And a note. 'Thought you might need this.' As soon as I turned it on, the messages started coming through. He says it's going to be beautiful, not to chicken out at such a crucial juncture. They'll never know what hit them.

skyward* says we have to do it now, immediately. Trigger the lightbombs, hit as many of the vaccine centres as we can. We can't let them submit. It's a trick. There's worse waiting for Ashraf and them than being arrested or disconnected. skyward* says they plan to ship them out to the Rural, put them into camps, detain and charge them as terrorists, even the kids. They might not come back. He says he never thought they would go this far, but isn't this the ultimate proof of what they're capable of, how fucked up the status quo really is?

But I'm confused. I thought it was a bluff. Not real. Not cause for concern, not reason enough for Ashraf to leave.

skyward* reassures me: yes, of course, but if they're so casual about inducing widespread panic, lying to us like this, then what else have they been lying about? We have to stop it. We have to expose the underlying tumour in our society. This is not the time to have doubts.

And then Zuko comes back, staggering in, half-fucked on glue, which would be a red card, but under the circumstances, I'll let it slide. Because he's a true believer. And there's work to do today, as skyward* keeps reminding me, the msgs coming in incessantly, like jabs with a sharp stick.

I don't know how he knew where to find me.

Lerato

An incessant bleeping with an undertone of tango drags me rudely from the depths of REM-sleep. I've been dreaming about cars loaded down on their axles with trickle castles, like the kind you make dribbling mud between your fingers at the beach, like Toby and I did a couple of years ago. Sturdier than dry sand, but still only sand, and when it dries out it all crumbles, like the castles on the cars, toppling around me.

At first I think Jane's accidentally set off the burglar alarm again and I'm going to have to fend off the security Aitos bounding in to the rescue, but then I realise home™ is playing Buster Mzeke's *Asphalt Sonata*, the song I assigned to work-related calls. I turn it off, roll over and go back to sleep for another twenty minutes. It is fucking Sunday.

When I get up, the apartment is oddly quiet. Jane is usually up by now, curled up on the lounger on the balcony with the Sunday papers and a chocolate hazelnut croissant fresh from the Communique bakery.

'Jane? You want some ultra?' I call, the volume of my own voice making me wince. On the Richter scale of hangovers, this one could have been responsible for wiping out the dinosaurs. I check her room. No sign of her. Maybe she got laid after her big meeting. What are the chances?

She left the TV on, the menu open to her catalogue of soaps, which means she was up all night watching them instead of getting laid. We're really gonna have to talk. I flick across to the cartoons while I wait for the coffee to brew.

But I'm feeling restless. I get up from the couch, go back to my room and throw open the cupboards. Soon I'm going to have to think about packing in anticipation of my brand-new life. I'll have to shed a lot of it; even Jane would notice if I started emptying my room. I'll take the special items: my music drive, of course, the Joey HiFi print I bought myself to celebrate my first-ever defection at the tender age of fifteen, the Miyazaki necklace a boyfriend bought back from Japan. Stash it all at Toby's apartment for the duration. The furniture I've accumulated over the last couple of years, the Twenties medicine cabinet, the Nash couch, my books and most of my wardrobe are going to have to fly. It's all about knowing when to let go. Because once it's official, I won't be allowed back on the property.

I'm not going to miss this place at all.

It's only after I've had my coffee and the greasiest protein combo the kitchen can deliver that I get round to checking my message. It's from Rathebe. Her hyperbole suggests some national crisis, without getting into any of the details. What I think is that it better be a new outbreak of the superdemic to force me into the office on the weekend. If it's some baby stroller issue, I'm going to flip.

Kendra

When the swivel grinds through its rotate to open onto the landing, there is an audio notice stuck to the outside of the door that activates as soon as it senses us.

'For your convenience, please find enclosed a digi map to your nearest immunity centre. This is a South African Police Services public service announcement.'

'Cunts. Jesus. Mother*fuck*.' Toby wipes his nose with his sleeve, rips off the GPS chip and scrunches it under his heel, only it doesn't scrunch. 'Fuck!' He picks it up and hurls it across the corridor, but it's so light it drifts to the left and ricochets off the wall with a dull plastic ting. He kicks the wall, then punches it for good measure.

He comes away shaking out his hand and still swearing. He looks shocking. His eyes are pouchy and bloodshot, and he's pale under his scrag of beard. I still haven't been able to face myself in the mirror. I'm grateful that I don't feel like he looks. He's already taken three painkillers this morning.

He cringes as we step outside the building, and tries to turn back for his sunglasses.

'There isn't time, Toby.'

'Are you chaffing me? We still got thirty-two, thirty-three hours at least. And if we don't make it, they can always come get us. They'll have a roving unit. Door-to-door delivery. Now that's servicing the community.' But he tags along anyway.

We still don't have a phone between us. When we tried to log in this morning, his connection was down. 'The cabling in this fucking building,' he muttered.

'Does it go down a lot?'

'Murphy's law, innit mate?' he says, putting on a jokey Brit accent. 'It's exactly the kind of crap that would go down today.' But I can tell he's unsettled.

Before we found the warning on the door, the plan was to find a public terminal, to get hold of his corporate friend, but now I don't know. We might just be bringing the shit to her.

'She can handle it,' Toby says. 'She's a big girl.' He spits a glob of phlegm onto the street in front of Truworths. A young house spouse coming out pulls her black leather handbag against her and steps pointedly around us.

'Yeah, fuck you too,' snarls Toby and starts coughing so badly, he has to lean against the window. Inside, there is a flurry of motion, and I grab his arm and pull him away before the security guard lumbers out to chase us away.

Glancing back over my shoulder, I catch a glimpse of my reflection in the glass of the window among the moto-mannequins in gleaming fabrics. My face is totally healed.

Tendeka

The thing is, transparency only works as a policy if you can still find a way to make the stuff you don't want people to see invisible – especially when it's out in the open. We're here to make sure there's no possibility of hiding what has happened.

Who would have thought that so many were ready to give it up, turn turtle before it even kicks in, before they even know it's going to kick in at all? Traitors to the cause.

And cowards, adds skywards* in yet another msg.

The emergency room at Chris Barnard Memorial is street level, a glass box beside the ambulance parking with a ramp that leads up and away to the parkade. There is already a queue of people outside, rumpled like they've been up all night, so everyone looks homeless. They're pale and shocked and some of the more

pathetic ones have convinced themselves
they're sick for real, doubled over and coughing,
psyching themselves out, buying in, pushing to
get to the front. There's no sign of the media.

But there will be.

There's been nothing on any of the newscasts, not even a suggestion on the alt channels,
which implies that the clampdown on info is already in force. There are probably S&D teams
working round the clock, scanning every blog,
censoring every streamcast. Suppress and destroy.

'Here?' Zuko asks. We're standing across the
road, at the edge of the parking lot for the chichi
restaurants in Heritage Square. He tosses a soccer ball deftly from foot to foot, ignoring the
carguard, who is beckoning that he must skop
the ball over here, have a little game, man. But
this is not the time for play.

We'll already have been picked up by the security cams outside the hospital, but I don't
think it's worth pointing this out to Zuko, who
is tensely eager underneath his cool, still fucked
on glue, and wound up from watching the
Grand Parade light up in pyrotechnics.

'Yeah. It's the most accessible.' We've already
checked out two other temporary vaccine loca-
tions, one in the CBD police centre, the other
set up at the main entrance to Adderley Station,

but there were dogs lurking at both of those, and they started barking when we came too close, picking up some residue of the chem scent.

No one will get seriously hurt. The explosive is low-capacity RDX. Limited 'blast phenomena' according to the instructions from Amsterdam. The nearest people will suffer flash burns, maybe. But they're right next to the ER. They'll be able to get medical treatment on the spot. Sometimes small sacrifices are necessary. It's collateral damage. And there is zero chance Ashraf will be here. He'll have gone to a more convenient clinic, closer to Khayelitsha. Definitely.

Zuko shrugs, always the team player, and strolls across the road, dribbling expertly, dodging a car, while still keeping the ball going, casually following it towards the ER doors, like goal posts. Just a kid messing around. The security guard is too preoccupied with managing the line to hassle him.

Zuko bounces the ball off his knees a couple of times, fearlessly, as if it were not packed to capacity with RDX, then lets it drop. Before it has a chance to touch the ground, with a swift and perfect sideswipe, he lobs it at the automatic doors.

The motion sensors pick up the ball and slide open to swallow it up.

I click the detonator in my pocket, subtly as possible, already walking away.

The bomb rips through the building with a shudder of glass and concrete.

I don't look back for Zuko.

Lerato

There is a weird vibe on the underway on the way in to the office, an undercurrent frisson even though there's almost no one around, just a few people coming home from partying, a couple of churchgoers. But the controlled clampdown means I'm oblivious to the reality, until I actually reach the office and find out what has gone off overnight.

Communique's offices are a study in controlled frenzy. The ultra-caffeine baristas are doing overtime. I don't even make it as far as the lifts before I am whipped away to join Rathebe's emergency task team, which has commandeered the boardroom and an additional coffee machine. There are twenty-three people crammed in with their laptops, all monitoring the datalines, killing the most damaging of commentary before it gets out, because anything is allowable when it comes to national

303

security, and the government is a big Communique contract. To my disgust, Mpho is already in the thick of it.

I pull up a chair next to him. I'm dying to slide into my backdoor to get the full story, but it's insanely risky with the kind of scrutiny going on right now.

When the first bomb reports start coming in, I don't have a choice. The techniques are so inventive, they leave me breathless and everyone else clutching for information and something to do with it, before it gets out on the newslines – and worse, the streamcasts. There's no way to contain this one, only spin it. We're shutting down large parts of the network with service errors to try and keep it contained. Later, we'll blame this on an underground cable being damaged by the bombs. Of course, I recognise the signature. Soccer balls and graffiti aren't exactly Terrorism 101.

I have to be circumspect.

Despite all the caffeine being consumed in the clean-up marathon inside, it's luck or fate that I'm the only one in the stairwell bathroom. The red mosaic tiles seem menacingly shiny, but I know I'm just tired and hung over and not thinking clearly. I take the third cubicle, in case the one on the end is too conspicuous and click my back-up SIM into my phone, which is not, surprise, surprise, coded to my identity.

Communique is willing to indulge us our whims and little vices, just about anything to appease the talent, lest we defect. But a fake SIM ID is serious contraband. Two years' jail-time if I'm bust with it. I'm mad to use it here.

The phone powers up on silent, logging on to the maintenance subnet which controls the building's cleaning bots. A neat little loophole I discovered by accident rewiring the VIMbot Toby stole from my apartment block. It doesn't work unless you can connect to a booster site to get the signal out of the building, but I already have that set up in every Communique bill-board Tendeka and friends have hit with their smear boxes.

It takes me a minute to track the reroute msg Tendeka sent out via a mirror in Singapore, trac-ing the trajectory all the way back to the Cheaptime Trip Bar in Little Angola, terminal fourteen, sent at 23h18. It helps that I know his hangouts, that I know who he was sending to, and can backwards engineer it. At least he was using a fake SIM. User ID chipped as Rutger Hoffman, German nursing student, twenty-four, resident in UCT's Slovo Res.

Still, can't be too many people hanging around at that time in Cheaptime Trip, and the cams would have picked him up in the vicinity.

Sloppy work: the guy shouldn't risk tech on his own. But it's not his solo ops that worry me.

It takes another two minutes to crack Cheaptime's time-clock database and delete all the records. I take their server down too, just for good measure. I just hope they're sufficiently small-time that they don't have back-ups, or at least that it will take them several hours to restore. It's a hack job, but there's not enough time to finesse it, with twenty-three other people in the room across the hallway, all on a similar tack, trying to dig out the terrorists, and it's only a matter of time. Although hey, if anyone does stumble across this, hopefully they'll just assume it's Tendeka and his pals trying to cover their tracks, that they're clumsy amateurs.

I consider sending Tendeka a warning via his loxion soccer club's fan board, something obtuse enough to be innocent, but I figure he's probably not smart enough to pick it up. I can't risk anything that will link me to him.

It's absurd how sloppy he's been, the sticky fingerprints he's left over everything. He accessed his banking at the Cheaptime Trip, wired cash from one account to another, so I follow the trail, closing down the links, deleting the cache, covering his tracks, because it's all here, an underway map of connections.

The Cheaptime leads to a soccer game, by way of his checking on the match scores, which leads to his underprivileged kids' soccer club in Khayelitsha, which leads, via one of the kids, Zuko Sephuma, to the sponsored graffiti project with street kids on Grand Parade, where a wall just happens to have exploded, causing minimal damage but a lot of fright. Enough to bury Tendeka, even if he's managed to miraculously avoid the cams.

Tracking that kid, Sephuma, who is the common denominator, leads to a streamcast on future*renovate, some anti-corporate community in Amsterdam, and the impenetrable moniker '10'. Christ, Tendeka.

Lots of postings from 10, IP address links back to the Cheaptime, couple of phone access logins, and back to the soccer club. Rants on the board, video clips of some of the 'hits' posted as instructional guides. I didn't realise he was filming any of it. I feel ill. And I'm running out of time, before someone else comes into the bathroom or wonders where I am.

It takes me less than a minute to crack his future*renovate email account. Penile enhancement ads. Newsletters from groups with dubious titles like WorldChanger or Guerrilla Corporatista, mostly unopened. Messages from fanboys and girls.

> \>> That was the sickest video yet, man!
> How did you pull that shit off? Props.

Zuko cropping up once again, quite the disciple. But the account is suspiciously empty, like he's been systematically trashing everything, taking some limited precautions here at least. I could get into the cache on the servers, but that would take hours, which I don't have. And I have to know if there's anything incriminating. Sent items and trash are cleaned out, but the schmuck didn't clear his IM conversations.

The bulk of the chats are with somebody called skyward*. What's with all the damn asterisks? Mostly bullshit, heavy talk about co-opting the revolution and other doggerel, but then I come across one which mentions me by name.

> skyward*>>how goes your tec contact? like
> to put her in touch with some of our other
> operations. she does good work.
> 10>>Lerato? Yeah, I only really know her
> through Toby, and he's too much of a prick
> to work with.
> skyward*>>pity.

I look up the IP address for skyward*'s email address, because now I'm going to have to hack into *his* email account and clean up there too. I feel sick at the thought of how much has to be done, how much time it's all going to take, the hundreds and hundreds of interconnections. I cannot believe he mentioned me by name.

The IP address is not in the Netherlands at all. And at first I think I've made a stupid mistake, an entry-level blunder. It can't possibly be. And then I catch on.

I eject the secondary SIM from my phone. My first instinct is to flush the incriminating evidence, but if I can get out of here, I'll need it. What I really need is my passport and the suitcase I haven't packed yet. There is a noise outside. I push the SIM as deep as it will go into my vagina.

I flush the toilet and emerge to find Jane leaning against the row of curved basins. The relief is mixed with irritation at her timing. I can't begin to imagine what she's come all the way up here for. Her office is in accounts, five floors down.

'Hey Lerato. I've been looking for you everywhere. Got a minute?'

'Jesus, Jane. Can't it wait till I get home? I'm a little tied up right now.'

'There's someone who wants to see you.'

'What? No. Rathebe will flip. I haven't even had a chance to process–'

She flashes a card at me, a visual ID. And at first it doesn't register. How can you live with someone for eight months and not know them at all?

I should have seen it coming. I should have guarded myself at home as carefully as I did at work.

She guides me to the lift. As I pass the boardroom, I will Mpho to look up, to help me. But he's panic stations like everyone else, head down, and what could he do anyway? Rathebe glances up, sees I'm with Jane, and gives a little nod of acquiescence that lets me know I'm really, really fucked, even before the lift doors open to reveal a security guy with two (!) Aitos flanking him, putting paid to the half-baked plan I suddenly realise I was entertaining, to take her down in the lift, still get away somehow. I take a step back, but Jane grabs my arm.

'It's okay, we can fit.' The guy whistles and the dogs press in tight against him, making space, but it's still a squeeze. I can feel the hot pressure of their breath on the back of my legs. Jane slides a card key into the control panel. I feel sick with stupidity.

I fucked a boy for a couple of months whose motto was 'It could always be worse'. It was just stupid. Of course it could always be worse. If you were buried up to your head in the desert waiting for the vultures to pluck out your eyes, someone could piss on you, fire ants could make a nest in your mouth, burrowing rodents could start eating your feet.

But this is bad. This is as bad as it could possibly be.

Because the IP address for skyward* comes back to Communique's corporate pipeline. To this building.

And the ID Jane flashed me in the bathroom had the logo for spyware controller. Internal Affairs.

Toby

Of course I've noticed that her face is healed. Think I'm a moron? When she stops to admire her reflection, I hustle her on. 'C'mon. Keep moving. You want to bring attention down on us?'

'But—'

'Yeah, yeah, I know. Lucky for you. Wish I had some nano to stitch me up from the inside.' The headache is eating through the painkillers, chowing down on the edges, and I'm itchy as fuck and my nose won't stop running, so I have to wipe it with the back of my hand and smear the snot off on my jeans.

'Charming,' she says, real helpful, and refuses to take my hand again. I hadn't even realised we were holding hands. I'm fucking starving, maybe even dying, and she's concerned about playing Ms. Manners. Which sparks me off on my moth-erbitch, and how the least she could do is download some cash so we can buy breakfast and a Ghost for K, who is jonesing bad, and maybe a pair of cheapnasty sunglasses so I can deal with the glare. I mean, what are parents for?

But the catch is that we're still phoneless. It took fifteen minutes just to get out of my apartment block, waiting for someone else's SIM to trigger the door so we could slip out. Pretend making-out in the hall, so we had an excuse to be hanging about.

I accost a pedestrian on the sidewalk, a man in a red leather jacket unlocking his car, one of the only people around.

'Hey, excuse me, sir? My phone is down and I was wondering–'

'No. I'm sorry,' he says, super-brusque in the brush-off, already getting into the car, adding, 'God bless you,' through the window as he zips it up, like I was some filthy riff. Like a riff could afford to be traipsing round town in a BabyStrange coat, even if it is fritzing, blurting random images from its memory. It did not take kindly to that power-up at the station. Shit. At this rate we're going to be walking to Lerato's.

It's the same story at the underway. The automatic doors won't fucking open to let us get into the station, let alone onto the trains. I don't see how they're expecting us to report to our nearest handy vaccine centre if we can't fucking get there. And no one will let me cadge a call.

K keeps touching her mouth, distracted, like she's making sure it really is all there.

'Do you think you could stop playing with your face and give me a hand here?'

'What do you want me to do?' she says, as if it's my fault that we're stranded, isolated. Disconnected.

'You're a girl. You're cute. Get someone to let you use their phone.'

'What do you want me to tell them?'

'That you dropped it in the toilet. That you were mugged. I don't care. Anything. Wait, here's the number you wanna connect,' and as I'm writing it down for her, I realise I don't know the fucking number. It's on autodial, pre-prog nine, starts 083-253 something something something. I don't know Lerato's digits either, or even that skank Unathi's. Which doesn't leave us much in the way of options. My stomach is knotting audibly with hunger.

Someone tugs on my sleeve. 'Buy me a bunny chow?' It's a street kid, wearing filthy men's shoes that swallow his feet, tufts of newspaper sticking out in ruffles, clutching a brown paper bag like his life depends on it, and faintly reeling already at this time of the a.m.

'Aw, c'mon don't touch the fashion. Not now, okay? Just piss off.'

The kid is nonplussed. He plucks at my coat again, skittering out of reach when I move to grab him, laughing. 'You should check, my larnie. Your fashion is fried.'

'Do I know you? Fuck off!'

'Toby.' Kendra puts her hand on my arm, and I'm so fucking sick of people touching me.

'What?'

'Maybe he has a phone.'

But the best the mangy street kid has to offer is a browning banana, which he proffers like a serious act of benevolence. Kendra takes it in both hands, like you're supposed to do with Japanese business cards. 'Thanks,' she says, as genuinely grateful as if it was the same fucking species of usefulness as a phone. So much for the black-market, the underground economy.

I grab it out of her hand and hold it up to my ear, feeling how it's already turned soft and squidgy inside its skin. 'Hello? Hello? Mom? Yeah, send the fucking cavalry already. What's that, you say? I'm sorry, you're breaking up.' This cracks the kid up, especially when I crush the banana in my fist so that the skin splits and the insides squelch out. 'You could do with an upgrade,' I say, examining the sludge in my hand. 'This one's fritzed.' I hand it back to him, but he declines, shaking with laughter. I shrug and chuck it into the alley, wiping my hand on my jeans, mixing the gunge with the dried snot. And it occurs to me, that's what my insides will be doing within the next forty-eight, liquefying inside this bag of skin. The novelty of being on the run is wearing off quick.

'We could have eaten that,' says Kendra-sweet, as I pull her away from the kid and down the street.

'Least of our problems.'

'Toby. I'm hungry. If I don't get something to eat–'

'Then what, buttercup? You might get hunger pangs in your tummy?'

'I'm hypoglycaemic, you asshole.'

'Oooh, so you're gonna faint on me?' She punches me in the chest. It's not a playful punch.

'Don't be an asshole.'

'Cos if you did, I don't know if I'd have the strength to pick you up and carry you. I mean, maybe you want to go back for that banana. You could scrape the leftovers off the pavement.'

She is near tears. I check off all the signs: her complexion gone blotchy, the liquid shine in her eyes. I hock another thick loogey of phlegm onto the pavement.

'Tell you what, baby girl, I got it all worked out. But I'm going to need you to take one for the team.'

'Toby, stop it. This is serious.'

'And I'm deadly serious.'

'You shouldn't spit. You don't know that it's not contagious.'

'You think I give a shit about these people?' I tuck her under my arm, crushing her up against me, aggressive, so I can feel the expansion of her ribcage as she grunts in surprise. I hope it leaves a big fucking bruise, but what would be the use, her nano would just clean it up, the same way it's sopped up the virus, like that bacteria that eats oil spills.

'I hope all these fuckers get it. They deserve it. And you know, I don't know why the fuck you give a shit either.' She squirms away, furious.

'It's not my fault.'

'Hey. Hey, I'm not holding it against you, sweetness.' I kiss her nose. 'Chin up, okay? We'll get you something to eat just as soon as. But first we need to get connected. We need help. You agree.'

'Yes,' she says, her face stormy-petulant.

'So we're gonna walk into that internet caff over there, and I'm gonna have a little chat with the guy behind the counter, and then you're going to offer to suck him off in exchange for some time online.'

'Jesus, Toby.'

'Or maybe he'll settle for a handjob.'

Her cheeks are flushed with outrage or humiliation. It's a good look for her.

'Although, you know, your technique could use some work. Speaking from personal experience.'

But I've gone too far. Something changes the channel on her expression. I wish my BabyStrange was still functional, cos it would have been great to capture the transition, kids: the twitch of muscles, that morphing of her expression from shock-wounded to contempt.

'Fuck you, Toby.'

'Ooh ouch. Like no one's ever said that to me before.' I stagger back a step, clutching at my chest, but she is already walking away, too fast, her shoulders as tight as if she'd been strapped to a coat hanger. Which makes me think of how those skinny blades jutted as she arched her back against me. 'And besides, you already did, sweetheart!' I shout after her, so that several of the pedestrians cock their heads in our direction. 'Remember?!' She doesn't turn around.

The shouting rasps in my throat and segues seamlessly into a racking cough as my body works overtime to eject what amounts to a thumbnail of sputum that blends into the street along with the pigeon shit and gunk. Hardly seems worth the effort.

Inside the caff, its windows dimmed to cut the glare on the screens, I dump the BabyStrange on the counter, which is still damp with the residue of cleaning wipes. Under normal circumstances, this would make me cringe in anticipation of the cost of dry-cleaning, which doesn't come cheap on wired fabrics. But I would hardly describe today as normal. 'Hey man, I'm going to cut to the chase. How many minutes can I get for this?'

The guy behind the counter is trying for too trendy for his age, with sideburns razored in sharp isosceles, a sideshow to distract from the thinning on top. Seems the blowout with K was pointless. Judging by the ripped pecs beneath the black vest, this one is more into boys than girls.

'This isn't a pawn shop, china. And even if it was,' he rubs a pinch of the BabyStrange between his fingers, the picture distorting, 'this thing is not well.'

'Yeah, well, neither am I.' And I know I check it too. I've got the shivers and the damp sweats and I can't stop scratching, like a junkie with no fix in sight.

'Man,' he sighs, with resignation, 'don't make me call in a defuse at this time of the morning.'

'Go right ahead. I don't have a fucking phone, my friend.'

He looks sceptical. 'Well, that's even more re-assuring. Do you know what kind of shitsville liability you are to me in here?'

'Come on. Give me a break. The quicker you let me use a machine, the quicker I'm gone. As opposed to standing in here, breathing my disease all over your establishment.'

He is unmoved, starts reaching for the phone.

'It's designer. It's worth thirty-k at least new, fifteen secondhand. Cost you maybe two to get it rewired. Five minutes, man. Doesn't sound like a raw deal to me.'

'How do I know it's not stolen?' He shakes it out, cursory, looking for bloodstains.

'Aw c'mon, like you care? And besides, I got the sneaks to match. You get a lot of colour co-ordinated scumbags in here hawking previously owned?'

'Okay, okay. Five minutes.'

'Thirty.'

'You just said–'

'Yeah, but I got stuff to do. Takes longer than five. And you only get the coat after.' Send Lerato a chirpy, check the newscasts to see what's already out there, upload my own footage off the BabyStrange while I've still got it.

'Whatever. Just do me a favour and take one of the consoles at the back.'

'So I don't freak out the paying customers?'

'Sharp as your sense of style,' he quips, pinching the sleeve of my coat with a proprietary gesture. I feel a twinge of loss. Or another coughing fit about to hit.

Kendra

Is it perverse to feel liberated? Not just ditching that asshole, just another Jonathan, but the grounding of being disconnect that separates me from the swirl of the city around me. The dissociation is real for once, not artificially imposed and filtered through my camera. I'm a stranger among the commuters and people opening up the storefronts. It's beautiful. And totally impractical, the squeeze in my stomach reminds me.

I realise I'm not so far from District Six, but without my SIM ID, the front door to Mr. Muller's subterr doesn't recognise me. It takes a long time for him to answer the intercom.

'Who's that?'

'It's me, Mr. Muller. Kendra.'

'Kendra! Why don't you just come down, my girl?'

'It's my phone, Mr. Muller. It's...' My voice

cracks. There is a brittle pause. I haven't seen him since the exhibition. I should have called, just to see if he was okay, but I've been preoccupied.

'Come down. I'll put on the ultra.'

By the time I get down, it's just starting to infuse. And he has food. A slightly stale bagel with peanut butter. But no Ghost. I wonder if I can convince him to get me one from the building's café, when he points to the news footage, which he has maximised so that it's playing all over the walls, tuned to different channels.

'Did you see this? The bombing?'

I haven't.

The footage focuses on the wall of the old city library, where a mural of a soccer ball and two hands forming a heart shape with the fingers has been painted. The words UBUNTU appear above it, spangled with glitter – no, lightbulbs, LEDs forming lightshow patterns. The soccer ball becomes a globe, a skull, a heart. And then the bulbs suddenly all pop, not exactly co-ordinated, with a noise like firecrackers, spraying twinkles of glass, so that people below cringe and duck.

A few of them sort of run away, hands up above their heads before they catch themselves and look back. The bulbs crackle and snap for another few seconds and then a thin drift of chemical-coloured smoke peels off, leaving the wall cratered and pitted.

'If they had an agenda, I might be able to understand, but this nihilism… Six dead, nineteen wounded. What are they protesting, anyway? Capitalism? As if there's an alternative. Where do they think their fancy technology comes from?' Mr. Muller is in full rant mode.

I'm not really paying attention. Most of the channels are playing footage from what looks like a warzone. Rubble, people screaming, broken glass and blood, a torn-apart car – like the truck in Mr. Muller's photograph.

'And don't get me started on the fantasy of economic equality,' he says. 'Society has always been structured by privilege. This is the best we've had it. You work hard, you put your back into it, you get to claim the rewards. Freedom is a state of mind, Kendra. How old are you? Too young to remember what it was like.'

The footage plays back in slow-mo. A line of people, with the desperate look of refugees or Rural, wait outside a glass box marked Casualty. There is a twist of tar leading up into the parkade, like a loll of grey tongue in a butcher's window, an ambulance parked outside. A soccer ball floats surreally towards the building and, more surreal, the doors slide open to let it in. A woman smiles, delighted and points. And then the building turns itself inside out. I sit down heavily on the couch. It's too much.

'Compared to living in fear, terrorised by criminals, the hijackings and shootings and the tik junkies ready to kill you, shoot you, stab you, for a watch or a camera, I'll take those modified dogs and the whaddayacallit, the cellphone electrocutions, any day. But these people don't understand what they're trying to achieve.'

Every channel comes back to it, on constant repeat. Like the chorus of a terrible song.

'Anarchy? Undermining our way of life? And what's that going to prove? More to the point, what's it going to change? This is only going to lead to more severe controls. But we need them, Kendra, I'm telling you, humanity is innately damaged. It's a flaw in the design code. We're weak. We're fallible. We need to be told what to do, to be kept in line.'

He notes me shrinking deeper into the couch.

'Forgive me, I'm ranting. You know what happens when I get started. What's this about your phone?' The sudden generosity of all his attention makes me want to weep with gratitude, so I fumble over my words.

'It's dead. They blew out everyone's phones. I don't know what to do.'

His voice takes on a sharp note of query. 'When was this?'

'Last night. The station. There was a protest. I guess it dropped off the scanner in light of… this.' I wave my hand at the overwhelming visuals cramming into the lounge.

Mr. Muller's face solidifies around his jaw. 'You can't stay here. You have to get to a, whatsit, immune centre. You're sick.' The word strikes me like an accusation. It's not only the associations of the superdemic; it feels like a personal attack on my genetic potential, the dark rotting tumour waiting to flower in my gut, like my father.

'But I'm not. The nano…' but suddenly it feels like too much to explain. And can I really explain?

'Are you part of this? Are you associated with those terrorists? I know what art school is like. And my God, that thing at your exhibition. You are part of this. If you don't leave my house immediately, I will call the authorities. There's a number. On TV. I'll call them. I won't be an accessory, Kendra. I'm an old man.'

'Mr. Muller, please,' I laugh, despite myself, at the quaver in his voice, at the absurdity. 'Look, whatever they said on the news, it's not the full story. Did they say it was a complete over-reaction to a peaceful protest?'

'Those kids had weapons. They showed it. Hacking up the dogs. People were next.'

'You talk about controls, but this wasn't control. This was a…' I cast around for the right word, and as soon as it's out, I know it's a mistake, the end of our rational discussion: 'A holocaust.'

He takes out his phone and starts hitting the keypad, his hand shaking so hard I'm sure he's going to drop it. 'I'm calling them, Kendra. I'm calling.'

It's more pity than fear that incites me to leave.

Toby

I leave a voicemail for Lerato. And send a msg. And an email. But there's no response. Of all times. The manager guy comes over. 'Hey, man, listen, I changed my mind. I really need you to go now.'

'What the fuck? I've still got four minutes.'

'It's on the news, china. You should… wow. You need to get medical attention.'

This is not exactly a revelation, kids, although I have to tell you, I'm feeling a little more up about the whole thing, probably due to ditching that little princess Kendra. Course, I'm gonna have to find her again, cos this is exactly the kind of shit I should be getting on cam. Documenting how the nano cleaned her up like a Catholic in confession. I scratch my beard.

'Fine. But then I'm keeping the coat. And gimme that whisky.' I say, pointing to one of the bottles up behind the bar counter.

'What? Hey, come on, man. That's not cool.'

'Neither is Marburg. Wanna risk it that it's really not contagious?' I cough for dramatic effect. He doesn't need to know it's faked.

I'm prowling the street, swigging openly from the Fish Eagle, trying to figure which direction Kendra would have taken, when the same damn street kid from before sidles up to me.

'You Toby?' he says, uncertainly.

'Look, kid. Seriously. Now is not the fucking time. Piss off.'

'Jussus. No need to be so rude, my larnie. I got someone wants to see you.'

'Oh, look. I appreciate the sentiment. But I got my preferred dealers. And I really don't like buying my illicit streetside, especially here with all the cams. Tell your friend he may want to consider relocating to a less heavily watched area.'

'Toby. You're Toby. Come with me.' The runt is so insistent, I follow him down the side street into a parking lot, half underground, quiet on a Sunday, with a CCVTV system that's looking a little fritzy, judging by the frayed wires swinging from the cam by the entrance boom. We go deeper in, between the cars, to find Tendeka huddled in a convincing impression of a bergie, a hoodie pulled low over his face. He looks like shit. It's the texture of his skin, sort of murky beige like clay that might slough off his skull. The street kid is on the point of tears.

'Okay, I did it. Can I go now?'

Tendeka waves, tired, dismissive. 'Yes, Whitey. Thank you. If you see Zuko. Or Ashraf... No. Never mind.'

The kid waits, squirrelly on the balls of his feet in those oversize shoes, to see if there's gonna be more, and then scuttles away, too fast to be polite. The motivation right there, kids? I'd say that was fear.

'He's frightened. I've lost everyone, Toby. I don't know where they are. When I saw you, across the street...'

'Jesus, Tendeka. You are pretty fucked up.'

'Not looking so great yourself.'

'You could hit me. That always seems to make you feel better.'

'I would if it helped. But it doesn't work. You're still a fucking prick afterwards.'

He smiles. And I know what will make it even better. I hand over the bottle. We get shitfaced. Not a bad way of killing a coupla hours, all told. Only catch is that while the cheap scotch makes me bouncier, it's bringing Ten down bigtime.

He says it's the end of the world. We've got a difference of opinion here. 'Sure, we might feel like death set on defrost,' I tell him. 'But how else are they going to make it seem authentic?

It's a bluff and I'm calling it. I'm not going to roll over and hand myself in at one of their immunity centres. Immunity from the virus supposedly about to chow down on my spleen, but not from the nice officers waiting to arrest me for illegal activities.' And I know it's a hoax because it's letting up, although I'm still itching like crazy. The inside of my wrist is red from scratching.

Tendeka agrees that we shouldn't go in. But see, this is where we part ways, because he's swallowed the hoax wholesale. He tells me it's exactly what they planned, him and his chomma in Amsterdam. He tells me he's going to die. Because that's the only way to expose it, for the outside world to know it's real. He yaks on about some bomb thing, can't believe I haven't seen the footage, but when have I had a chance to kick back with TV? So he set off this bomb, cos he says if it's just him dying from this bug, they can cover it up. But the bombs will focus attention on this thing. It'll stop people getting the vaccine. They'll die. In the limelight.

He's fucked. It's hilarious. So when he asks me if I'll come with him and bring the BabyStrange, cos his camera-phone's fucked from the station fry-up, and he needs to get this down, who am I to say no, kids?

Kendra

It's not so hard. Without Toby looking sketchy and virtually dying at my side, it only takes four tries at sugar-coated grovelling to get someone to let me make a call.

'I dropped it down the stairs,' I tell the lady at the bookstore, who flutters in the stacks nearby to ensure that I don't make a duck with her phone. As if it would be any use to me without her unique bio-sig. I dial Damian's number from the flyer he gave me. I'll be damned before I phone Jonathan.

Vix answers. She seems less than stoked to hear that it's me. 'You didn't rock up, hey?'

'I know. I'm sorry. Please can I just speak to Damian? It's urgent.'

There's a scuffle and then Damian comes on, sounding sleepy. 'Hey, Ghost girl, you missed out.'

He hasn't heard about the bombs or the station 'incident', as they keep referring to it on the news. He hasn't even got up yet, and it's already afternoon.

It takes a lot of work to convince him to come pick me up and take me to Andile. And when his car pulls up outside the bookstore, a classic Ford Anglia done up with decals of skulls and bunnies, Vix is sitting in the passenger seat.

She turns round in the seat to look at me. 'You don't look sick.'

'Well, we don't know that until she's been checked, right?'

Damian puts a hand on her knee.

'And you're sure it's not contagious?'

'I don't know. I'm sorry. They said it wasn't. It would be crazy to unleash an infectious disease. They'd never recover from the bad press.'

'Sounds pretty crazy as is,' she says. 'You do seem to attract drama.'

'Victoria!' Damian shoots her a scandalised look.

'I'm just saying!'

Outside the world seems removed, glancing past the windows of the car, which are rain-pocked, like dusty fingerprints. The inner city is usually quiet on a Sunday, but today there are road blocks and reroutes, blue and red lights flashing around the diverts near the hospital. Everything is coated with a layer of grey dust. The emergency workers in their biosuits look like ashen alien yetis.

Initially, they won't let Damian's car into the Inatec car park. The security cop is steadfast that there's no chance, his Aito padding round the car, sniffing intently. His logic is sound; if we had a permit, the gate would have accessed us already.

Vix takes charge. 'Would you just call, what's his name?'

'Andile Cwane,' I contribute from the back.

The security guard takes a long time checking the register. 'Sorry, no one by that name works here.'

'No, sorry, of course not. I'm an idiot. Dr. Precious. Can you call Dr. Precious?'

'Precious de Kock?' There is a note of surprise in his voice, and Vix seizes on it.

'Yeah,' she pipes up, 'call Dr. De Kock. Tell her it's about the sponsor babies, and there's a huge issue that would upset the Prima-Sabine company greatly. She'd want to know about this. You'll probably get into trouble if you don't call.'

The security guard doesn't seem too sure, but he steps back into his booth and dials someone, maybe Dr. Precious, maybe higher-level security. His Aito loops around the car.

'Can you do up the window, please?' I ask.

'Why? I'm just going to have to unwind again when he comes back,' Damian complains, when the dog jumps up against my window in the backseat, its breath huffing against the glass, claws scratching against the bodywork.

'Shit!' Damian grabs for the handle and rolls it up as fast as physically possible.

I don't flinch. The dog is so close to me, through a millimetre of glass, I can see the black sheen of the gums around its teeth, the Braille of its tastebuds on its grey-pink tongue.

'Get down! Get down! Dammit!' The security cop bats at the dog, which whines in agitation. 'Okay. She's on her way. Forty minutes. You can go through and wait in the parking lot. The silver Chrysler Spitfire. That'll be her.' We sit in awkward silence, until Damian clicks the radio, loads a sample from Kill Kitten's new album.

'It's not the final mix,' he says, by way of apology. And I try to listen, I really do, but I'm distracted watching the main gate.

'Are you even into new spectro, Kendra?' asks Vix bitchily, but then a gunmetal shark of a car pulls into the parking lot and I don't have to answer.

Dr. Precious emerges from the Chrysler with Andile in tow. He chucks me on the shoulder, playfully. 'Woah, hectic mess you landed in, babes! Real history stuff. Don't worry, we'll sort

it out. You didn't get caught up in all that ugli-
ness, did you, Dame? No? No antibodies
required for you, then, china! Well, come on,
Kendra!' Andile ushers me giddily towards the
doors.

Damian and Vix are standing, hesitating at
the car.

'Should we, uh… Do you want us to come in
with you?' Damian asks.

'Ag, no! She'll be fine! Really. You'll be bored.
All the scans and samples. Nothing serious. Just
procedure. You know what it's like. No point
waiting around. We'll get her home.'

Damian looks concerned.

'It's cool, Damian,' I say. 'Seriously. Thanks
for getting me here. I don't know what I would
have done.'

'No. I think we should come with,' he says,
slowly.

Dr. Precious moves over to him, and says
something really quiet. Vix gives me a sharp,
quick glance, but the way Damian studiously
doesn't look at me is more alarming.

I smile uneasily. 'Is there something I should
know?'

'No, we're good, come along.' He hustles me
in through the doors. 'Precious, she's just living
up to her name. Doesn't like people hanging
around when she works, especially civilian

hangers-on like Dame's little girlfriend. Doesn't really have the clearance to be here. You know she applied for the sponsorship, right? Didn't make the cut.'

The sound of a car door snapping shut makes me look back.

'I think she's jealous of you,' Andile shakes his head ruefully as Dr. Precious walks in behind us. Beyond the glass doors, the Anglia reverses into an inexorable parabola and out of the Inatec parking lot.

Tendeka

'So what are you gonna do with all your worldly after you're gone? Donate it to the street kids? Auction it off? Martyr relics get top price on eBay.' Toby bounces beside me, facing backwards on the street, so that he nearly crashes into a flower-seller struggling with two plastic buckets bristling with bouquets.

'I'm dying,' I tell the flower-seller, who is cursing at Toby, by way of apology. She recoils behind her buckets and the flowers. I can't tell what they are. The colours blur when I try to focus. 'No sir, I don't got no flowers for that!'

'Too dramatic,' Toby muses. 'Cliché. Flowers. Bad. No. I thought you planned all this meticulously. You can't go whimsical all of a sudden. And, besides, you're frightening the lady.'

'She should be frightened. We all should be. Can your friend hook us up? Lerato?'

'To what?'

'Remote link-up. So we can transmit your coat's cameras to the billboards? The city is going to bear witness.'

He looks uncomfortable. 'Yeah, about that.'

'You can back out. I don't mind. Go running to an immunity centre, get your life-saving shot and your arrest warrant all in one, let them fuck you, let them fuck all of us. Just leave me with the coat.'

'Jesus, all right. Don't get so worked up.'

'I'm fine,' I say, ignoring the smear of bright red on the back of my hand when I wipe my mouth. 'You still don't believe it, do you? We're dying, Toby. Both of us.'

'See, here's the thing. I don't feel like I'm dying, as a matter of fact, I... Jesus motherfuck.' He catches me as I list forward, bracing me against his chest and his shoulder, laughing. I hadn't realised how skinny he is.

'This shit does not agree with you, Tendeka.'

'It's my fucking asthma. Accelerating the virus. Fuck, it's the steroids in my meds. I'm immuno-compromised.'

'Didn't Che Guevara have asthma?' chirps Toby. 'What is it with you revolutionaries and lung issues?'

'I can't be the only one. What about the kids who were there? Old people? This is happening

way too fucking fast. Bastards. Fucking bastards.
They didn't think it through.'

'Hate to blow your big momentous revela-
tory, but whatever it is, you're going to have to
get to a hospital.'

'No.'

'Okay, well, then we have to get away from
here. People are staring.'

'I want them to. They should see.'

'But you don't want the cops to come ruin all
your fun, right? You don't want to premature,
not on your martyrdom. Trust me. Come on.'
He slips in under my arm and we slope down
the street.

'I'm fucking dying!' I scream at two young
men, about to step into Steers. 'Pay attention.
Open your eyes!'

'And I have fucking leprosy!' Toby shouts.
'And scabies!'

'Stop it! This is real. Stop fucking around for
once in your goddamn life.'

'Hey, Ten, can you walk on your own?'

He shrugs me half-off, leaves me unbalanced
for long enough to admit that I can't.

'Thought so. C'mon. Let's find a locale appropriate to making your last stand.'

I'm forced to sling my arm over his shoulders
and stagger on.

Lerato

'You've violated company code, Ms. Mazwai.'

Jane sits sprawled on the couch, her arms across the back, smug, patient. I don't say anything. Her casualness is what's really terrifying, more than the dogs panting in creepy tandem, or the man standing behind me with an AK-47, subverting the cosy domesticity of our little scene. I have to confess, I was expecting a blank interrogation room, not a lounge on the penultimate to penthouse floor. I smile, carefully cultivated, loose and easy, slightly rueful. The punch of adrenalin in my gut sharpens everything.

I consciously echo her pose, cheap tricks of body language. She notices and leans forward, irritated. 'Don't you have anything to say in your defence?'

I shrug. Laugh, a little. 'You bust me. What am I supposed to say? I'm sorry? I didn't think

341

it was such a big deal. Is all this…' indicating the man with the gun, the dogs, 'really necessary?'

'What were you doing in the bathroom?'

I stare at her, amused, puzzled, ignoring the uncomfortable edge of the SIM digging into me, inside. Then spell it out, as if she's a moron. 'Okay. If you really want to know, I was taking a dump.'

She waits, lets the silence draw out between us, the loaded kind. In spite of myself, I plunge into it.

'Bad chicken. Last night. Upset stomach.'

'So why isn't this a big deal? Being bust?'

I shrug, look away, bored with the proceed-ings. 'Like you've never had a little sugar. In fact, as I recall, you smoked that joint with me.'

'You think that's what this is about?'

'Why don't you tell me what it's about, Jane? This terrible thing you think I've done.'

Another silence, fraught and frigid. Like Jane herself, come to think of it.

'Do you have to keep doing that? It's really tacky.'

'Does it bother you?'

'I've read the same books you have, Jane. The manuals on intimidation techniques. Please. It's too tedious. Can we just skip to the bit where you accuse me of the heinous crime?'

'Intention to defect.'

Shit. I knew Stefan was a fucking plant. I knew it. But still, it's not so bad, not irrecoverable.

She lets a long pause play out before she adds, 'Corporate sabotage.'

'What?' The adrenalin ratchets up a notch. But I don't let it show. I am the incredulity distilled, made flesh.

'One count direct involvement. Four conspiracy. Eleven aiding and abetting.'

'You think I did what?' I am standing up now, radiant with outrage, doing the maths in my head – they're way over, which means, maybe, that it's a bluff. Or that they're trumping up the charges. The Aito at my knee grumbles a bass warning. 'This is absurd.'

'Sit down, please. We have records. Instant messenger chats. Phone calls. Photographs. Our last conversation.'

'Of what?' Both dogs are growling now, but I stay standing. I am righteous indignation personified. I am the wrath of the falsely accused.

'You violated Communique's trust, your contract.'

'Please. Where's this evidence?'

'You aided a terrorist.'

Fuck. Still, not like I wasn't expecting this one. I shake my head in pained disbelief and sit down with a sigh. 'These are pretty hectic allegations, Jane. Where is this proof?'

'Are you denying them?'

'I want to know where your proof is. You're accusing me of... insane stuff, conspiracy against the company, corporate sabotage, and as for terrorism! That kind of crap could lead to serious jail-time, disconnect.'

'Execution even.'

'I'm sorry?'

'We're thirty-two storeys up.'

There are employee suicides, occasionally. Wall Street Crash syndrome, even though those reports of executives throwing themselves lemming-like from tall buildings in 1929 were apparently severely exaggerated. Today, it's usually because someone can't hack the pace, typical burn-out, but sometimes it's because they've realised there's no get-out-of-jail-free card when they get bust siphoning off funds or selling proprietary information to a competitor. But then, windows in skyscrapers are usually designed not to open. Jane catches me looking.

'You have to break through. Hell of a momentum required. Sometimes we toss a chair through first.'

'I want a representative.'

'Would you like to see–'

'A lawyer? Yes. I would, actually.'

'No. The evidence.'

She picks up a remote control for the wall2wall display, taps it against her lips.

'You sure you want to go here? It's not too late.'

'No, no, I want to see.' How bad can it be? How much can they have? I wrap my hands around my knees and lean in. I am the anticipation of vindication.

She hits the button. The wall powers up on a folder system I recognise immediately as our central home™ cache, accessed remote. I relax imperceptibly. I'm careful about cleaning up, about auto-deleting, running shells and re-routes. If this is all she has... but then she clicks through to another folder entirely, her stash of Mexican soap operas. Episode 212 of *Ángeles de la Calle*. Which is not, when she presses play, the story of love and life and death and betrayal in the favela. It is a recording of every transaction I've ever performed on my cell phone, which means they chipped it, downloaded it direct, every message, every time I connected to the triplines, probably every one of my calls. Jane smirks.

I have nowhere else to go.

'You've been an awful bitch to live with, you know that?' She blinks, and I lunge to the attack. 'You're boring. You're anal. You have no imagination and almost no talent to speak of. This…' I waft a hand at the dogs, the man with the semi-automatic. 'Why doesn't this surprise me?'

'You're not taking this very seriously, Ms. Mazwai.'

'You're a pathetic gutless bureaucrat who couldn't hack it in the real world, Jane. I always wondered how you got to this level. Are you even genuine Internal Affairs, or just some nasty little snitch spying on your colleagues? And cut the "Ms. Mazwai" crap. I've shared a bathroom with you for over eight months.'

'This isn't helping you.'

'Get me your superior officer. Now.'

'We've been watching you.'

'Who is it? Rathebe? Mogale? Give me a name.' I pull out my phone. The man with the gun shifts behind me, causing the dogs to stir. She makes an impatient placatory gesture, waiting me out.

'How do you think you got away with this?'

'This is bullshit. This is not company policy. This is fucking intimidation. Give me a name.'

'You think you're that good?'

'Fuck this. Fuck *you*, you crazy bitch.' I speed-dial reception thirty-one floors down, entertaining visions in my head of someone, anyone charging upstairs to my rescue.

'Did you really think we wouldn't notice?'

'Thembi? Hey, it's Lerato. Can you put me through to Internal Affairs? Someone senior. I have a situation.'

'We *let* you.'

I look at her blankly for a moment. I lower the phone. I am a crumpling façade.

Toby

Once it breaks, it's kif deluxe. Total 360, matter of, what, an hour? From spitting up blood, to an endorphin overload equal to a bliss hit. I wonder if that's intended, designed to make you more willing to hand yourself over, flooded with goodwill and lush happiness, or if they fucked up the formula one time. Maybe it's the whisky, the bug burned up in the alcohol content we just poured into ourselves. Maybe they didn't factor that in, didn't get the lab rats loaded before they made 'em sick. Course, the bottle we sunk between us is starting to catch up with me. I smack my tongue against my parched palate.

Tendeka is looking savagely grim, but it'll wane soon soon. It's cos I'm thin, I tell him, fast metabolism, but he's still on his apocalypse trip. He's still trying to explain it away: 'It's your body's natural response. It's an old evolutionary trick of the mind, flood your system with happy chemicals when you're dying.'

'You don't understand, buddy, I'm flying.' I lug him towards my apartment. Despite his good intentions, I'm not going to hang around the street corner while he waxes lyric about the repressive regime and rights and clampdowns. Not when I've managed to avoid the cops, being arrested, the freaking Aitos prowling outside my door. And by the time all this is over, I will have wangled a new phone, found a legit excuse for why mine was stolen or schmangled, and everything will be back to normal.

Tendeka slurs something.

'What? I can't understand you.'

'Alcohol. Adrenalin.'

'Alcohol and adrenalin what?'

'Why you're feeling better.'

'Yeah, yeah. You'll see. Wait till it hits you. Any second now. It's not the booze.'

'My tongue is swollen.'

'That would be the whisky talking.'

'No, it's…' He wrenches forward and kotches a thick splodge of blood onto the pavement. There are globby bits in it. It's seriously vile, and maybe I'm underestimating how he's handling. Lucky then, kids, that his primitive hackjob of a key works perfectly on my apartment block's door. We have to swipe it a few times over the door scan, which squawks in protest, but just when I'm ready to concede, the override goes through and it clicks open. It's a handy thing to have, and when Tendeka doesn't ask for it back specific, I pocket it.

He's badly delusional by the time I lug him onto the roof of my apartment block, going on about getting skywards and future renovations, as if this were the time for home improvements. It's very pretty up here. I should come here more often.

'Is it casting? Is Lerato hooking us up?'

'Course, man. Would I let you down? Oh, there I go.' This is a joke, kids, cos I'm easing him down so he can sit, only he sort of keels to the side, so he ends up lying on his back instead. And then he curls half-foetal on his side.

'Nice position,' I say. 'There's a reason people lie on their sides like that, we covered it in first aid. I'm not remembering what it was, though. But it's good. You got it right.'

'Where's the camera?' His eyes dart around, hunting out the lenses in my coat.

'All over. There're like a thousand of them embedded in the fabric. Miniature. You can't see 'em.'

'Okay, tell them…'

'Tell 'em yourself. You're going out live. Just speak into the coat.'

He looks up and grits his teeth, focuses. 'My name is Tendeka Mataboge.'

'Excellent start.'

'I'm thirty-two. I'm dying. It's the only way to show... I've been infected with the M7N1 virus as an act of government-corporate censorship. Repression. This is human rights violation taken to its worst. They are wilfully killing their citizens. It's... It is casting, right?'

'Yeah, yeah, yeah.' I'm getting bored with this whole shebang. 'Oh hey, I can see it from here.'

'Where?'

'No, no, don't sit up.' I point and watch the LG billboard flashing through its routine. Smiley models selling consumer electronics and cars. 'Trust me. It's going out all over the city. I'm surprised they haven't sent out the helicopters yet.'

'Good. That's good. That's...' he feels for my hand, 'important, Toby.'

I grasp his hand in both of mine.

'Do you think Ashraf is watching? Will you tell Emmie? It's, it's... I'm doing it for the baby.'

'China, I don't know what you're on about. You just hang in there, Ten. Get your strength up, then you can finish the cast.' He looks up at me with painful gratitude.

I'm so looking forward to him pulling out of this whole dying swan mode, and how stupid he's going to feel when he does. On a whim, I hit record on the BabyStrange anyway. It might just record something. Keep in mind, kids, it's always good to catch humiliating moments live.

Tendeka

Fuck. Fuck. Fuck. Not so bad, not so bad. Had food poisoning once. Worse. Like someone twisted my guts round a fork. Like spaghetti. Can't open my eyes. Too bright. Light hurts. Climbing into my head. Breath is liquid. Can't find my pump. Where's my fucking pump? But it's casting already. If I could open my fucking eyes. If. I could see the fucking adboards, hundreds of them. All fucking casting already. Casting us dying. Capturing our death. Captive audience. Me and Toby, of all people. Everything clenches. Jesus fucking motherfucking Christ! Every muscle. Squeezing. Doing damage inside. I can feel it. My muscles spasming. Too fucking tight. Too. Christ. Toby, I've changed my mind. Toby. FUCK! I've changed my mind. I want… Toby's wrist is glowing green. Try to grab it. Show him. Tell him, cos I've figured it. What was I–? The cast. The cast. The fucking cast. No one will be able to ignore or suppress it. Going out. Not this. Not anymore. FUCK! I have to chill, I have to relax. I have to fucking relax. Fuck fucking fuck. I have to relax. The spasms in waves now. Clench. Un. Clench. Something rips free inside me. Mouth full of molten copper. I can taste the light. Force my eyes open. The city is shimmering. Red and blue and green, like Christmas. Like skyward* said. Worth it. It's okay. Ash's gonna be so proud.

Lerato

'Are we done fucking around now?'

It's the first time I've ever heard her swear, and she does it so level, so cold, not even bothering to raise her voice, it's like a slap. They've played me, given me just enough rope to loop around my neck.

'I won't testify.'

'You don't have to. That's taken care of.'

'I don't understand.'

'Everyone involved in the *incident* has handed themselves in already. And those that haven't...' She doesn't even bother to shrug, as if that would commit too much energy. 'Well, they've made that choice. Now your choice, if you want to call it that...'

A door opens across the lounge and Stefan strolls in. Behind him, I can see a bank of monitors, a screen showing the inside of the lounge. He's been watching all along, the whole show. Defeat tastes like sour milk.

Jane takes some unspoken cue and stands up. The deference in her manner makes me suddenly, badly scared. I didn't know it was possible to be even more scared. She snaps her fingers impatiently at the man with the gun and he turns to follow her out, along with the dogs.

'Good luck,' she mouths at me, as the lift doors close, leaving me and Stefan alone. The SIM is starting to get really uncomfortable now.

'No papaya mojitos today, I'm afraid.'

'So, are you Mr. Wall Street?' I glance at the window. I would stand up to face him, but I don't trust my legs to support me, or for that matter, my heart not to burst.

He laughs. 'I'd very much like to hope we're beyond that stage. We haven't come this far with you to... waste your potential. No, I'm the closer.'

'Ah yes.' My mind fails to come up with a snappy comeback. 'And here I thought you were in recruitment.'

'You could say that. You're an exceptionally bright woman. We're quite in awe of your work – and your arrogance. It borders on pathological. But you're remarkably inventive: the faked phonecalls for spyware, the backdoors in the adboards, circumventing the diagnostics report-back feed! Unfortunately you missed the obvious. The oldschool search function – or didn't you know admin could request info at any time? It was fluke, of course, a random inspection that did you in. You got around all our security systems, but not a human being. You see, you're not the first to try to steal data, siphoning it off through the backdoor. Although you're the first to get our own technicians to install it. That was ingenious, we all agreed. Your only mistake was thinking we wouldn't notice.'

'What would I say that would make a difference at this junction? I still want a lawyer.'

He nods to himself, a tight little nod, as if he's decided something. 'Let me lay it out for you, Lerato. You keep your job. Things carry on exactly as per normal. Three months from now, you will be transferred to Mumbai, into another department. Your contact with your former co-workers and Zamajobe and Siphokazi will dwindle away. You'll be too busy to correspond, and within a couple of months, they'll stop bothering. It's not like you have any meaningful relationships anyway.'

'I don't understand.'

'You're being promoted. Unless you'd rather…' He tilts his chin at the window and smiles. He's smiling because he knows that even though I can't refuse – considering the unscheduled flight that would entail – I wouldn't anyway. But I'm still apprehensive.

'What would this reassignment be?'

'It's sensitive. Government linked. But you already know that. Doing what you've been doing, all that subversive stuff you so perversely enjoy. We feel we haven't been challenging you sufficiently. We feel you're ready for more responsibility.'

He hands me a page of twelve names. I recognise one immediately.

Tendeka would too.

Stefan sees my face and smirks. 'Defusers just aren't enough any more. You know that, with your little workarounds. But any action is justified in a state under terrorist threat.'

'You just have to create your own terrorists.'

'Smart girl. You'll be running several identities, posting, inciting, organising. Whatever is required. Let's just say you're on the up. Heading skywards.'

And it makes perfect sense. The process has to be managed. Fear has to be managed. Fear has to be controlled.

Like people.

Kendra

It's not a toothpaste commercial. The Inatec building is clinical, military, with double doors for gurneys leading past wards and theatres, the corridors painted a cool mint, and rows of metal cages like you see at the vet, all standing empty.

'Prisoners out on parole?' I say to defuse the silence bristling under the hum of machinery and the muffled clop of our shoes on the polished floors.

'Ha.' Andile snickers. Dr. Precious sniffs daintily.

I persist. 'Kinda creepy, though. Where is everybody?' But what I'm really thinking is, where are the dogs?

'Sunday, babes. Or are you on a different schedule? Ah, here we are. Come on.' He makes scooting motions with his hands towards a small theatre with a biohazard sign on the door. There is a cubicle to one side, with a curtain the same colour as the walls, a catscan machine and a sonogram, and other equipment I can't readily identify.

Dr. Precious goes over to a metal basin outside and starts washing her hands methodically. Andile holds open the curtain for me. They're both so tense.

'Put on the smock, please.' His voice has taken on a flavour of detached authority.

The cubicle barely has enough space to manoeuvre. I fold my clothes on the bench and reach for the green smock hanging on the back of the door. 'Front or back?'

'Doesn't matter,' says Dr. Precious. 'It's procedure for the scan. You can put your clothes back on when we do your blood work.'

'How serious is it, doctor?' I call out from the cubicle, fastening the gown at the back. 'Am I heading for the big kennel in the sky?'

'Really, babes,' Andile says, aggrieved.

'Can't say until we've got the results.'

'I wouldn't stress it too much, babes. Dr. Precious already put in a request for the vaccine from head office, so when it gets here, we can do everything at once.'

'When?'

'When what?'

'When did you put in a request on the vaccine? I didn't hear you.' I throw open the curtain, ignoring the undignified vulnerability of the smock.

'When Murray phoned me from the gate. I called it in immediately,' snaps Dr. Precious.

'Babes, you have to chill out. You've been through a hell of a time, but we're on your side. Now take it easy. I'm not the doctor here, but you don't seem to be showing any of the symptoms. I'd say your sponsorship has paid off.'

'Can you sit up here, please?'

'I think… I know. I want it out. Now. Get it out.'

'Out? Babes, you know it's permanent. You agreed to that. Got your DNA signature on that.'

'It's not permanent in the dogs.' I am near hysteria and I don't quite know why. I feel like I'm no longer in limbo. As in, I've hit the water and it's closing over my head.

'Different technology, I told you before. The Aitos are on a more basic system. It wears off in the dogs because it's pure tech, the nanobots have a limited lifespan. Maybe ten years before they wear out. Your nano is much more sophisticated. It latches onto your own cells as a power source. It reproduces itself.'

'Andile. I can't do my job if she doesn't co-operate.'

'Babes.' He opens his hands, but I know he's not the one armed with the syringe. I get up on the table, obediently, and push up my sleeve for the good doctor. She straps a blood pressure sleeve over my wrist, shoves it all the way up to my bicep.

'Pump your fist for me, please.'

'What happens to the dogs afterwards?'

'They put them out to pasture.'

'So you can't adopt? Or use them as guide dogs or something?'

'I've never heard of–'

'Impossible,' says the doctor. 'It's our intellectual property. It's very closely guarded. They put the dogs down.' She sees my face. 'But don't worry, they don't feel anything. Just a prick. Then it's over.'

She positions the needle against the crook of my elbow. 'Make a fist for me.' Normally, I look away, even though I don't mind needles so much, but this time I'm watching as the slim metal head bites into my skin.

She pulls back the plunger a fraction, so that blood swirls into the chamber, like ink in water.

I look up and see that she is watching me intently. 'See,' she says, 'just a little prick.'

Still holding my gaze, she pushes the plunger all the way in.

The world tilts to the right, and then everything swarms up to meet me in a surge of claustrophobia. Suddenly I'm scared. I struggle up through the tightening darkness, sealing in on me, like the crush of water.

'Don't fight it.'

My eyelids flutter, letting in snatches of light like a strobe, snapshots of movement. Dr. Precious pushes my shoulders, holding me down. Andile's mouth twitches. He looks away. I can't keep my eyes open. I can't move my arms. I try and push up, through the dark, which is wide open, too open, so I'm drowning in it, fighting.

Then calm.

It's just like diving.

Following the bubbles up, knowing that soon I'll break the surface.

Toby

When do I finally tweak what's happening? Not when he snatches my wrist, so tight I can feel it bruise. Not when he starts shaking violently or when his eyes roll back and his jaw clamps and he starts making hideous sounds through his teeth, wet, viscous shrieks.

No, kids, the indicator for yours truly that this is some serious fucking shit is when he starts bleeding from every exit point. At first I laugh, cos I can't help it. Because it's so overboard gruesome, total B-grade horror, and so badly done, it starts oozing out in thick dark runnels, and then it's pouring out, gushing, and I try to pull my hand away, and he won't fucking let go. It's like someone turned on a liquidiser inside him. And I cannot get him to let go.

'Tendeka,' I shake his shoulder, but he just continues dissolving onto the rooftop. It's soaking into my shoes. The hem of my BabyStrange is dipped in the mess ebbing out from under him. Jesus. I'm frantic to get away from it. I'm wrenching his fingers. Bending them back. Gagging. And then he squeezes once more, convulsive, and lets go.

I tumble backwards, clutching my wrist, and fall in the blood, the soles of my tackies squeaking in it, so I leave tracks and a handprint. And now I do vomit, kneeling in Tendeka's insides. When my stomach stops contracting and there's nothing left except spit, I look down and see this muck mixing with his blood, and I try and brush it away, scoop it up with my hands, so it doesn't, because I can't handle this, can't handle him pooled around me, can't handle how I've violated his remains. Please. Jesus. Motherfuck.

'C'mon Tendeka.' I'm whispering, rocking on my heels, forwards and back. I want to shake him, scream at him, even though I know it's pointless, that he's not teasing. That it's not some hoax, a bluff. I can't touch him. And oh Jesus motherfuck, if it's not a hoax, how long do I have? I can't. Not like. Jesus. I can't even look.

I fall onto my knees again, dry-heaving some more, my hands over my mouth so I don't do it again, and somewhere the heaving turns into sobbing.

The coat. The coat. The fucking coat. I check the playback. But there's nothing. Static. Blur.

White noise. I rewind, fast forward and there! It's bad quality, but it's there underneath the fritz. 'Human rights violation–' and my snarky comment, overlapping.

Oh fuck, Tendeka. Fuck. I'm sorry. Maybe it can be cleaned up. If I can get it to, I dunno, someone, upload it to some geek site, let them clean it up. And get to a clinic. Get the vaccine. Turn myself in. How long do I have?

I look up for helicopters. But it wasn't casting. I'm okay. They're not looking for us yet. I hit save. I sprint down the stairs. I don't look back.

And it's only when I'm back in my apartment, with the door double-locked and the fridge up against it, already uploading the files to my machine, not that it's gonna do me much good with my connection down, that I notice my wrist is glowing green, a pale jellyfish phosphorescence shining through. I switch the channel on my screen to mirror, and stare at my face. I look incredibly healthy. I close my eyes, probe how I'm feeling. Freaked. Definitely. But not sick.

It gets worse. Tendeka's on every channel on the TV, his face dominating the screen, Osama, coupled with some kid, Zuko Sephuma, who's already been arrested.

My first thought is how much shit I'm in. How I need to just set fire to my entire apartment and all the evidence and walk away, disappear. What flammables do I have at handy?

Or.

Or I have the total sony exclusive on the untimely and grotesque death of a terrorist.

Or a martyr. Depends on who's paying.

I can't stick around here, though. They've already been here once. And they're sure to notice Tendeka's corpse on the roof. Hard to miss with all the splatter.

I stuff the coat, spare clothes and my laptop – and fuckit, the VIM, cos wherever I'm going, I'll still need a clean-up – into my bag.

I step out of the door into a whole new bright world, feeling exhausted and exhilarated.

And thirsty.

Acknowledgments

Writing may happen in isolation, but books don't. I'd like to thank a long list of people who helped make *Moxyland* what it is, from its original South African incarnation to its assimilation into the Robot Army.

Thanks to Marc Gascoigne and Lee Harris at Angry Robot for their boundless and bounding enthusiasm and easy-going candour – and my agent, Ron Irwin, for getting the book into their hands.

The University of Cape Town's MA in Creative Writing programme gave me the creative space to start the book and a grant from South Africa's National Arts Council gave me the financial freedom to finish it. Thanks especially to André Brink, Stephen Watson, Ron Irwin and Jenefer Shute.

Maggie Davey, the publishing director at Jacana read the manuscript on the plane to the

Frankfurt Book Fair and by the time she'd landed had decided to give *Moxyland* its first home. Jacana's Russell Martin, Bridget Impey, Emily Amos and especially Pete van der Woude (most passionate punter of books and deft ringmaster of book launches) helped make it a critical success in South Africa.

Sam Wilson, Sarah Lotz, Matthew Brown, Tinarie van Wyk Loots, Alex van Tonder, Lindiwe Nkutha, Padraic O Meara and Wynand 'Munki' Groenewald were the first readers who helped panel beat the early drafts with their feedback.

I owe much to Helen Moffett, my brilliant luddite editor for midwifing this unwieldy bastard, and Dale Halvorsen, aka Joey Hi-fi, the most inventive cover designer a girl could ask for (twice).

My family and friends provided love and support, both fiscal and psychological.

And lastly to my husband and best friend, Matthew, thank you for everything (most especially our daughter).

About the Author

Lauren Beukes is a writer, TV scriptwriter and recovering journalist (although she occasionally falls off the wagon).

She has an MA in Creative Writing from the University of Cape Town under André Brink, but she got her real education in ten years of freelance journalism, learning really useful skills like how to pole-dance and make traditional sorghum beer. For the sake of a story, she's jumped out of planes and into shark-infested waters, and got to hang out with teen vampires, township vigilantes, AIDS activists and homeless sex workers among other interesting folk.

She lives in Cape Town with her husband and daughter. He next novel for Angry Robot will be the (very) urban fantasy *Zoo City*.

www.moxyland.com

Moxyland's Stem Cells

Moxyland was inspired by a DNA remix of many influences, from *BoingBoing* to Stephen Johnson's Emergence to Theo Jansen's incredible evolving mechanical Strandbeests. It riffs off surveillance society and the Great Firewall of China, bird flu and the threat of terrorism, the cult of kawaii, RFID chips in passports, virtual rape and refugee camps in *Second Life*, and real-life murder over a virtual sword in China.

It developed from 12 years of working as a journalist, from stories I worked on for *Colors* magazine where I spent many weeks in Cape Town's townships with photographers Marc Shoul and Pieter Hugo, interviewing electricity cable thieves, paramilitary vigilantes and people dying of the twin pandemic of TB and AIDS and learning how to make smileys or boiled sheep heads.

Of course, it also grew out of the legacy of apartheid: the arbitrary and artificially applied divides between people, the pass system and the insidious Special Branch – a secret police operation to rival the Stasi that infiltrated activist organisations, used wet bag torture to extract 'confessions', threw troublemakers out of fifth storey windows or blew them up with letterbombs and plotted chemical warfare and sinister bio-experiments. Don't let anyone tell you that apartheid has nothing to do with South Africa now. Those roots run deep and tangled and we'll be tripping over them for many generations to come.

But really, the stem cell that developed into *Moxyland* was Lucky Strike. Or, rather, the hush-hush underground parties British American Tobacco organised for their brands when the South African government outlawed cigarette advertising in 2000.

They seduced hip young things to be brand ambassadors for the price of free cigarettes. They staged provocative theatre at bars and restaurants like a faked strip poker game with models. And they dropped millions on the most outrageous events, from Peter Stuyvesant's swanky mansion pool parties to Lucky Strike's private concerts, flying out international rock acts and house DJs for one night only. The height of the debauchery was a million Rand party train with multiple dancefloors and five different bars, snaking through the Cape winelands on its way to a secret destination for a luxury picnic. If you'd missed the ARG-style clues, subtly disguised in a Lucky Strike target with only a phone number stuck up at the back of a bar, you missed out.

I wrote a story on it for *The Big Issue* and then transmuted it into fiction with a short story called 'Branded', about a girl who turns sponsorbaby for a soft drink company with a dubious agenda. It blossomed like a tumour from there, mutating into interesting directions I hadn't anticipated – and a full-blown novel four years later.

It's been fascinating to see real-world correlations develop since the novel made its debut in South Africa in 2008. Some of them are strange and wonderful, others are deeply worrying to me. And the best of it is stuff I couldn't have invented.

In the last year, for example, Portugal has launched wave power generators, cell phone wallets have been rolled out and there's now proof, after all, that subliminal advertising can work, if paired with some kind of reinforcing reward – which might well include feel-good neural feedback in the future.

South Africa's national energy provider, Eskom, *has* announced its intentions to open up its own proprietary university (not, as yet linked to an AIDS orphanage); a Seoul National University team created the first transgenic dogs that glow in the dark thanks to the addition of an anemone gene; and the Pentagon put out a brief for military contractors to develop a 'multi-robot pursuit system', ie, packs of robots that could 'search for and detect a non-cooperative human'.

There was a real bio-engineered artwork that caused a controversy in 2008 when it was exhibited and then 'killed' at MoMa in New York. 'Victimless Leather' was a small living jacket made up of embryonic mouse stem cells, but it grew out of control, clogged up its incubation system and had to be 'put down', to the apparent distress of the curator – all of which, purely coincidentally I'm sure, generated a whole lot of headlines.

But the scariest synchronicity with *Moxyland* was something an electrical engineer friend told me – that a cop buddy had idly asked him over a beer if there was any way to SMS an electric shock to a fleeing suspect's cell phone, you know, because it's a pain in the ass to chase them wearing a heavy bulletproof vest. Luckily, my friend says that even for the purposes of bar talk, it's an impractical idea, especially without buy-in from the cell phone companies and government. Impractical. But not impossible.

The thing is that it's all possible, especially if we're willing to trade away our rights for convenience, for the illusion of security. Our very own bright and shiny dystopia is only ever one totalitarian government away.

Further reading

Antjie Krog's *Country of My Skull* about the Truth and Reconciliation Commission Hearings that exposed some, but not all of the atrocities committed under apartheid.

Jonny Steinberg's *Thin Blue* and Andrew Brown's *Street Blues* about the harrowing challenges of police work in South Africa.

The Bang Bang Club by Greg Marinovich and Jaoa Silva – the true story of the four news photographers who risked their lives during apartheid. (Kendra would have loved these guys.)

Fiction

A Dry White Season by André Brink
Black Petals by Bryan Rostron

LB, Cape Town

SPREAD THE WORD!

Moxy is our mascot, a symbol of defiance to the powers that be. Use these nifty stencils to get the word out to people just like YOU!

Photocopy or scan and print the stencils onto stiff card. Blow 'em up real big if you want to.

Cut out the shapes, then spray in the order given.

Your finished Moxy should look a bit like this:

WWW.MOXYLAND.COM

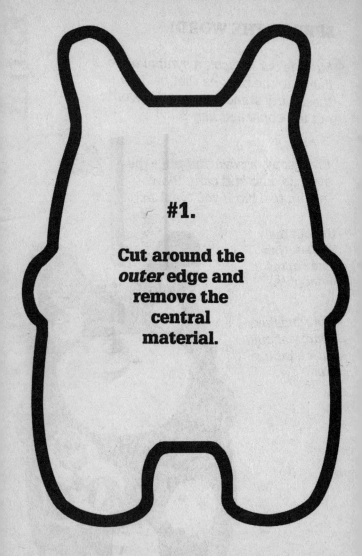

#1.

Cut around the *outer* edge and remove the central material.

WWW.MOXYLAND.COM

#2.

Use a different colour to create eyes, mouth and detailing.

#3.

Final stage, small but important: back to your first colour to add eyes to that ghost thing Moxy carries.

Or do 'em a different colour. No one's gonna tell YOU what to do, right?